22,213

amB

Three-Core Lead

Three-Core Lead

CLARE CURZON

A CRIME CLUB BOOK
DOUBLEDAY
NEW YORK   LONDON   TORONTO   SYDNEY   AUCKLAND

A CRIME CLUB BOOK
Published by Doubleday, a division of
Bantam Doubleday Dell Publishing Group, Inc.
666 Fifth Avenue, New York, New York 10103

DOUBLEDAY and the portrayal of a man
with a gun are trademarks of
Doubleday, a division of Bantam Doubleday Dell
Publishing Group, Inc.

Library of Congress Cataloging-in-Publication Data applied for

ISBN 0-385-41139-1
Copyright © 1988 by Clare Curzon

For our friends in Prague.
Na brzkou shledanou.

Three-Core Lead

1

Swaffham completed his illegible signature with a neat, backhand underline, adding his designation, "Government Official." He looked up to find Whittle's ripe gooseberry eyes gleaming at him through their thick lenses.

"I had wondered how you describe your function." His tight-lipped smile was just short of familiar.

"It covers a multitude of—activities," Swaffham said, heavily noncommittal. He hooded his own eyes lest the other man should read dislike too clearly in them, capped his gold fountain pen and replaced it in an inner pocket. Then he swivelled the document for the next signature.

Whittle picked up the ballpoint provided and propelled it over the paper. Swaffham watched impassively. What kind of parents called a baby Adrian? Overnice ones, expecting too much? Was that one of the earliest clues to the man's unappetizing personality? he asked himself. But no, he was placing too much emphasis on his own prejudice against the name: there had been distasteful precedents. The antipathy he experienced at present was instinctive, had a genetic source: it was a case of body chemistry signalling strong incompatibility.

When it came to job description in Whittle's case, he was equally bland, inserting "Factor," after a smirk at the other two to indicate he was aware of their attention. He offered to pass on the ballpoint to the woman, but it was declined.

The third signature wound out like a line of mohair knitting pulled off large wooden needles, the letters loose, squarish and frequently overlapping. Reading it upside down, Swaffham worked persistently through it from start to finish, as with some maze puzzle in a magazine. The characters were indeed all there, the Ariadne clue having created its own intricacies: "Hilary D. Manton-Jones. Occupation, Secretary."

"I am most grateful to you both," Swaffham said urbanely. "Hilary, my dear, you must let me ring for the car. I fear it is inexcusably late."

"In fact, we completed only just inside the dateline," Whittle pointed out with oily smartness.

The other two turned to look at the cherub-decked timepiece on the creamy marble overmantel. It responded with twelve clear bell-notes, across which Whittle brushed aside the need for any hired conveyance. He had his own car. He would be honoured if the lady . . .

She appeared to hesitate.

Smiling, Swaffham reached for the antique tapestry bellpull and gave it a relaxed tug. Something jangled distantly in the house. Almost before its echoes died there was a knock on the door and a uniformed chauffeur stood there, cap under elbow.

"Forbes, my guests are about to leave. Will you escort the lady down?" He turned to Whittle. "Thank you for the offer, but everything is taken care of." He lifted a sable coat from the settee where the woman had dropped it on coming in. He arranged it over her shoulders with no more than an avuncular caress. Whittle observed that they did not kiss.

The uniformed chauffeur closed the door quietly behind the two of them.

"Let me offer you some brandy." Discreetly Swaffham omitted the word "more," advancing with the decanter. Whittle subsided again in a padded chair. Swaffham poured for them both.

Balked of comparing notes with the woman while he drove her home, Whittle reflected that hers was an uncommon enough name. Even if ex-directory, she must surely move in circles to which he could obtain access. Certainly she was something more than a secretarial aide. Her name had never appeared on any list of the department provided by his researchers. Nor on his personal dossier for Swaffham. A dark horse, this man. His secret mistress, then? But it had been a slip to use her now as witness to the extra-departmental agreement. Better perhaps not to let Swaffham suspect that a follow-up on her might provide Whittle with a hold over him. Softly, softly, after all. He relaxed, and permitted himself to be detained.

Possibly Swaffham had dismissed her from the range of Whittle's curiosity from no more than old-fashioned courtesy towards what he would fustily consider the gentler sex. Unless, of course, there was some private matter he now wished to raise once the two men had no third party present.

The round, gooseberry eyes lifted to meet Swaffham's flat, near-black ones which gave nothing away. Swaffham allowed him the bare time needed to down his final drink before the atmosphere of mine-host-of-the-local-at-closing-time showed through. And then, dismissed, Whittle found even such fine brandy was little compensation for temporarily losing track of the woman, although Swaffham's last words as they shook hands reassured him. "I'll put a photocopy of the document in the post tomorrow."

"Splendid," Whittle said, and meant it. The addresses of the signatories had been typed in when the document was prepared, leaving a space for each of them to add name and profession. They had not been included in Swaffham's careful reading-out of the content. And, covered by the excuse of using an ink pen, Swaffham had kept a sheet of blotting-paper over that part as Whittle checked the single page of text and signed. It might have been intentional secrecy, or merely the habitual caution of a creature long-conditioned to the demands of Security.

What it wasn't was accidental. Not that Swaffham had ever exactly been a field operative. The information that Whittle had acquired on his background had been leaked by a retired SIS-man: "The best bloody interrogator the country ever had since Burghley!" A specialist skill, and it meant that one needed to watch one's tongue in his company. But surely nothing to *fear* now that officially he was at the end of his useful days.

Whittle took leave of the man at the street door and went, smugly satisfied, out into a warm May night shiny with recent rain. Cruising towards the street end, he realized that it might not be necessary to wait for the next day's post to check on Swaffham's mystery woman.

Through the net swags at an unlit window, Swaffham watched expressionlessly as the blue Mercedes pulled away from the kerb. He had several little tidying jobs to perform before recovering his charcoal-grey overcoat from the otherwise empty cloakroom and abandoning the Mayfair apartment rented for the occasion. Seventeen minutes after Whittle had left, he himself stepped out into the deserted street. From the direction of Hyde Park, where all night long the hum of traffic never ceased, came the purr of the black Rolls, pulling in beside him. The driver nodded, confirming that Ms. Hilary D. Manton-Jones had been dropped at Paddington Station cab rank precisely as per instructions. He added a few words that made Swaffham smile in gratification.

"Take the short route then. No need to let the grass grow under our wheels."

Forty-three minutes later the Rolls was turning in through the gateway of a Berkshire country house, headlights catching diamond-facets of rain on the glossy leaves of rhododendrons walling the driveway. When he stepped out into the fresher night air, Swaffham caught the reeling scent of wistaria blossom which hung in heavy clusters like pale grapes above the porticoed door.

Inside, they were waiting for him. He handed over the document, the enveloped ballpoint pen which Whittle had made use of, the exposed film and the reel of audio tape. In return he received a sealed package containing currency, passport and flight tickets.

Then he seated himself at a small table and repeated, with a new supporting cast, the same scene as in the Mayfair apartment. This document, however, was slightly different in certain details, the names below his own being added by the two men present. He added the date, smiling to himself as he checked it against his discreet Rolex wristwatch. When all was satisfactorily completed, he folded the document neatly in three and slid it inside an envelope which he handed to the grey-haired man wearing fine latex gloves.

Swaffham wished the others good night and was shown to his suite. There, when he emerged from a steaming bath, he found a tray of smoked salmon sandwiches and a chilled bottle of hock waiting on a table near the bed.

It was pleasant to have one's little preferences remembered, and good to ease one's aging limbs at the end of a demanding day. Above all, it was an agreeable way to begin one's early retirement. He removed the gold Rolex from his wrist, observing that he had now been his own man for an hour and fifty-two minutes.

At breakfast some ten days later, Detective-Superintendent Mike Yeadings of Thames Valley Serious Crime Squad based on Maidenhead grunted and refolded the newspaper with the obituary notices uppermost. Nan peered at him round the coffee pot. "Refill, love?"

Mike pushed his cup forward, still reading. "Thanks." He shook out the paper as a preliminary to conversation. "Do you remember Howard Swaffham? We ran into him two years back, down at that hotel at Paignton."

"Special Branch or something, wasn't he?"

"Something similar. Spooks, they call them now."

"What has he done?"

"Died. In Prague."

"Anything sinister in that?"

Yeadings hesitated. "Not necessarily. I'm a little surprised he chose to be there at all. He wasn't an undercover operative or anything like that, and his department would have been quite uncomfortable about his taking a holiday behind the Curtain."

"Because he knew too much, you mean? A risk to them, if anyone took liberties with him?"

"Decidedly."

"So why advertise the fact of where he died? They could have had it suppressed: merely, 'Suddenly, abroad . . . ,' couldn't they?"

"You have a point there, love. If I get a moment today I might look into who sent the death notice in. I don't recall that there would be a vengeful widow determined to embarrass his late masters. And if they inserted the information themselves you may guess it was for some devious purpose. In any case, it wouldn't have been 'suddenly' at all. He was a sick man even when you met him. It just doesn't seem in character for him to have gone to the Czechs as to an elephants' graveyard."

"What kind of man was he, then?"

"And what kind of question is that? I can't give a one-word answer. On him less than on most security men I've known. Well, *complicated:* there's your word. At the same time, a simple man without obvious quirks. A quiet man who weighed his actions and others' words. A decision-maker who tried to be just, within the confines of his loyalties. I suspect he was a man of some sorrows and, as you've probably gathered, one I admired as far as I knew him."

"And how far was that, Mike?"

"Our paths crossed twice officially. Once on a case of mine in Windsor in which he showed an interest, and once when he whipped a killer out of my hands and left me hog-tied in red tape. But by then I knew better than to protest. He had the courtesy later to intimate what the risks had been to national security. Much later, when I was offered a position in a department similar to his, I asked his personal advice. And, duly grateful, followed it."

"Which is why you're still a policeman? For which I'm thankful too."

"Even as an Aunt Sally for militant police authorities? The Fascist lackey of corrupt capitalism?"

"That talk's beginning to sound outdated, thank heavens. But I'm glad you're not a spook. So much duplicity must put a strain on any man, and on his family too. You said Swaffham had no wife?"

"There had been one. I don't know what became of her. He struck me as too single-tracked professionally to have room in his life for personal relationships. But you can't really tell; he was human underneath."

Mike darted a glance at the kitchen clock, shrugged expressively, downed his cooling coffee and pushed back his chair with an appalling screech on the ceramic tiles. "Must go, love. Take care. Tell Sally I love her. You too, of course. 'Bye."

Heading for Amersham, summoned to give evidence at a resumed inquest, Mike Yeadings found the dead security official intruding disturbingly on the summary of evidence he was mentally rehearsing. Halted at traffic lights, he actually turned his head as if to check that the passenger seat was empty, so strong was the sense of another presence.

Howard Swaffham, man of many secrets, extinguished. Poor devil, finally at peace. And then that thought brought its own unease, because it revealed an aspect he hadn't faced before. Swaffham, the watchful, the seemingly detached while totally committed, surely had a seething centre under the unnaturally still exterior. Had that seething ever found time to subside, or had he gone unsatisfied as ever to his grave?

Yeadings shook his head, engaged first gear and pulled away in the triple line of traffic, impatient with his own fanciful curiosity.

Yet the presence stayed with him. The compactly stocky figure in the charcoal overcoat and immaculate bowler, features negatived by the dark-rimmed spectacles, continued to haunt the seat he had filled some fourteen months before, at their last, unexpected meeting. It was a ghost needing to be exorcised by action, otherwise present official demands would get swamped.

He pulled up at a public telephone, checked it wasn't vandalized, noted its number, then radioed Reading Control to have DI Angus Mott ring him there. He had three minutes and forty-two seconds to wait for the summons, then his inspector's voice came through, warily cool. "Guv?"

"Bit of a delicate private matter, Angus, but you might avoid a brush-off it you mention my name." He told Mott about the "Deaths" entry in *The Times*. "I'd like to know who placed the notice and what family the man had. To date he's existed for me *in vacuo*. And in view of his job, I'd rather it wasn't widely known we're interested."

"Can do," Mott assured him. "I have a *Times* contact. Any chance you'll be back by midday?"

"Doubtful. There's new medical evidence since the adjournment, and they'll have to recall most of the witnesses. I'll put in a plea for business elsewhere, but I suspect it'll be a long morning of examining the ceiling."

Despite this prediction, Yeadings was anything but glazed as he waited to give evidence. The room's bland and characterless interior of pale, polyurethaned wood and vinyl might have been part of any modern public building—clinic waiting-room, church vestry, non-denominational crematorium chapel. Significant, how his mind continued to dwell on matters funereal. Not entirely because this was a coroner's court, but because there were other questions popping up in his mind like targets in the butts: died how? with whom? why there? And all of them referred to that dark, contained man; that secretly *distressed* man, Howard Swaffham.

Distressed. Yeadings had never applied that word to him before, but he knew now that it was the right one. It covered the enigma of the quiet man's seething centre. And with it defined, it could now go into deep freeze.

He was at last free to settle to the matter in hand. The coroner weighed straight in, sifted the chaff from the grain and had the open verdict he'd been after by a quarter past twelve.

Yeadings headed for Maidenhead again, drove downriver towards Boulter's Lock and sat by the water to eat the sandwiches Nan had given him; one Stilton with cucumber spread, the other ham with mustard. Some like it hot, he reflected ruefully, guessing that little Sally had lent her mother a generous hand in preparing them.

It provided an excuse for a lager and lime at the hotel opposite, and a few words exchanged with some cheerful pensioners waiting for an excursion boat downstream. One of the old codgers called him "lad." Silly, how a thing like that perks you up when you're feeling a trifle lived-in. He set off in lighter heart and made it to his office by a little short of 2:40 P.M.

DI Mott's contact at *The Times* office had already produced the information that Swaffham was survived by a daughter, Felicity Marlowe, whose authority had appeared on the death notification. A follow-up at Public Records next day unearthed the further background of the man's early widowing, and the girl's divorce prompt on a teenage marriage. She would at present be twenty-three. The London telephone directory gave her name in full and an address at Fulham. Yeadings rang her from home at six-fifteen that evening, hoping to catch her between work and play.

The immediate reply to his ring was an impersonal "Hullo," without any repeat of the number: the mark of a lone woman on the defensive. He gave his name and professional rank.

"How do I know that?" the quiet voice demanded, unimpressed.

"Wait five minutes, then ring Maidenhead police and ask for my home number. I'll arrange for them to give it to you."

There was a short silence, then, "What's your car registration?"

He told her.

"That will do just as well. How can I help you, Superintendent?"

"I should like us to meet," he said, feeling his way with caution. Despite the controlled tone, there was something feral about the girl. He sensed that one sudden move on his part would send her leaping off into the undergrowth.

Felicity Marlowe gave a short, unamused laugh. "That's more or less what *he* says, my heavy breather. Then adds unattractive inducements. You're lucky to get me at this number. I'm having it changed tomorrow."

He made no comment. "Well, I'm a very ordinary policeman, with no inducements of any kind. Just curious, though." He paused, then risked, "Concerning your father."

Her reply came back at once. "In that case we have something in common. Where shall we meet, Superintendent? Can you make it tonight?"

They made it a mid-point between them, at an old coaching inn fashionably updated to suit a yuppie clientele. The bar was thronged with their Quant clothes, vodka martinis and loud, Young Conservative voices. Back at their corner table, Yeadings and the girl were unobserved and their conversation usefully jammed by others' babble.

In appearance Felicity was quite unlike her father, being slight, average tall for a woman, her fair hair dressed simply with an unusual centre parting which emphasized the uncluttered look of her pale, perfectly oval face. She wore a cream linen suit and matching shoes, light coral lipstick and no eye make-up. The short, sandy lashes made her look vulnerably young. Yeadings supposed that to any curious onlooker their rendezvous must look like a baby-snatching operation, and was amused.

He brought across their drinks—his pint, her white wine—and, seating himself, asked, "Did you really know my car registration in advance?"

She looked at him evenly, raised her glass in salute, sipped and set it down. "I have a short dossier on you. My father supplied it. In case we ever met."

"Ah."

"Ah, indeed." She had placed her black, boxy handbag on the table, and now behind it she passed him an envelope which she'd held in her lap. He covered it with his large hand and pocketed it while searching about for matches and miniature cigars.

"We both knew he was dying. He left this letter with me in case you wanted to get in touch."

"And if I didn't?"

"I was to wait six months and then destroy it."

Yeadings hummed between tight lips. So his intuitive urge to probe had been right. Or had the remarkable Swaffham contrived to project himself from beyond death into the policeman's mind, insisting he make the contact? "Is this the only note of its kind he left with you?" It came out almost humbly.

"Oh yes. It was you or no one." Her voice was sharp, with a sardonic edge to it. The couple at the next table looked up with amused eyes. But Felicity was smiling at Yeadings. It was a sad smile, and for the first time he saw her father in her, despite the femininity, the pale transparency.

"It was you who put the notice in *The Times*," he prompted her.

"To replace the one his old department submitted. They were a little put out by my interference, I understand. But the better newspapers are quite receptive to grieving relatives' requests. And all I added was 'Suddenly in Prague.'"

"I wonder why."

"You know why. It worked, didn't it? Made you curious. I knew he was up to something devious. Oh, he had retired, just a week before, but at some personal level he was still functioning, driving in the same direction. He was determined to—use himself up to some purpose. He didn't confide in me, and I didn't expect him to; but now I want to know. I wanted you to feel equally curious and do some digging. So will you?"

Yeadings buried his nose in his glass, giving himself time to think. "How did you discover where he died? Hadn't the department stepped in by then and covered things up?"

"I told you, he was freelancing. He'd an agreement with the hotel manager where he was staying. The man rang me to say Daddy had died. I asked him to seal up my father's belongings, return them to me direct and I'd refund all expenses. They're rigid about bureaucratic details like that in the Curtain countries. Everything would have been minutely examined, of course, before release, but they wouldn't permit anyone unauthorized to lay a hand on them. They were flown over next day. I'm still waiting for the body to be released."

"Perhaps you would let me have a look at his things."

"Why not? But there's nothing there. His passport shows he entered the country four days before his death. It has his photograph, and its made out in the name of Francis Day Maskell." She looked at him with a vertical frown line between her eyes. "You haven't said yet if you'll take it on."

There was a lot he could say. The obvious way out—"I'm a very busy man"—was insulting, but the fact remained that each day had no more than twenty-four hours, and most of them mortgaged to his job's demands and his very special family commitments. "Time," he warned her, "is the enemy. I'm not a free agent, and this has to be unofficial, at least until we've a reason to make it otherwise. Your father obviously meant it to be that way." That was as near as Yeadings dared get to implying there could be trouble with Swaffham's old department. If it got wind of the civil authority taking an interest, it would jump on them from a great height. Special Branch, SIS, MIs 5 and 6 were sharp thorns in the flesh of the humble Plod.

"It's what he did mean to happen. He wanted you to be curious. Otherwise why did he prepare me for your getting in touch?" She was quietly insistent. Yeadings was horrified to see a drop of water, squeezed from between her closed lids, run slowly down her cheek. She was forcing her voice to stay level. "There was something he wanted you to dig into. Perhaps me too. His last wishes, in a way: a dying man's request. We have to comply. Maybe the letter he left for you will be explanation enough for us both."

"Perhaps." Yeadings doubted it. Swaffham had never been an obvious man. He wouldn't have believed in explanations that could be covered in only a page or two of words. Yeadings had the conviction that the man's whole life, his reason for being, were involved in this matter and requiring scrutiny. He was subject now to that semi-psychic sureness that came with some of his more bizarre cases, pointing him in the right direction, a sensation that began physically, at the nape of the neck, with the fine hairs rising as if in response to an electric charge. ("My old Welsh granny giving me a dig," he'd excused it once to Mott, and they'd laughed. But he wasn't laughing now, and he wasn't going to promise the girl any sixth-sense assurances.)

"Perhaps," he said again, meaning that anything might come of looking into it. Or nothing.

2

Felicity hadn't required him to read Swaffham's letter there and then. Perhaps she suspected, even as he did, that its full meaning would require some working out. It seemed enough for her at the time that he took it from her, and thereby left himself open to further obligation. And once it was out of her hands she seemed to become more vulnerable, as though realizing she had now given up the last part of her father along with the charge he'd laid upon her.

When Yeadings saw her into her car, she wound down the window and apologized for her weakness. "It's just that somehow you remind me of him," she admitted surprisingly. "Not in looks exactly. You're bigger. But so sort of serious and comfortable. As if you wouldn't really mind how silly I was."

He stood looking after the tail lights of her car as they disappeared eastward. Swaffham—comfortable! That was an aspect of him quite unknown to Yeadings. The father figure: the man had brought up his daughter as a single parent, however much housekeepers or boarding-schools had helped. Perhaps her early marriage, rapidly cancelled, had been an act of rebellion, a look-I'm-here challenge to an authoritarian figure who'd failed to notice she'd become a woman. Whatever the case, the two of them seemed to have found each other later, together had faced the growing knowledge of inevitable death and final separation.

And then she had to recognize a similar figure in himself! It wasn't enough that he should be required to pick up whatever complicated trail the man had left behind, but now he must become involved personally with this youngster who grieved. He was sure of that; grieved silently, with dignity, but none the less deeply.

This, if any, was a case when he needed to call on Nan's wise experience. He spent some time that evening considering Swaffham's letter before he read it aloud to her. Listening, Nan set up her ironing board and, late as it was, began to press Sally's little cotton dress and one of his best shirts. Her excuse was that the familiar smoothing movements made thinking easier. Mike knew this and waited patiently for results to issue, like printouts from a trusted computer.

"Read it again," Nan commanded at length. "Slowly, and let's air our impressions as you go."

" 'My dear Yeadings,' " Mike repeated. " 'I have reached that stage of life, common to all men, when we need to record some progress, to justify—if we can—the mess we find on our hands; and in so doing tend to ponderousness. By the time you receive this I shall have passed beyond even that state, and qualify perhaps for your forbearance.' "

"Stop there. Can you hear his voice saying that?"

"Clearly. Rather droll, self-parodying, but covering up real feeling, I'm sure."

"Yes, I see. Go on, love."

" 'I was not, as you must know, a creative person, so I leave behind no positive achievement. My function, as for many who cannot paint, or write, or compose music, or produce anything of lasting worth, has been demolition. And in this I have achieved some considerable success.' "

Nan made a little humming noise between closed lips. "You notice the tense he uses. '*Was* not a creative person.' He's seeing himself as already dead. And he doesn't count his daughter as any positive achievement. Isn't that rather curious?"

"He knew death was just round the next corner. I can't speak for his attitude to his daughter, but I guess he was too modest to regard her possessively. She's spirited, delightfully her own woman. It's likely he thought of her that way himself."

"And what did he actually die of? Had he been given a specific survival time which he must work within? Mike, I think it could be worth talking to his doctor. Or getting Felicity to find out the detailed prognosis. With some diseases it's possible for experts to pinpoint the end with great accuracy."

"You have a point there, Nan. He goes on, 'As well as the need to counter corruption, what I most regret is the unavoidable wasting of some good along with the bad. It is inevitable that when we execute an evil man we also deprive the world of his potential usefulness. Yet in tolerance extended undeservedly, we become part of what we should destroy.' "

"That's in a much more serious vein. People don't talk like that any more. Not outside the pulpit. Even there, 'good' and 'evil' are distinctly old hat."

"M'm. I never heard him speak on those lines, but it might well be what he privately thought. It is his *state of mind*, after all, that he's trying to explain. And he began with that warning about sounding ponderous.

"Nan, when you were still nursing, you talked with people who were slowly dying. Didn't they say things like that?"

"No. Mostly they wanted you to go on saying they'd get better. Some, more realistic, wanted reassurance that we'd stay with them and help them through the worst pain. Maybe they saved other thoughts for their priests. Can that be how Swaffham saw you?"

"Surely not. We were professional parallels to some extent, and when I had the chance to move into work more like his own, he advised against it."

"To keep your hands cleaner than his own?"

"There may have been some consideration like that."

"So perhaps he needs you as the independent adjudicator, a member of the jury sitting on his case?"

"I would never give a verdict on the man."

"Even if he's desperate for it?"

"Nan, I'm a simple policeman. All this philosophy, or ethics, or whatever, has nothing to do with me."

"Are you sure? He knew what you are. And, according to the girl, he was up to something at the end. Possibly it *is* as a simple policeman that he needs you. This letter is to point you in the right direction. Go on to that bit about the device he'd invented."

"That's figurative, love; not an actual bomb or machine. Here it is. 'With this in mind, then, I have contrived a device which shall go some way to balance the account. It requires only that someone should fit plug to socket and switch the thing on. To this end, I have provided a three-core lead, with myself as the yellow and green wire.' "

"Yellow and green. That's the earth wire. I've replaced enough fuses to know that. He says he's the earth."

"And in another sense, the earth because he's in it, dead."

"But the earth *lead*. That means there are two others, two other cores to the cable, apart from himself. Two other men, then? If so, why doesn't he say so plainly, and give you the names?"

"Because it isn't the man's way," growled Yeadings. "And he knows it's not mine. Tell me something dodgy and I have to report it to higher up. It gets logged, discussed, and maybe looked into if anyone's interested. But *puzzle* me, dammit, and he knows he's got me hooked. And, what's more, I'll have nothing I'm obliged to pass to higher authority until the whole mystery's blown open. Crafty bugger! He's laid a treasure trail for me, and this is just the beginning." Yeadings growled his disquiet.

Nan disconnected the iron and snapped the tubular stand shut. "Speak only good of the dead," she chided, but her lips were smiling. "Let's consider this afresh in the morning. So late, it begins to sound like student whiffle."

So the Swaffham puzzle was relegated to a back burner for the moment, although during the next day Nan at least gave the mixture an occasional housewifely stir and a sniff at the contents. When Mike rang her at midday from work, she had a suggestion to make. "Love, this Felicity Marlowe—do we know what she does for a living?"

"No. I didn't get much farther than discussing Swaffham with her."

"I wondered, since it's a personal connection, a purely unofficial interest, whether you'd care to invite her here for a meal?"

"I'll think about it. Thanks, Nan." It did seem a solution to the stretched-timetable problem, and Nan's direct involvement could well provide a new dimension to the pursuit. Yeadings discussed it with her that evening, after Sally had been put to bed for the third time. Her first reappearance downstairs was to report a non-existent mosquito in her room; the second, to demand a glass of water which she would probably leave untasted.

"Did something go wrong at the Friendly Club today?" Mike asked, after he'd firmly shut the door on his final good nights.

"Not more than usual. Some of the children there are always a little fractious. No, I think she's picked up our vibes. She knows we're a bit unsettled."

"It's the Swaffham thing intruding. Maybe you should ring his daughter as you suggested. Get her here, air the whole business. I've written out her new number. Do it now, Nan."

But Felicity Marlowe was tied up for the next three days, so it was Sunday lunch they agreed on. "We might go for a family picnic if it's fine," Nan warned her. "So wear something that won't spoil."

"Did you explain about Sally?" Mike asked anxiously.

"No. Sally's used to people doing a double-take. If you make a fuss about it, newcomers think Down's syndrome is worse than it is."

Casual Nan, protective at a wiser level than himself with his overt anxiety, Mike thought. Fortunately no one needed warnings about baby Luke. At four months he was milky and docile, just beginning to chortle, a plump, bald, perfectly normal young Yeadings.

If he had feared that the family atmosphere might overwhelm the lone girl, Mike was proved amply wrong. Initially shy with Nan and a little uncertain as Sally took her by the hand for a tour of the garden, she was soon chatting to her, bending to catch the monosyllabic answers, peer into an open paeony or stroke a fuzzy leaf which the little girl brought to her notice. She admired Luke bouncing in his harness, suspended from a doorway like a miniature parachutist in his red jumpsuit.

A sudden heavy shower killed the picnic notion. "It's no pleasure driving miles to sit in the car to eat," Nan decided.

"No problem. We'll scout out somewhere dry, won't we, Sally?" Mike countered. He handed her the little basket with the thermos flasks, picked up the cold box and they tramped several times round the lounge, hand-in-hand. It was clearly a much-practised operation. Sally grew more excited with every second. Yeadings suddenly stopped. "Where, do you think?"

Sally pulled her hand free and pointed to the centre of the room, deposited the basket, tore off her sandals and swooped on the carpet, rolling in glee. Before Nan could intervene, Felicity had removed her own shoes and squatted alongside. "Cloth first,"

Nan reminded them, shaking it out of its folds. Everyone fell to, setting out the feast.

"This reminds me of school," Felicity said, half-way through the meal. "Midnight junketings in the junior dorm, with smuggled goodies."

"That must have been fun," Nan responded. "We missed all that at day school."

"Fun. Yes, it was, at first." Felicity sobered. "Until we were fifth-formers. Then there used to be illicit guests, boyfriends shinning up the drainpipes. I suppose it was mild enough, but we thought they were absolute orgies. It spoiled a lot of friendships. We split into those who did and those who didn't. Quite apart from sheer funk in case Authority discovered what was going on, I just couldn't. The others convinced me I was frigid."

"When you simply felt private?" Nan seemed to understand completely. "Is that why you married so young?—to prove you were like everyone else?"

Felicity nodded. "And to get back at my father. He seemed not to need me, so I was giving him some of the same. I didn't understand then that we were both essentially shy people, both private in the same way."

"And it didn't work out, the early marriage?"

Felicity pulled a comic face. "Later, we dismissed it as Further Education. I came out of it tougher, and a little more cautious, I think."

"Someday you'll try it again, for different reasons."

"Maybe, but a long way ahead."

"And meanwhile, what do you do? Workwise, I mean," Mike blundered, fearing she'd think him curious about her sex-life.

"I took a drama course. I get little jobs—TV adverts, some modelling on film. Now and again I'm offered a real stage part with actual speech. That's the dizzy heights! It sounds unlikely, after I've admitted I'm shy, but I'm really happy on a stage. Being someone else releases me from being myself. It takes away my inhibitions." She smiled, mocking herself, and again Mike thought he saw her father in her.

The sun came out and dried off the white-painted garden furniture on the steaming terrace. The party moved out through the open patio doors. Sally scrambled up to see the miniature lakes in

Nan's hanging baskets of fuchsias. While baby Luke snored gently on in his carry-cot, Mike, lingering over his coffee, was crimping and moulding his fingers between parted knees.

Recognizing familiar symptoms, Nan said, "You want to get at the garden, don't you? Well, why not?—so long as we others are allowed to be lazy."

He grinned apologetically and accepted his dismissal, reappearing in deplorably baggy cord trousers and rolled-up sleeves at the far end of the left-hand fence, wielding a garden fork.

Nan explained about his battle with the weeds. "We get nettles coming under from next-door. While the soil's damp he can pull them up by the yard."

"Nice, having a garden," Felicity envied.

Later, Mike set up his powered "mangle" to chew up the weeds for his compost heap. He ran the cable back to his shed and held up a warning finger to Sally before switching on.

The child cried out, "Ooh, ooh, *ooh!*" and shook her fingers violently.

"That's to show us she knows she mustn't touch," Nan explained. Mike switched on the power. Nettles, dandelions, chickweed and the odd bramble came noisily spewing out of the machine in a homogeneous chopped green salad.

Smoking his pipe in the dusk, after Felicity had driven off, Mike said to Nan, "Know what I was thinking, working on the garden? All that destruction, grubbing up weeds: the sort of thing Swaffham did with people—terrorists, traitors, moles. I appreciate what he meant about some good being wasted along with the bad. You can't help it at times. Pruning's the same. With gardening you've got to be ruthless. Underneath all his skill and deviousness, Swaffham had a gentle conscience. It made him melancholy. But he did a good job, for all that; made the world a safer place."

"Felicity was very fond of him. She's desolate that he's gone," Nan said quietly. "We talked quite a bit once the children were in bed. She's going to see his GP, ask him just how long the specialist had given him."

"Thanks, love. It's a start."

That night when Yeadings began to dream, it was about his own hands in heavy gardening gloves, groping among the yellow roots of nettles, but as he pulled they came out as yard after yard of snaking, plastic-sheathed cable. He followed one to its end and there was Felicity holding the three-pin plug to Mike's own weed-mangler. She tore it off and showed him the separated wires inside. "And that's me," she said loudly, showing him one, but he couldn't see which because it had started to rain, and then everything dissolved into green pulpy refuse.

Next day all was suddenly activity on the crime-busting front, after a lull when statistics had deceptively implied a higher moral tone prevailing in Thames Valley. Yeadings was called out to an overnight break-in at a bonded warehouse where the thieves had escaped with a fortune in liquor, leaving one guard hovering between life and death, his skull smashed in by a pick handle.

Within two hours of his return from the scene of this crime, a car was reported half-submerged in a quarry off the A4, with the decomposing body of a girl in the boot. Then the following morning a crazed middle-aged man with a shotgun held two women and three small children hostage in a semi-detached on a housing estate at Earley.

Serious Crime had had to call on uniform branch for support on the first two investigations and, already thin on the ground, now needed marksmen. The gunman was meeting all attempts to talk him out with bursts of wild firing, and appeared to have unlimited 12-bore ammunition. A neighbour who knew the house where they were holed-up reported a well-stocked freezer there in the scullery off the kitchen. It could be a long and demanding haul if reason was to prevail and the hostages be safely recovered.

Yeadings consulted with the Home Office psychiatrist sent to advise him, and spent much of the next day and a half cramped in a communications truck in a parallel road. From time to time when the gunman refused to continue their telephone conversations, Yeadings would come out in the open, megaphone in hand, to parley and risk being peppered with shot. It was really the job for a more junior officer, but he had dealt with hostage situations twice before and experience counted. Between sallies he snatched the odd pub meal brought him on a tray, stretched out on a folding bed unsuited to his thirteen stone bulk, and stone-walled against the theoretical approaches suggested by various members of his team.

In the end he triumphed over the dog-handlers, tear-gas enthusiasts, SAS fans *et al.,* by stomping out unshaven in jeans and stained pullover, waving a far-from-white handkerchief to gain admission and obtain a close meeting free of media and public attention.

As he'd hoped, what won the day was his closeness in age to the man under pressure, and a similar capacity—when not amplified for all to hear and titter at—to beef gently about his own (fictional) hard lot. For a little over two hours, inside the siege house, the two men talked their way through crisis and back to near-normality, Yeadings from time to time showing his broad back at the upstairs window on which the marksmen had their 7.62s trained.

The break came at a little after the thirty-fourth hour of the siege when Yeadings slowly approached the open window and dropped out the shotgun. At the same moment the front door opened and the two women edged out, the children in a bemused huddle between them. Even then there was more waiting while the man faced up to this new failure after the immediate relief of giving in. He still needed Yeadings as his contact through the formalities, until he was accorded the blessed chance to sleep.

Nan had avoided the television all that long day, for fear of news flashes alarming Sally. She relied instead on incoming phone calls, when either Angus or another of the DIs on the case could find time for progress reports. She knew, as darkness came on for the second night, that this would be the crisis. Either Mike would bring it off or the police would have to move in. Whichever way, the man's nerve might go, and she could be a widow in an instant.

But, with Sally asleep and the baby given his last change and feed, she was free to see the second half of the ten o'clock news. And there it was, coming over live: Mike's bulky silhouette against the square of yellow light; some long object being dropped into the dark garden below; the front door slowly opening and the escapers huddled there a moment, then running into the arms of other dark figures springing up from among the bushes.

"Thank God," Nan said fervently, willing the cameras to turn again on the upstairs window, but they only gave her the close-up of the fastspeak commentator, smugly on-the-spot, proudly recapping the success as though it was all his own doing.

Well, for Mike it wouldn't be over for quite a long time. Maybe by dawn he'd make it home to his bed.

When he came in, heavy-footed and bleary-eyed, he simply kissed Nan and grinned at the steaming kettle. "Tea and a bath," he said. "My idea of heaven. Then bed."

"And the man?" Nan asked.

Yeadings rubbed his chin, shrugged. "Stress," he dismissed it. "There's a lot of it about, but he'll get some sort of help now."

3

There had been little progress in the other two main inquiries while Yeadings was tied down in his endeavour to prevent a further homicide statistic. Now that the Earley siege was over, and the incident logged as an aggravated domestic one with medical overtones, he could pass it on to others—notably the psychiatrist and local uniform branch who would follow up the unlawful discharge of firearms and whatever they made of the hostage business. Given some luck, good counselling of the mother-in-law (or rather mother-out-law, since the man had never actually married the younger woman he held at gunpoint) plus Social Services' help with the children and in offering some ultimate hope of employment, the problem could now be carried on the broad back of the taxpayers.

Less could be done for the dead girl found in the boot of the partly submerged car in the quarry, although sightings would doubtless be reported from as far away as Exeter and Oban now that the artist's reconstruction of her face had been prepared for the national press.

The preliminary report from the pathologist gave manual strangulation as the immediate cause of death. No surprise to anyone who'd been obliged to view the body as discovered, Yeadings considered. What was startling was her previous condition. The girl had also suffered severe bruising, a badly torn left leg and a dislocated ankle, consistent with a fall from a height. There was plenty of room there for surmise on how she had come to fall and on to what kind of surface. She had been fully clothed except for shoes, and there had been no sexual interference. She was—comparatively rare for a teenage female victim of violence—*virgo intacta.*

At the report's end Galbraith had scrawled, "To be continued in our next," with his initial; for all the world as if it were the first instalment of a serial romance. The superintendent grunted. For him the prime query was why she had had to be killed at all when in such a pitiable state. Because the girl's arrival at a hospital must reveal some criminal's identity? Because undoubtedly she would talk when questioned? Or simply because she had to be killed in any case and her earlier injuries had resulted from an attempted flight from her murderer?

He was getting a strong impression that the murder wasn't a crime that stood on its own. There was no element of sex, so to some perverted criminal mind this taking of a young life could be merely a part of the whole, an attempt at cover-up by removal of a witness. It could still be a domestic case—the majority of violence against the person, whether officially reported or not, came from within the family. The Incident Room had been set up in the mission hall of Ledster village, with Chief Superintendent Faraday as senior investigating officer. Yeadings quickly checked on the state of other outstanding cases before working through the reports already accumulating on the murder. Eventually he looked up from a welter of paper and sighed. " 'Make a précis,' they used to tell us, and they'd chuck us the second leader from *The Times:* O-level stuff. We'd cudgel our brains over reams of waffle, to find there was only one solid sentence in the lot. The rest was verbal polystyrene."

"Good training for police work," Mott grunted back, plotting a route over an ordnance survey map.

"Not so good, because here, although you can reduce the verbiage, facts are the main body. They proliferate, breed like fruit flies. Mothball one and that's bound to be the very thing the case hangs on."

Mott lifted his head and looked reflective. "Mothballed fruit flies. Sounds like a Far Eastern delicacy."

"A Thames Valley potential error," Yeadings retorted darkly. "And watch it, lad. Since that law degree of yours you're a damn sight too literal. Which prompts me to ask, how's the delectable Paula?"

It wasn't the non sequitur it sounded. Paula had taken her London LL.B. at the same time, but as a full-time student, while Angus slogged more lengthily in his precious free hours. They had met at the degree ceremony just over a year ago and now were engaged to marry.

"As you said, Mike, delectable. And flourishing."

Yeadings *hrrmp*ed. "I wondered, would it upset things if I diverted your attention to another young lady? Not an official interest, although it might eventually become so." He paused a moment. "On the Met's patch."

Angus was watching him, alerted like a dog who scents a promise of walkies.

"The Felicity Marlowe you traced for me to a flat in Fulham. She's a young actress. As I told you, I knew her father, recently dead. Had her to the house for a meal last week. I'd like to know if she's quite the innocent she appears. D'you think you could casually run across her?"

The young DI tapped his front teeth with a ballpen. "Devious, aren't we? Suppose I get Paula in on it. Any risk? They could meet up in a more likely way, living in the same area. Two girls at the laundromat or whatever; then, enter the fiancé, profession unspecified, and all off together for a drink?"

"Sounds about right. No overtime in it for you, but I'll cover any expenses myself."

"What, pay for Paula's smalls to be washed? Over my dead body! But any time Nan's short of takers for her pot roast—"

"You're on, both of you. Give Paula my best respects, will you? Meanwhile, back at the break-in . . ."

They went on shifting paper, typed-up summaries from computer printouts, Yeadings cagily redistributing in his police-issue chair middle-aged muscles stiffened by the long, cramped wait in the van during the gunman's siege. He would have liked to take a few days off, get Nan, Sally and the baby down to the sea while the weather stayed warm, but the workload wouldn't permit it. Nevertheless, if nothing startling came to light before five-thirty he might well steal away while the routine moves of the murder inquiry rolled, and do some necessary thinking on the patio at home, a long glass of something chilled in his hand.

It was there, with the sliding doors to the lounge open and Nan inside half-watching some American soap opera which he professed to despise but was careful to keep up with vicariously, that he heard her urgent call. "Mike, quick! It's Felicity!"

It was an intervening advertisement for shampoo, and a slight blonde in diaphanous veils was floating in slow motion through a fairy-tale wood dappled with sunlight, her long, golden hair streaming out erotically behind.

"Can't be," was his instant reaction; then the policeman took over. "Of course, with a wig . . . If it is, it's downright deception," he complained.

The nymph-girl turned full-face, threw back her head and ran her hands sensuously up through her hair. The creamy strands floated slowly apart, shining like polished wood grain. In close-up the cameras and lights were doing everything but putting star-filters on it.

"It's not technically fraud," Nan said in her practical way. "Nowhere does it claim that's real hair, or belongs to the model it's shown on."

"Nor has it been shampooed by this Glynt stuff? But when you know it's a put-up job, would you go out and buy it, Nan?"

"Might well do. It's a form of welcome flattery to the pedestrian, housebound nappy-washer. Oh Mike, your face! I'm not serious!"

"I'll bounce you, madam!" he threatened, reaching for her. "When did you ever have to depend on fantasies?"

"Actually," she admitted, when she had recovered from the smothering between settee cushions and Mike's hard chest, "there's a bottle of Glynt up in the bathroom cabinet. I thought I'd give it a whirl, but I hadn't noticed before who the girl on the label was."

"I do believe you're right, love. I guess I'd better give Angus a buzz. He's going to fix it for Paula to run into Felicity, and this might provide an excuse to start the conversation rolling."

Nan pulled back and scanned his face. "With what in mind, Mike?"

"I was curious, that's all. Even more so now that I've seen her in her war-paint. It will help to have a contemporary's opinion, and I value Paula's. And I'm afraid I've let you in for standing Angus and Paula a meal on the strength of it."

"Any time," Nan said cheerfully. "They light the place up. And they have fun bathing young Luke while I put my feet up. Mind you, the bathroom's awash at the end of it, but it does tire the little beggar out ready for bed."

Familiar music blared to introduce the late news, and they settled to hear the headlines. The strangled girl's body from the car boot had been demoted from national to Thames local items, for want of fresh details. "Tomorrow," Mike promised, "we'll get special coverage when the artist's impression is issued."

"And no one's reported her missing?" Nan said sadly. She had come across many cases of family neglect during her nursing years at the Westminster, but it never failed to move her to pity. It was partly for Nan's sake that Mike attempted to switch off his profession when he reached home.

In this particular case it wasn't easy, because of the frustration of knowing that further scientific tests must be run before there could be any fruitful investigation. Nor was there yet any indication of where to start looking for a height of the sort the girl could have fallen from. The quarry itself was no more than a shallow, water-filled gravel pit which, in this dry period, accounted for the car not having disappeared completely from view. There were no nearby church towers or two-storeyed houses, and the only high ground was the rounded Chiltern hills.

The car itself provided their main hope of determining the route it had taken to reach the gravel pit. Efforts were being made to obtain its identification, made more difficult by the use of false number plates belonging originally to a red Renault written off after a motorway crash near Newport Pagnell two months previously. The murder car itself was an eight- or nine-year-old tan Cortina partly resprayed and poorly maintained.

"How long had the girl's body been there?" Nan asked, cutting across his musings.

"Further tests on the car may determine that," Yeadings told her. "But the preliminary estimate is that she'd been dead between twelve days and three weeks. It's imprecise because the lab people can only make educated guesses at temperatures inside the car boot, due to so many contributory factors—a period of warm weather, the cooling effect of static water, food taken, the action of body gases. You know how it is."

"And you can't pinpoint any local girl of that age group disappearing so many days ago?"

"We're not short of young females on the UK list of missing persons, but no one similar from nearer than Bristol or Morpeth."

"So possibly no one has yet noticed she's missing. But a sixteen-year-old? She'd hardly be a recluse."

"Sixteen-year-olds can be bloody independent, announce one intention and then go off in the opposite direction. If the parents have split up, each may assume she's staying with the other. Anything can happen before they think to check up. Or if she's into flat-sharing, she may have gone off with a boyfriend. Her buddies certainly wouldn't want to start a hue and cry. Play it cool is the recognized fashion. Which is what we should do ourselves, Nan. How about a dram and a sandwich before we turn in?"

Half-way through their snack the demands of the dead girl were overtaken by those of a living one. The phone rang, and it was Felicity Marlowe, impatient at the lack of progress in solving her father's puzzle.

"I've made up my mind," she said abruptly. "I'm going to Prague. It seems the most likely place to start."

"Don't be hasty," Yeadings counselled. "It's not what your father would have wished."

There was a brief silence while the girl considered this. "Well, anyway, I shall apply for a visa on Monday. As a tourist. It will take a few days to come through, I expect, which gives me time to rethink if anything comes up at this end."

Yeadings rounded off the conversation with a couple of paternal platitudes and replaced the receiver with a wry expression. "She's threatening me. 'Get on with it, or else!' I'd better warn Angus to put Paula on to her right away."

He made the call and was assured that Paula was ready and willing. She had even improved on the original laundromat plan. Felicity habitually shopped at the local supermarket on Friday evenings, paying by cheque. This information came easily from the manager when Paula produced a leather purse with three pound coins inside and suggested who might have dropped it in Hollywood Road.

Today being Thursday, Paula would attempt the encounter next evening, tackling it on her own since Angus was tied up with the body-in-the-boot case.

Yeadings had his doubts, but Nan was full of confidence. "Paula's very enterprising," she claimed, "and her head's screwed on the right way. Felicity couldn't make a better connection."

But she was her father's daughter, and Swaffham had never trusted anyone without a rigorous examination of his motives, Mike remembered.

Paula had her scenario roughed out. It involved the use of an abandoned shopping trolley with a bent axle, which had missed being thrown out and stuffed at the back of a dark cupboard. With a little effort she was able to remove one wheel, then sandpapered the shaft to a shiny perfection that would ensure the thing's coming apart at will, with minimum tilt. She practised up and down the vinyl flooring of the flat's kitchen until she was sure she had complete control. The only difficulty she met when the encounter actually came off was in keeping the thing in one piece, loaded with groceries, until the moment of impact as Felicity Marlowe left the supermarket, letting the electronically operated door swing back and create chaos.

The line she had decided on was one of slightly flustered reassurance that no lasting damage had resulted. Felicity was civil but detached. Without absolving herself verbally, she managed to imply that it was primarily the fault of the moving door. "It should have been a sliding one," she arbitrated.

"A design fault." Paula seized on it, nodding. She pulled a wry face. "I sometimes think I'm a bit of a one myself." She proved the point by fumbling as she picked up a bag of long grain rice, putting a fingernail through one corner and causing a stream of small white seeds to go bouncing around her on the pavement.

"You'd better get yourself a carton," Felicity suggested drily. "They're in a bin just inside. I'll stay here and watch the rest of your stuff."

Getting in by the electrically operated Out door gave Paula further scope for borderline inadequacy. Mustn't overdo it, she warned herself, stepping round a buxom woman, heavily laden, who appeared to suspect she was bent on some improper action against the check-out points. She made sure that the selected box had a firm bottom, brushed off the offer of help from a sympathetic shelf-loader and returned to where Felicity waited, her own carton of supplies at her feet. They both retrieved the scattered goods and packed them into the new box.

"What will you do with your trolley?" Felicity inquired, sounding amused despite herself.

"Ah." Paula glanced round with comic furtiveness. "Charity, don't you think? Suppose I just park it, would someone with practical hands benefit, do you think?"

Felicity smiled. "One man's junk—"

"—is another man's treasure. Precisely. I honestly feel that it and I are totally incompatible."

"My car's opposite," Felicity offered. "On the double yellow lines. We should just have time to pull away before the traffic warden gets back."

After that it was easy. When they reached the street door to Paula's top-floor flat, she expressed her thanks. "Look, one thing I don't make a mess of, and that's coffee. Will you take your chance?"

It would have been rude to refuse, even with frozen goods left in the sun-warmed car. "Maybe a quickie," Felicity said, and went up with her to the flat Paula shared with two final-year engineering students, then fortunately away.

She was easy to talk to, and sincerely interested in Paula's brief account of her career to date. She admitted to being a small-time straight actress. "Between resting," she offered wryly. She went on to describe various parts she had taken and the reasonably important role she was rehearsing at present. "A series for Yorkshire Television, due to be screened in the autumn. She's rather dizzy, this character. A sweet spanner-thrower in others' good works. A minor part, but it has to work to make the story credible."

She shrugged, modest and rather throwaway about her own efforts. Then she cocked her head and challenged, "As an up-and-coming barrister you must be a character actress yourself to some extent."

"Any good, do you think? As one professional to another."

"I can't tell on such a brief meeting."

Paula got up and turned to the window, frowning in thought. She had this urge to level with the other girl. It could be fatal, but there was a chance it might earn her some respect, make them closer as a result. She turned back, head tilted assessingly, arms folded, hands cupping her bare elbows. "You should be able to tell. I set you up, you see. We didn't meet by chance at all."

She saw alarm spring up in the other girl's eyes and put out a steadying hand. "With the best of motives. But I don't want to go on deceiving you. Let me come clean."

"Go on." The voice was low, apprehensive.

Paula held up her left hand. "I'm engaged to a copper. A detective-inspector, Thames Valley force." She saw Felicity's dawning realization. "Yes, his boss is Mike Yeadings. They thought I might be of some use to you, seeing we're almost neighbours."

"He told you . . ."

"In strictest confidence. He isn't at all happy about you going to Prague."

Felicity was quite still, considering this. "But out there, they won't have any idea who Felicity Marlowe is. All the correspondence I had was as Miss F. Day Maskell. The same surname Daddy was using."

"Have you applied for your visa yet?"

"I'm going to do it on Monday."

"They'll check up on you. It doesn't look right, someone like you travelling alone behind the Curtain as a tourist."

"My passport says I'm an actress."

"How many actresses do you know who would take a non-package holiday alone, where there are no sunny beaches, they can't speak a word of the language and no one ever gets royalties out?"

"I must go, Paula. I'll just have to take my chance. They can't do me any harm, even if they find out who my father was. He's dead, and they know that. He never let me have restricted information about what he was involved in. I'll merely be there for family reasons, retracing the last days of a man I was very fond of."

"They'll suspect something ulterior. If you're really determined to go, you need a cover story first which will keep them thinking of you as Felicity Marlowe, Actress. Something linking you to Czechoslovakia."

"There is no connection except my father."

"Then we have to make one. Supposing—" She narrowed her eyes, searching her memory for an elusive name. "That's it!—the Winter Queen. There was a book by Carola Oman about Elizabeth Stuart, daughter of James I and VI, who reigned for a year as Queen of Bohemia before the Habsburgs drove them out."

"It sounds vaguely familiar, but how does it help me?"

"It's going to be your great chance for a star role! Let's think. The working script hasn't been issued yet, and you're over there in advance to get the feel of the place, do the round of the old palaces, have a look at whatever regalia remains."

Felicity nodded, catching on to the idea. "Get Cedok enthusiastic about it—that's their Intourist equivalent—and maybe they'll give me a little red carpet of my own. Paula, you've got something there! Only who shall I say is writing the play? They may check on whether it's true."

"You'll think of someone. It would make marvellous TV anyway. Maybe Superintendent Yeadings could use his influence to leak the story to the theatre-gossip press."

"I could do that myself. I know the right people. If I really think, I'll probably find the very person who could write a script if I can manage a résumé. But first I have to get hold of the book and learn it off. Give me the title again."

Unaware that Paula, instead of restraining Felicity's intention to follow in her father's wake to Prague, would even gallop alongside and put a spur to the project, Mike Yeadings was over with Forensic, poking into matters that were of specialists' concern. One of the scientists raised his head from a microscope long enough to recognize him as he entered.

"Packet of photographs for you on my desk," he volunteered.

Yeadings went across and emptied them out. They were enlargements of parts of the clothing the dead girl had been wearing.

Several showed a flat background with long, curving stems across it. "Horse hair?" he queried.

"Dog."

"Any particular breed?"

"Very particular. Nothing less than an Afghan hound. The dead lass had friends with upmarket tastes. Thanks to my own daughter's fanatical interest in dogs I've built up a comprehensive set of micro-slides for recognized breeds."

It sounded like a case where the Kennel Club could give help. If they provided the address of the breed society's secretary, he could be pressed for the list of registered members. Since it concerned the murder of a minor, he would hardly refuse to cooperate.

Yeadings went out into the enclosed space where the abandoned Cortina was being given a minute going-over. Angus Mott was hunkering beside the headlights. "Seeing it's been tinkered with, let's have a look at the back of the number-plates, Joe."

They waited while these parts were removed. The police mechanic laid them out on the inspection bench. He grunted. "Wrong first time round," he said sourly, pointing to the reverse side where bright marks scored the dirty surface. "It's not a simple swap of plates. This one's been jiggered. Look at them scratches."

"How so?"

"Letters and figures rearranged. Not all of them. These two and those there. Anybody do anagrams?"

Angus copied the possible combinations into his notebook. "Could even have been taken from a car of the current registration letter." He underlined one number on the page.

"I think you've got something there. That would account for the good condition of the metal. It hasn't had the wear and tear of the car by any means."

Yeadings watched as the DI walked over to their Rover and radioed the new registration through for the National Police Computer. Almost as soon as he had his pipe alight and pulling well, Angus was back with the information.

"It could well be the one. It's from another car reported stolen ten days ago. Blue Mercedes. Owner's an Adrian Whittle. Address in Highgate."

4

It was left to the Met to contact the owner of the blue Mercedes, but Angus Mott went along to observe. The house in Highgate was the end villa of a three-storey Victorian row, with a ten-foot brick wall separating its driveway from the narrow side street. The tall, bent iron gates stood open, and a patch of untended grass indicated that this was their normal position. An indifferent selection of shrubs, grown into a solid green mass interrupted only by the long windows, masked the dark red brickwork of the ground-floor exterior for its full depth. Beyond that point the driveway took a right-angled turn, and a faded, blue-painted timber door hinted at the first of a block of rear garages serving the entire row of houses. It struck the Thames Valley man that any craving for modernity that the resident had must be channelled into the car reported stolen.

The sallow-faced housekeeper who opened the front door informed them that Mr. Whittle was expected back for lunch within half an hour. The Met detective-sergeant announced his intention to wait, and they were shown into a gloomy book-lined room with two long sash windows overlooking the drive and side wall bounding the property.

"Rather quiet out here all day, isn't it?" Angus asked ingenuously, smiling at the woman. "Don't you have a dog for company?"

She declined to thaw out, turning on him tragic, shadowed eyes which reminded him of that TV actress who did concentration camp victims and French Resistance parts. She gave considerable thought to what answer to give him. "Mr. Whittle is not fond of animals," she admitted at last. "All the doors and windows have very good locks." She waited, unsmiling, for any further demands or queries and when they failed to come she reached for the door-handle and went quietly out.

"They are good too," Sergeant Mepham agreed, running his hand up and down the window-frames. "Plus the best alarm system money can buy. She's taken us for Crime Prevention officers."

Mott grunted and began reading titles along the library shelves. Little-used hardcover editions of the sub-classics. Nothing eye-catching, but then they weren't looking for a porno-type. The girl hadn't been interfered with. Just "decently" strangled. And if she'd picked up the dog hairs in this house the beast had since been removed. There hadn't been a single bark when the doorbell shrilled.

Ten minutes short of the expected time of Whittle's return, a red Peugeot turned in from the road, passed under the windows and parked at some invisible point at the rear. Distant voices sounded inside the house, coming closer. Then the door was flung open and a man came bouncing in on his toes. He was tall, with angular, forward-thrusting shoulders, and he was literally rubbing his hands with glee. "My car? You've found it? Thank God. This one I'm using is a swine."

"Mr. Whittle? Mr. Adrian Whittle?"

"Yes, yes. Of course I'm Whittle. I suppose I'm expected to go and pick it up myself? Or is it damaged?"

"Your car, sir, reported missing. Can you give us its registration number?"

The man frowned. He pushed forward his flat, curiously blunt-featured face and Mott saw that his eyes, magnified by thick lenses, were the green of ripe gooseberries. He reeled off the number. "Well?" His eagerness was tinged now with tetchy impatience. "Where was the car found? I take it it *has* been found?"

"Not all the car, sir."

"So they've vandalized it! Or was it in a smash? What's missing?"

The two detectives were watching expressionlessly. "Most of it, sir. All we have is the licence plate."

The man stared, mouth agape. One hand fluttered towards his chest, stopped there, fingers spread hopelessly. "Well, what good is that? I can't drive a bloody number-plate! Still, if they threw it away, fixed another one, the car had to be sometime where you found the thing. Can't you—"

"—guess where someone went joy-riding in it? It's not that simple, sir. And the licence plate went runabout too. You wouldn't really care for the car we found it attached to."

"Oh, I see. So you haven't any good news for me after all?"

"Not unless you know anyone who's lost a tan-coloured Cortina, eight or nine years old, partly resprayed."

"I don't think so. Where did it end up?"

"In Berkshire. A little place called Ledster."

"Can't say I've ever heard of it. Well, that's disappointing. We haven't been much help to each other, have we?"

"Early days yet, sir. These things take time. Eventually some observant garage mechanic may spot your engine number—if it hasn't been spirited abroad already. That's mostly what happens to quality cars."

Superintendent Mike Yeadings continued to check on progress at the Incident Centre before driving back to divisional station to set in motion the Kennel Club inquiry. He had put a "not for publication" restriction on paperwork concerning the discovery of dog hairs on the girl's clothing. It could pay to keep some details under covers, especially with the press shadowing young coppers on unaccustomed plainclothes duty, offering to stand them rounds from apparently bottomless pockets. Another fact the public hadn't yet access to was the girl's physical condition prior to the strangling. His secret hope now was to tie in an Afghan hound with a house which had a broken balcony above a freshly laid macadam drive. Tar streaks had marked the striped blouse and blue skirt the dead girl had been wearing, but there was no broken glass that might have come from a window.

"Well?" he demanded, when Inspector Mott returned from the Highgate interview.

"Three-storey house, gravel drive and shrubs below, no dog," Angus said succinctly.

"And the man Whittle?"

"Hopeful, impatient, apprehensive, disappointed. Got it all in the right order. No reaction to description of the tan Cortina. Claims he'd never heard of Ledster, which isn't surprising."

"So we can safely scrub him?"

Mott hesitated a moment, and Yeadings looked up, scanning his thoughtful face. "I guess so."

"But—?"

"Caught a glimpse of him in the driving mirror as I pulled away."

"Ah. Not glum enough?"

"Just momentarily, and I'm not even certain what I saw. But I thought—a touch smug, that's what."

"Any reason why he should be? Had he delivered himself of an anti-Bill spiel, flexed any political muscle?"

"No. As I said, his reactions were reasonable enough till then. Might have some private reason for wanting rid of the Mercedes, I suppose. Could find the insurance money came at a handy moment. He's running a much cheaper car in the meantime. Large house, old and rather dreary, good security locks, middle-aged housekeeper. Maybe he'd overstepped in buying a new Merc. Do you want us to run a further check on his background?"

"Let it ride for the moment," Yeadings decided after a moment's thought. "We're too thin on the ground for chasing will-o'-the-wisps. See what else turns up first. Log it, though. Add a small query."

Felicity Marlowe hadn't been idle between rehearsals. She had gone straight to work on the film fiction. As Angus Mott was driving away from the Highgate interview, she was being shown into an upstairs office in Wardour Street. "Benny," she said directly, "do me a favour, will you? I want to mug up some period stuff at the British Museum Library. I need someone with weight to sign my Reader's application."

He made the expected quip about weight, rolling himself in his chair from one fleshy buttock to the other, but his eyes were shrewd. "Period?" he queried, signing without question where she pointed. "Something in the wind then? Who's your backer?"

"It hasn't got that far. But there's a screenplay in the making, and I want to be on my marks. It's something I could do really well."

He ran his eyes swiftly over her body, but not licentiously. "First Napoleon stuff? Ancient Greece?"

She crowed with laughter. "Not drapery. Ruffs and farthingales. Big satin sleeves stiff with pearls. Velvet riding-habits, ostrich plumes. Lines with some character in them. How do you fancy me as a Princess Royal?"

"The young Elizabeth," he guessed gloomily. "It's been done too often. Give it a miss."

"Not Tudor. *Stuart!* Daughter of James the First, married the Count Palatine from Heidelberg, briefly the Winter Queen in Bohemia."

The little eyes almost disappeared in their fleshy wrinkles. "Yeah. Mother of Prince Rupert, no less! Thirty Years War," he said. Benny was a European all the way, however ignorant of specifically English history. "Exiled and widowed in the Netherlands. Rhineland locations. Who's handling the script?"

"Benny, I can't tell you. It's deadly secret. But he thinks I'm right for the young bride. It's a tremendous story, and I want to go deep, dig for the character. That's why—" She waved the slip of paper. "Promise you won't tell. It could be my big break, and I don't want anyone beating me to it. You'll be the first to know *if,* I promise. And anyway you'll look after my contract, won't you?"

He promised to not to let it go further, but she was confident he would. Just enough of the rumour to get it around, with no names mentioned except her own; all others—surmise. And if, *when,* she was challenged about it, she would act flustered, deny everything, admit only that she had discussed it in outline with Benny but it was deadly, deadly secret. That way, something was sure to show up in the theatre gossip columns. With luck, enough to back up her visa application.

She went to Cooks in Berkeley Street for travel information on Heidelberg and Prague. Once she'd convinced them that she didn't want a package tour she was taken to a young man with a positive mania for exclusive arrangements. He knew all about Eastern Bloc hotel bookings. "They make the decisions," he told her. "You can state a preference, but it doesn't guarantee you'll get it. If your visa application makes you sound like a VIP, a journalist or an author you'll probably be sent to the Alcron, just off Wenceslas Square. If you're TUC it will be somewhere more matey, in with the comrades. In Western Germany you have the normal choice, subject to availability, of course."

He seemed quite confident that her visa would be granted. "If they've any doubts about you, they just watch all the harder when you get there," he said happily. "What they really want is our sterling."

She gave him the dates she wished to travel and he laid out the timetables like a game of patience. To boost her story of the film part she decided to go first class: fly to Frankfurt, by train to Heidelberg, two days there and then by train again over the frontier. She hoped five days would be enough for all she needed to do in Prague, finally fly home direct. That last service, the Cooks young man told her, hadn't a first class. Class just didn't exist behind the Curtain. "We'll book it BA," he compromised, branding himself a patriot.

At the British Museum she was photographed—not bad for instant colour—and had her bag searched before they let her loose among the books. She spent almost two hours listing the titles she needed and skimming through volumes not easily obtainable outside, then took a taxi down Charing Cross Road to pick over the material on offer. When she arrived home, loaded with purchases, there was a note from Paula pushed through the letterbox, inviting her to eat out if she could confirm by 8 P.M.

She rang the number, to discover that Paula had been stood up by her fiancé and didn't see why she should cancel the table. Angus, who was supposed to be part of a Serious Crime squad, had a sudden rush of urgent work. "It was pretty garbled," Paula complained, "but from what I could gather, he seems to be looking for a lost dog!"

They agreed to go Dutch over the meal, use Felicity's car and return to Paula's flat afterwards. One of the students there had a renovated photocopier which would be handy for running off passages from the books.

They set up a programme of intensive study to keep Felicity occupied between rehearsals for the next four days. After that she had a whole ten days during which she wasn't required to appear. If the visa came through in time, that was when she would get away. Her provisional flight was already booked.

In the early hours of Sunday, Yeadings awoke in a cold sweat, to pitch dark, shaken by a frightful face in a nightmare. Nan, disturbed as he threw off the covers to grope about the floor for his slippers, mumbled some query. "Swaffham," she heard him say distinctly, and she sat up too. "What's happened?"

"I've been a fool. Had my mind too full of other matters." Even to Nan he couldn't put into words the horrific presence of the man in the dream that had woken him. A face of such open and raw passion, yet this was the man he had known as unnaturally controlled, distanced from humanity. It was as if he was now urgently demonstrating that all his lifelong suppressions were channelled into those last vital days before death, and all remaining energies directed towards one end, some act of reparation for an admitted wrong. All that psychic violence concealed in a laconic letter, and Yeadings had been too preoccupied to know it for what it was—the most poignant cry for help ever to be made to him. So he hadn't found time to comprehend, let alone formulate some way of dealing with it.

He sat on the edge of the bed, with his head in his hands, seeing still in his mind the agonized face of Swaffham from his dream. It was a fortnight since the man's death and no move made towards solving the puzzle he'd left behind. "I'm going to ring the girl," he said uncertainly.

Nan didn't try to dissuade him; she had met this before, his intuition breaking through logic and routine; the paralysing conflict as he tried to rationalize a seemingly senseless urge.

"I have to ring Felicity," he said, this time firmly. He reached for the receiver and pressed buttons.

Two-seventeen A.M. Nan, glancing at the clock-face, was aware that he hadn't paused to recall the girl's number. It was a complete boil-up of the subconscious. At any other time he would have had to search around for the note he'd made of it.

The call was answered on the third ring. Felicity's voice was low and calm. "It's all right," she assured him as he apologized for the hour. "I'm still up. Working at my history. The Elizabeth Stuart background." She hesitated, put on a touch of mock-modesty. "You know there's this film part I've been offered?"

She was being cautious, perhaps even afraid her line might be bugged. Well, with the security services alerted to Swaffham's death in Prague, it might well be the best course.

"Yes, I wanted to congratulate you. It could be something big."

He was glad she had recognized his voice at once, so he hadn't needed to give his name. "I don't know much about the lady in question, but it's a fascinating period. Protestant-Catholic struggles in Europe, and the Thirty Years War. Does your script start with the court of James in England?"

"I haven't seen the final screenplay. Don't want to before I've a firm idea what Elizabeth herself was like. But there's to be a child actress to start off, and I come in where Elizabeth is betrothed to the Count Palatine, and then the action moves to Heidelberg."

"Nice place to be on location, but the castle's only a shell now." He was filling in, following her lead.

"I guess we'll go across for some shots of the Rhine, but they'll do a studio mock-up here and outdoor shooting in Wales or Scotland, I expect. I'm trying to lay my hands on some of Elizabeth's correspondence, and I hope to make a flying visit to see what they've got in the library of Heidelberg University. All the portraits are there too, for the age and period I need."

No mention of Prague. She was still being cautious while gushing over the role supposedly on offer.

"Well, if you're soon to be off researching, I hope we get the chance to meet beforehand." He managed to sound regretful and slightly besotted.

She laughed casually, the pretty butterfly accustomed to evading would-be collectors. "We'll probably bump into each other. I'll give you a ring sometime, shall I?"

Don't ring me, I'll ring you. It couldn't have been plainer.

"Be sure you do." Sounding hopeful, but not confident, just one of her handful of admirers. He wished her good studying and then good night.

"Will she ring, d'you think?" Nan asked, having overheard most of the conversation.

"I'm sure of it. Before I'm down for breakfast, from a call-box where she can't be overlooked. That young lady has her wits about her. Wouldn't be Swaffham's daughter otherwise. All the same, I'm utterly opposed to her going behind the Curtain. She's working up a plausible reason, especially if her main visit is made to appear Germany, but they aren't fools in the old man's department. If they get to hear, and they could be agog already, it's bound to strike them as curiously coincidental."

"Switch off, Mike," Nan said softly, "and leave it till she rings."

He grunted. "I don't feel like sleep. Fancy a cup of tea? I'll go and put the kettle on."

She let him bumble about and trail off down to the kitchen, knowing that action of some kind was necessary for him before he could finally throw off the moment of startled waking and settle his unease.

5

Felicity rang at three minutes after seven, from the shop where she regularly bought fresh croissants. "Hi," she said briefly. "Where and when?"

"Same place as before," Yeadings suggested. "The coffee bar, ten-thirty?"

"Fine," she told him, and rang off.

This time she was at the inn first, seated in the low-beamed coffee lounge with the padlocked cage of the bar as background. She had chosen a family-sized table by a lead-light window and had watched him cross the forecourt, hidden herself by the chintzy curtain. There were two other tables occupied, one by a tight-faced young couple in the throes of a suppressed marital tiff. Over by the brick ingle-nook a three-generation group stood round their chairs, loaded with cameras, extra cardigans and tourist information, while they waited with crushing North American patience for someone to emerge from the kitchen with their packed lunches and coffee flasks.

"I've ordered our coffee," Felicity said casually as though they had been together for some time. "Ah, here it comes."

A slender lad with swarthy skin and long, pharaohesque eyes performed balletically with a tray and she thanked him with a smile before squaring up the cups and pouring. "Help yourself," and she nodded to sugar and cream jug. "I was going to get in touch with you myself. I've been to see my father's medical consultant."

"Was he helpful?"

Her mouth twisted wryly. "He meant to be. He saw it as his duty, to 'assist me in the process of grieving.' A digest psychologist as well as officially a leukaemia expert. The important thing was that he had given Daddy eight weeks. In fact he lived only three. That's a lot of difference, when a professional is so certain that he commits himself to quoting the precise time anyone has left. He was surprised himself, and embarrassed. He said in some cases you can almost name the hour, and he'd thought this was one. He had prescribed tablets for the whole period. I checked at the chemist Daddy always used, and he'd had the order made up. There was nothing left behind at the flat, so he must have had all he needed with him when he went abroad."

Yeadings nodded. Planning forward for eight weeks, but time running out. That surely meant leaving things unfinished, he allowed; but Felicity was still frowning over her coffee cup, following up the detail of the drugs. She shook her head. "But there was nothing of the sort in the things parcelled up and sent home from Prague. I sealed them all up again for you. They're in the back of my car now."

"Thank you." Yeadings reached inside his jacket for Swaffham's letter and smoothed it out on the table between them. They stared at it in silence, then he tapped one line with an index finger. "The date. May 1st. What's significant about that?"

"The day he went abroad. The day after he retired. He wasn't wasting any time. Not like me. I've let the grass grow for two whole weeks. Listen, I'm sure the real clues are out there. He never even came to say goodbye to me. Just as soon as he could get clear of the department's work, he was off."

"The department's work," Yeadings repeated. "And you wouldn't have any idea what that was, his final act for them?"

She looked at him steadily, through him to something beyond, as if she hadn't quite made up her mind, and he waited. "No," she said at last.

Because she was an actress, he couldn't be quite sure she had lied. "Well, perhaps when you've thought about it some more, you may be able to make a guess."

"He never confided in me. It was completely against his principles. He would have considered it compromised me."

Yeadings looked at her heavily. He knew how to make silence oppressive, but it didn't force her to the mistake of rushing in to fill it.

In fact she was exhibiting too much restraint, chary of himself who was supposed to be the ally. There came across this intimation of a political skill few girls of her age should have mastered. If only she hadn't been trained to the stage, reading her would have been easier.

He let a sigh escape him. "It could simplify things if I knew where he spent his last hours before leaving, who he was with, where he was, for example, when he wrote this letter to me, and how—if you never saw him that day—he managed to get it into your hands."

"He posted it from the airport, with your sealed envelope inside one addressed to me. There was no covering note. Instead he rang me before the plane went out. That's when he explained what to do. You were to have the letter if you came asking questions. Otherwise I was to wait the given time and destroy it."

"The given time being six weeks?"

"Six months."

"Ah yes. As you told me." He sat hunched, brooding over his own large hands as they went on pressing the fold of paper flat. "Before he caught the plane for Prague." It sounded like recapping, but he was still questioning her. The pause before she replied was sufficiently marked for her to hurry the start of her sentence.

"Actually, no. He flew Lufthansa to Frankfurt."

"He told you that himself?"

"No." Her voice was low, confessional. "I heard the public address system calling the Frankfurt flight and he said he had to go."

"Did you try to check his name with the airline afterwards?"

"No. I looked up the timetable, and it was the only suitable flight going out then."

Yeadings rubbed one wide-spanned hand over his eyebrows, making them stand up in black tufts. "There's something I don't understand here. Swaffham—your father—was about to do something of such importance to him that he took precautions to leave clues to it with us for use after his own death. But the note for me is anything but explicit, and he left writing it to the very last. Then the vital instructions about its delivery were *phoned* to you at the very moment of departure. Now tell me, what would have happened if he hadn't been able to get through? If you'd been out, or in the bath and not bothered?"

"There wasn't much risk. There would always be one telephone in use at Heathrow." Her voice had a touch of resentment in it. "And we had an arrangement. I was to be all morning at a certain house with an ex-directory number. That was the way he preferred to say goodbye. No tears, no fuss."

Her head was lowered, which muffled her voice. All he could see now was the pale, smooth hair falling symmetrically to either side of her forehead, and the central parting, its severe perfection marred at its end where a few strands had gone endearingly astray, erect from a little whorl like a calf-lick. Yeadings felt almost total father, but cynical enough still to recall that other girl with the synthetic hair, the Glynt nymph floating in slow motion through a sylvan dreamworld. If she could put on such a show for shampoo, how much more for something she was deeply involved in? How devious, in fact, must he believe her to be? How deceptive?

"Would there be another cup in that pot?" he asked bluffly.

She looked up, shocked, and he thought he glimpsed real pain before her confused apology for neglecting him. He went on staring as she poured, and recognized the signs of last night's late studying, mauve shadow faintly under the eyes, a single vertical line incised between the brows as though her head was far from clear.

"So now," Yeadings said, every inch the Old Bill, "you are off on the trail, with this spurious story about a film part you want background material for. How often does an unknown young actress chase a moonbeam like that?"

The girl pulled a face and pushed the filled cup towards him. "She doesn't. But the idiotic thing is that it has actually taken off, this idea Paula and I had. There really is a script being written, because I just happened to approach the right man at the right moment. He was boiling up to a creative high and he hadn't anything to work on. He's done some good work on a series about the Wars of the Roses with a research team's back-up for the historical material, and one pilot excerpt for a projected life of the first Duke of Marlborough. He'd just heard it was to be scrapped in favour of his arch-rival's romanticized life of Sarah Churchill, and in despair half-decided to have a go at the *Decameron*.

"Then I gave him a nutshell rundown on Elizabeth Stuart and he simply left the ground, went into orbit. He started straight in on it. Rushed to Granada with the synopsis and a sample scene. They've promised him an unspecified advance and a research assistant. I've offered to nip across to the Rhineland and Prague to see what's on offer there while he works on the script. When the casting comes up he's going to press for me to get the lead."

Yeadings would have sworn the enthusiasm was genuinely spontaneous, except that the lucky break had arrived so conveniently. "How is this romance going to stand up to examination?" he asked cynically.

She shook her head at this doubting Thomas. "Mike, it's real. It just is." It was the first time she had used his name since he suggested it, and it came out convincingly, as if they'd been familiar contemporaries. For some illogical reason that tipped the balance for him. He began to believe that the screenplay was truly on its way to becoming fact, and the girl might launch her serious career playing the Winter Queen.

"When do you leave?" he asked.

She gave a satisfied, closed-mouth smile. "On Friday. My visa's due Thursday from the Czechs. I've told them what I'm looking for and they've even offered to help. It's not a period of history the Commies are mad keen on, but they may put me in touch with some inspired academic when I get there. I hope so. As for Heidelberg, I've been given two names, one a professor of seventeenth- and eighteenth-century history, the other the head of the University's *Handschriften Abteilung* which looks after the documentation."

"And who was your source for them?"

She smiled serenely. "London University. I just walked into King's College in the Strand and asked if anyone in the history department had a contact in Heidelberg. Paula put me up to it."

"And they simply fell on your neck and started writing out addresses?" Yeadings marvelled. "What it is to be young and have charm!"

It was difficult to see what he could do to help anyone so confident and capable of fixing her own contacts. It remained for him simply to voice warnings, stressing that once it became apparent her quest was other than the historical one she advertised there could be trouble from two directions. First, the Czechs invariably resented any form of investigation into their contemporary practices. There was so much kept secret there, as yet unaffected by the mistrusted Russian *glasnost,* that by poking around she could unwittingly unearth some quite deplorable skulduggery. Even to seem ready to do so could provoke an incident. And secondly, even if Swaffham's one-time department wasn't already laying traps to keep her off some scandal of their own which he had been bent on bringing to light, they would have the added embarrassment of reclaiming her from the offended Czechs. She could end by being *persona* most definitely *non grata* almost anywhere you cared to mention. And there was always the chance that political relations could suddenly turn ugly for quite unrelated reasons and she be used as a pawn, with very uncomfortable consequences. It had happened to others before her, and there was no reason to suppose the world was suddenly a more genteel place.

"You don't need a policeman to tell you that it's only too easy to break the law even in the UK. Over there, there will be laws you don't know about, so be doubly scrupulous. Help no one, trust no one, carry no parcels, buy no purchases except at official agencies, guard your tongue at all times, make sure no one gets near enough to plant things in your pockets. Be careful where you eat and drink, preferably among plenty of neutral onlookers. Expect to be overheard at all times. What more can I say? Polonius act now over." He sat deflated, staring at her, aware what an owlish, aging object he must appear to her, and so not truly valid to her own experience.

She puckered the edges of her mouth, like a small child trying not to cry. "I told you before," she said accusingly. "You are like him."

"Did you ever tell him lies?" Yeadings asked, genuinely curious.

"Sometimes."

"And did he believe them?"

She stared back, round-eyed. "I never knew."

They went on facing each other out, neither sure what the other thought, but both suspecting. And suddenly Yeadings felt himself grinning, saw merriment come into the girl's eyes and then they were laughing aloud together.

"Look," he said, "two things. I want you to spend the last evening with Paula, at her place, before you go. I'll send her a list of coded messages for you to learn. It shouldn't be hard for an actress, just a few more lines. Write a postcard every day to some names I'll give you. A few extra if anything untoward happens. If you're determined to go through with this, then at least we'll have some idea what you're up to and if you need help.

"The other point is this. I need to know every move your father made in the last three or four days before he went abroad. He was a government official right up to then, and I need to know what most occupied his mind, if only to ensure that as a mere Plod I'm not caught interfering in affairs of state.

"Now you had recent access to him as a person, and you're pretty perspicacious. There must be things you observed without necessarily registering at the time, people he was seeing, places he went, arrangements he made. I need a clear picture of all this, because, don't forget, he claimed he'd 'contrived a device with a three-core lead,' and up to now you and he are the only leads I have at all. The earth wire, he said, was himself, and you are going after that one. But from somewhere in his recent interests you have to help me turn up another. Will you think about that and get in touch again? Before you go, ring me either at home or work from a random call-box."

She looked uncertain again and very young. He wondered if there was any way at all he could still persuade her not to pursue her search abroad, but already it was too late. She was pushing back her chair, standing up. "Thank you for everything. I have to fly now. There's the visa to pick up from the Czech Embassy, and I have to find a dress first for the part."

She must have caught some questioning look in his eyes, because she laughed and added, "Bourgeois starlet, stage-Queen Presumptive. I couldn't go looking like this."

" 'This' looks perfectly all right to me."

She shook her head. " 'This' is the negative, anonymous me, avoiding involvement, playing safe and unmemorable. Something quite different is required now. I want to create such a positive impression as the ambitious young actress straining after the big time that no one will ever see me as anything else. Acting for real.''

She reached up and gently kissed his cheek. "Love to Nan, Sally, Luke. I'll be ringing, as you said." She turned, fluttered her fingers from the door and went springily across the forecourt, pale hair bouncing on her shoulders, and never a backward glance.

She had forgotten the things parcelled for him in her car. Paying their bill, he watched her straighten as she put in the key, turn and look back towards the inn. "Spoilt your exit," he said flatly when he reached her. She pulled down the corners of her mouth, opened the rear door for him to help himself to the leather grip and the cardboard carton.

His arms loaded, he had a sudden impish desire to kiss her but refrained. "You'll be ringing," he reminded her and she nodded, slid into the driving seat, fastened her seat belt, switched on the ignition. " 'Bye, Polonius," she said saucily, tipped her chin and grinned. She went off like a rocket, with a teenage spurting of gravel under her wheels. Alternative exit. He wondered what she felt like inside.

"Well?" Nan softly demanded when he arrived home that evening. Both children were in bed and she had waited to have her own meal with him.

"Long day," he said, deliberately misunderstanding. "Not a lot of progress. Lions fifteen, Christians three."

She silently observed that that was a little more favourable than official police statistics, currently at eighteen percent solution rate for serious crime.

"And Felicity?"

"I wish I could decide how involved she is. She's set on stalking Swaffham's ghost, and all she burbles on about is this TV film part."

"Working herself into it," Nan assured him. "Has she a set programme for the trip?"

"Heidelberg for the background, with a couple of academics to contact at the university there. Then on to Prague."

"How?"

He considered her. She had paused before lifting a casserole from the oven, her hands enclosed in a continuous oven glove. "Yes, that's something I should have asked."

Nan continued with the serving of dinner, talking to him over one shoulder. "I had a look at the atlas this afternoon. Heidelberg has no airport. The most reasonable choice is Frankfurt, if she's decided to fly. Then she could go on by train or road. Would she hire a car, do you think?"

He had to admit to himself that because he had been so opposed to her going at all he hadn't allowed himself to imagine the detail as Nan had subjectively done. "I know nothing beyond the fact that Cooks in Berkeley Square are making the arrangements."

"If I rang them early tomorrow," Nan said slowly, "just to check they were making progress . . ."

She meant claiming to be Felicity herself. "You'd look silly if she'd already collected the tickets today."

"I doubt if there's been time to fix everything. They don't issue the bookings piecemeal. They wait until everything is complete and hand the whole thing over in a smart little folder. It's worth a try, Mike."

He grunted. "Can't do any harm."

"You don't have to know anything about it. I'll wait until you've gone to work."

"I'd be glad of your help about something else," he invited, and told her about the coded messages he'd promised to provide the girl with. "Things that read innocently off a postcard. I'll try to cover all possible situations that may arise. We can work it out together after the meal." He sniffed the rich aroma of the casserole. "What is it?"

"Lamb fillets done the Greek way. Just as well, seeing they've been in the oven over five hours!"

Nan was in luck when she rang up because the young man at Cooks who dealt with Felicity's bookings was in conference. The woman who gave her the information was unaware how well informed Miss Marlowe would be and so gave her the report in detail. The tickets themselves were ready to be picked up. Nan thanked her and left the notes she had made on the pad beside the telephone.

She had arranged for Sally to be met after Friendly Club that afternoon by a neighbour, and was to meet Paula at a coffee-house near Middle Temple at noon. Luke, being blessedly placid, made no demur at being strapped into the Vauxhall's rear, together with a lop-eared rabbit, and totally ignored as ballast. The M4 exercised its habitual effect on him and he awoke only for decanting into his pushchair on the Embankment.

As Nan had hoped, the unaccustomed presence of a small child among the wigs, robes and briefcases at the coffee-house ensured that their table was given a wide berth. She spread their belongings on the two spare chairs and composed herself to wait for Paula.

She was seven minutes late and came at a run, muttering imprecations on some anonymous litigious oaf. Nan felt she had strayed on to the set of a Rumpole production.

With her customary acuity Paula latched on to the arrangements for Felicity. She scanned the list of coded sentences. "Nothing difficult there," she agreed. "I'll check she's word-perfect. I've kept tonight free, and if she agrees to stay over, there's a spare bed."

She tucked the paper into her briefcase pocket, glanced at her watch, grimaced and swallowed her coffee too hot. When she had gone, again at a gallop, Nan bought two doughy buns to share with Luke and the birds in the Temple Gardens. Her small part of the action was over. Now all that remained was to wait, hope, and see what ensued.

That evening Mike was phoned from a call-box. Felicity sounded abrupt. "My flight is on for Friday. I still haven't been able to find out anything about those final days before my father left. I called at his Pimlico house on the morning of his last full day and he was just leaving by taxi. Didn't say where he was off to, but then he never did. Formally dressed. I supposed he was on his way to the office. No unusual conversation, but he asked if I was all right for money. He'd do that sometimes, a sort of left-over from seeing me off to boarding-school."

"Did he usually take a taxi to Westminster?"

"As far as I know, yes. Anyway it was raining quite steadily."

"Didn't he offer you a lift?"

"No. I was staying on to clear out some books of mine. He'd

given them their marching orders because he intended closing the apartment down while he was away. That was why I'd called, at his request. I had the feeling he was waiting there until I turned up."

"So where are they now, these books?"

There was a slight pause. "In my flat. Do you want to inspect them?"

"No stone unturned, no avenue unexplored," he said in a comic drudge's voice.

"I'm leaving the keys with Paula. Feel free."

"So that's it, and goodbye?"

"Auf Wiedersehen."

"Perhaps even *'auf Wiederhören'?"*

He made the suggestion on the spur of the moment, and afterwards he wondered whether possibly he'd sensed she'd not been completely open with him and had her own doubts about its wisdom. Whatever the reason, he'd said the right thing because she did ring again. It was on Friday and from Heathrow, like her father's last call to her, but although Yeadings strained to listen he could hear no background announcement of her flight. Later he had a WPC check on the air timetable and it was thirty-five minutes before the Frankfurt take-off.

"Something I've remembered," Felicity said hurriedly. "That last morning at the house, he asked me for a friend's new telephone number. Danny Norman. He's an actor, but he can turn his hand to anything, wallpapering, gardening, even a bit of Cordon Bleu cooking. He'd worked for Daddy once before, when we had the house in Surrey. It may mean nothing, but you could try. He's in my address book at the flat."

"I'll look him up. Everything okay with you, Felicity?"

"Fine. One odd thing though. Those books I mentioned. I had a quick look through them when I picked up my luggage this morning. They're in the box just where I left them, but there's something else been put in with them which I know nothing about. Would you take a look, please?"

"I'll see to it. I mustn't wish you luck, I believe."

"God, no! Tell me to break a leg. We're a superstitious lot."

"Break a leg then, and hop back soon."

"I will. Thanks, Mike."

6

Nan Yeadings, checking her shelves before shopping to restock the larder on Friday morning, lifted the bottle of sunflower oil and remarked the sudden lowering of the liquid level. Bracketed with the disappearance of an empty screw-capped half-pint bottle from the kitchen windowsill, it could mean only one thing. Mike had gone forearmed on a drinking sortie. No spree on his part, however; strictly business. And sometime today, she knew, he intended driving to London.

Yeadings ran his quarry to earth shortly before noon in the third bar he looked in on, but before revealing himself he headed for the gents and poured a quantity of oil carefully down his throat. Then he sat down and took measured sips until he felt the balance right, midway between nausea and total coating. Peering into the mirror, he loosened his tie, smoothed his hair down, rinsed his hands, finally binned the almost empty bottle. As he emerged he called across the fast-filling room, "Well, well, well! Charles, I do declare!"

From solemn contemplation of the mahogany-finish bar counter, Charles Maybury raised a long, grooved, witty face the colour of unbleached linen to give a swift, salutary grimace.

Yeadings knew how deceptive appearances were. The man's meagre vein of humour had long been worked out. The facial tic and the sudden lighting of the eyes were due, like the tint of the coarse-textured skin, to chronic dyspepsia, alcohol-inspired. No one ever saw Maybury drunk, but equally nowadays never notably the reverse. His mind too had attained a neutral state, incapable of work commensurate with his Civil Service grade. Little restricted or urgent information came his way as he dog-paddled the last two years towards early retirement. The only sticks now thrown him to retrieve were routine personal inquiries regarding colleagues. His concerns covered pension rights, leave of absence, disciplinary reports on alliances useful or undesirable. The days when Yeadings had been peripherally of service to him were over, but Maybury would still remember them, and with any luck might be moved to indulge in a little nostalgic reminiscing.

He inquired, conventionally and without real curiosity, after Mike's family, quivering barely visibly at news of the latest addition.

"At my age, imagine! Enough to make my hair drop out." Get the topic over quickly, Mike warned himself, recalling Maybury's tragedy of five years back—wife and both boys in a multiple car crash on the M1; two killed outright and the youngest horribly mutilated.

It wasn't done to ask for progress reports. Maybury would volunteer as much as he wanted you to know. He grunted now, and it could have been from sympathy or something else. "You saw that about old Swaffham, I suppose?" and there they were, straight into it, without Mike having to plan an approach.

Maybury, if anyone, would have known what cases Swaffham had been involved in during his final phase with the department, even if he didn't know their import. He would have seen the man coming and going almost daily, would have known the composition of his teams, might even, as a fellow semi-melancholiac, have had some idea what was getting at him, what misjudgments at the very top had set him on the path of reparation. Reparation, or retribution—which was it? Smelling something definitely off, in any case, and intending to clean it up the minute he got free. And that, surely, meant something wrong inside the department, which couldn't be tackled while he was a part of it himself.

Mike kept the doubles coming, spied cartons of apple juice behind the bar and from half-time, when it was his turn to fetch, switched to that for himself, indistinguishable from scotch with a dash of soda in. Maybury took some tanking up, but it would be a mistake to overdo the treatment and have someone make inquiries when the man got back to his desk mindless. Yeadings didn't need any security department checking on him and his motivation just now. "Take a turn in the park?" he asked vaguely. "Get a healthy sniff of the petrol fumes?"

They walked down Dover Street, crossed Piccadilly and turned into Green Park. Maybury seemed in no hurry to return to his desk. He stretched out on his back under a tree, hands clasped under his head, and seemed strangely contented. "We did some good jobs together, Howard Swaffham and I," he recalled. "Cool wasn't the word for him in those days. He seemed set to go right to the top, DG, no less. We thought we'd all move up with him, on his coat-tails, but it didn't come off."

"So what happened?"

"I never knew. I was away for some months. When I got back things had changed. Swaffham had moved sideways, was controlling a new operational team."

That would be at the time of the car smash, Maybury's breakdown, with almost a year's sick leave.

"For that matter, nobody really knew. They supposed some policy disagreement with our masters, but I wondered . . ." His voice died away as his eyes closed. His breathing went deeper, and Yeadings admitted he could have plied the scotch too well.

Then, suddenly, Maybury sat erect, straightened his glasses by the ear-pieces, patted his pockets, almost brisk. "My desk calls, Mike. Gotta go, I'm afraid. Enjoyed the little chat. Have to do it again, eh? Make a night of it sometime." He rose to his feet, his dark suit crumpled, with here and there fragments of cut grass clinging to its surface.

He stood looking down at Mike. "Leave you to sleep it off, eh?" and the facial tic almost seemed to imply that Mike had been wrong in denying him any remnant of humour. As he turned away he said something more, almost under his breath. It sounded like, "Never got over young Harry, I guess." Then he was walking away, back towards the roar of traffic, and Mike was left thinking that perhaps apple juice went worse with sunflower oil than its equivalent in scotch would have done. He would have to drop in at the Ritz, for a quite unritzy purpose.

It was only in the car later, heading for the Temple Chambers where Paula worked, that he had sudden photographic recall of the single wreath lowered on June Maybury's coffin years ago. White roses and a plain card, "June and Harry, from Chas and Johnny, sorrowing."

But that wasn't right. He puzzled over it, circling to find a parking place for the Rover. He was sure the card had said "sorrowing"; an unusual way of putting it, but simple and true. Then, again the white card flashed up, clearly. "June and *Phil*, from Chas and Johnny . . ."

No Harry anywhere in it. So Maybury's parting mutter hadn't referred to himself grieving over his son. He'd still been talking about Swaffham. It was Howard Swaffham who'd "never got over young Harry," some five years back. And Mike had let Maybury get away without demanding, "Harry who?"

At Chambers Yeadings presented his official card, to ensure he had instant access to Paula. She joined him in a consulting-room which the senior clerk vacated for what he assumed would be a minatory interview. "Old Thompson's getting ready to bail me out," she told Mike with a whimsical smile. "He's accustomed to pupillage petty crime. What brings you here? Is anything wrong?"

Mike told her of Felicity's last-minute phone call from the airport that morning. "So being in London later on another matter, I hoped you might have the keys to her flat with you. If so, may I borrow them for a while?"

"I have, and of course you may. They're a spare set. She did stay over with me last night and was going home to pick up her luggage this morning. That must have been when she looked through the books again, because she didn't mention anything to me about an extra object among them. Didn't she give any clue to what it was? Or was it wrapped and she didn't care to open it up?"

"I've no idea at all. She hadn't time to say much. She was due to be through Passport Control. I'm going across now to see what she's found. Her father's clothes and things sent back from Prague were innocent of any message. I had Forensic go over them, just to be sure. It does look as though Swaffham was cut off before he completed what he went there for."

"So her journey will be useless?"

"She may be all the safer for that. If it became known whose daughter she was after he'd pulled off a *coup* things could turn ugly for her."

"And if she draws a blank, at least she'll know she did all she could. We'll have to make it up to her when she gets back. I only wish Angus had a brother. She deserves something of the sort."

"Yes, I could do with another pair of hands on the job," countered Mike, deliberately misunderstanding. Paula made a shooing gesture at him with her black robe and he shot her a wide grin before holding the door ajar for his leave-taking. "Thank you for your help, Miss Musto. Your observations will certainly help my inquiries." He was conscious of a sudden and impressed silence in the room he passed through. He left Paula's imagination to provide the details the others would be avid for.

Although only two streets apart, Felicity's flat and the one Paula shared with her student friends had little in common. He let himself into a first-floor vestibule matt-washed in a cool, pale grey with ceiling-high leafy bamboo stems hand-painted at several points. The three rooms beyond were similarly pale and furnished with an almost Japanese economy of detail; one soft peach, one willow green, one faintly blue. Expense had been matched by taste, but to him they weren't rooms to live in. Never home. But for Felicity, perhaps a backdrop, a scene easily adapted to whatever drama she chose to develop there.

At first it left him vaguely uneasy, because he couldn't be sure of the essential girl behind the actress; but wandering about, touching objects, opening cupboards, he became gradually reassured. It was the sort of background natural to a cultured girl of reasonably wealthy parents, probably the apartment decorated and furnished professionally at her father's expense. And she lived there, tidily, without leaving any considerable mark of her own on it, just as she could be negative in what she let you see of herself. A daughter brainwashed to Security, aware of possible dangers, the wild creature he had once sensed ready at a flash to disappear back into the undergrowth. Yes, this was Felicity's habitat all right. Now where would she be likely to hide away her books?

There were none on the glass shelves of the living-room; only ceramics, two or three figurines of twisted steel, a Swedish glass vase and a stuffed cloth hedgehog showing signs of wear and stuck all over with pins. The kitchen cupboards held the usual equipment, if of exceptional quality. In the bedroom, two floor-to-ceiling mirrored doors slid back to reveal the girl's wardrobe. The third opened on to a fitted desk with electric typewriter, record player, radio and tape-recorder. Above it were shelves tightly crammed with books, many of them paperbacks. A scarred lacrosse stick leaned in one corner, and beside it an opened carton which presumably was the one she had brought from her father's apartment.

On the dozen or so books inside lay something smaller wound in a plastic bag. Yeadings unfolded it carefully, to expose a three-inch floppy disc. Well, of course, what more up-to-date way to leave information behind you? All Mike had to do now was find a compatible machine to read the thing on. He was no technocrat himself, but he had experts to advise him. All the same, something warned him it wasn't going to be plain sailing. The third wire of Swaffham's three-core lead wasn't itself a bit of electronic software but a person. He was sure of that. This recorded information was only part of the live wire Felicity represented. There was another lead yet to find and follow.

How about that name she had remembered, the actor her father had tried to get in touch with, the one with a new telephone number? Danny Norman, presumably ex-directory. So where was Felicity's address book? It had to be here. And it was, in the drawer of her bed-head.

Danny Norman had an address in Kilburn. Yeadings made a note of it and of the second phone number under the deleted one. It was too late to follow him up now when things were so urgent back at Division. Danny Norman would have to wait.

Mike Yeadings went out into the afternoon sunlight. Above the steady traffic hum was the drone of a jet overhead, stacking to land at Heathrow. Watching it pass over, he thought of Felicity already in Germany, probably even now gazing up at the rose-red, fairy-tale castle of Heidelberg, working on her own fairy-tale of the hopeful young actress offered the part of a queen.

They had brought her a chilled Morning Glory and a choice of perfumes; only a sample-size bottle but it made her feel the part. She had never before drunk champagne for breakfast. Part of the jet-set fantasy, she supposed, accepting the offerings in her twice-removed persona, as tribute for a princess royal, soon to be Queen of Bohemia. The stewardess also slipped her a pocket-sized phrase book. She wondered how much German Elizabeth Stuart had had at her command.

Would she address her bridegroom as Friedrich or Frederick? How could she get free of all those stifling Gravines-in-Waiting?

Could the young lovers ever escape to run off hand-in-hand into the forests on that prolonged ceremonial journey up-Rhine?

"Fair and fresh-cheeked"; "Well-bred and handsome . . . tall for her years . . . gentle . . . rather pensive than gay": that, from contemporary records, was the bride of Frederick V. Well, Felicity could be all that herself, and mischievous too, even act rapturously in love for the first time. She was already so much committed to the part that she half-expected to be reunited with her lover at journey's end, a strongly built young man of medium height, swarthy, dark of hair and eyes, with a bold cavalier moustache and well-turned legs in their close-fitted hose . . .

In the event Frankfurt proved drably grey under a felty layer of cloud, and there was no one to meet her. She checked in her historical role together with her luggage at the Central Station. She had chosen not to approach her father's colleagues about his contacts here, but she recalled a name, a personal friend he'd once quoted as representing the rational post-war German. Hansrudi Frühling, 17 Kornmarktgasse.

He had been across to London twice in the past ten years, and although she had never encountered him she had seen letters for her father on the hall table with that address on the reverse. If her father had begun his last European tour at Frankfurt then he surely would have looked up his old acquaintance Hansrudi, who might, or might not, have known who else he intended visiting, and why.

She took a taxi to the narrow street's end and then continued on foot to No. 17. It was all quite un-English—the vast, double street-doors with their glass panels protected by heavy iron scrollwork, the piercing shrill of the electric bell and, as she was let in, the strong scent of an unfamiliar wax polish, the hollow echo of her steps on floor tiles. The woman who waved her in would be about thirty, handsome in a gaunt, Nordic way, wearing a short tunic of green cotton and straw-coloured espadrilles. Her hands were damp as if she had rinsed them to answer the door and not bothered with a towel. From deeper in the house there escaped the warm smell of fresh baking and children's voices.

"I will see if he iss in, the Papa," she said, and bellowed between funnelled hands up the stairway in incomprehensible German, prefaced by the single screech, *"Pa-pi!"*

She turned to Felicity. *"Frau Mahrloch, ich spreche gern Englisch, aber—"* she began, her words cut across by a distant handbell's silver notes. *"Ach, er ist zu Hause.* At home, *nicht wahr? Bitte*—please go up. He waits."

Felicity saw why, when she started up the final flight to the third floor. He was a small man, not a dwarf but perfectly proportioned. Yet there was something wrong, because he leant on a blackthorn, with one foot drawn back behind the other, resting on its toe.

"An English lady, my daughter says," he greeted her almost shyly. "I am truly delighted. Please forgive my manners, and come in."

She moved past him into a high-ceilinged, square room with ivory-washed walls, close-boarded waxed floor with silky rugs, and a few pieces of distinguished furniture. The overall effect was one of elegance and space. Between two high-backed chairs in one of the long windows was a fine, rosewood table with ivory and ebony chessmen set out on their board. Across the other window stretched an enormous desk, its surface completely covered with stacks of old books and clips of papers.

"I hope I don't disturb your work," she said. "My name is Felicity Marlowe . . ."

"Then you are the daughter of my good friend Howard Swaffham." Herr Frühling nodded, taking both her hands into his own.

There was moisture in his eyes, but he was an old man and it could have been rheum. She was in no mood to trust anyone.

"My *late* friend," he said softly, and the pressure on her fingers was slightly increased. "I cannot tell you how sorry I am. For you, and for myself also. It was a relationship I valued highly."

"You know, then? I thought I might have to break the news."

"I read the continental edition of *The Times.* I would have written had I known my name meant anything to you. At my age one is wary of being a nuisance to the young. It might be another unwanted message of condolence to answer. An unnecessary task, to accommodate a stranger."

She regarded him steadily and his grey eyes didn't waver. "My father once spoke of you to me, and I remembered your address from the back of your letters. I think—you saw him quite recently when he flew out from England." It was less a question than a hinted accusation.

The little man still had hold of one hand and he led her now over to the chessboard. "He came here, yes. This is how we left it. To be continued, if it was in our fates to do so. Do you play chess, Fräulein?"

"My father tried to teach me, years ago. I never worked at it enough to give him a good game." That wasn't strictly true. She had even taken part in the Hastings tournaments as a schoolgirl, but lately there had been no time to keep it up. She looked at the board now and tried to recognize her father's strategy.

"He was White," Herr Frühling offered, discerning her thought. He waved an arm to indicate a stiff, brocaded settee across the room. "Please sit down. My daughter will be bringing you coffee and some of her excellent Kümmelkuchen. I hope you like caraway flavour. The English regard it as a rather Victorian taste, I believe."

"I look forward to trying it," Felicity assured him. "I wish I spoke German just half as well as you speak English, Herr Frühling. I should never have taken you for anything but British if we had met in London."

"I had the advantage of perfecting the language as a prisoner-of-war," he said wryly. "Working in a market-garden widened my vocabulary and left me with a curiously unsophisticated accent, but subsequent meetings with your father and his colleagues provided the opportunity to correct this. I continue to read in English, but seldom have the chance to speak it nowadays. I think you must find me perhaps rather stilted. What is the young persons' word at present for being behind the times?"

"Fuddy-duddy," she offered him and he seemed to light up. It would have been cruel to mention that his age qualified him to the title of "Crumbly."

The coffee and Kümmelkuchen arrived on an immense, elaborately laid tray inside a small goods lift. There was crockery for three, and Herr Frühling's daughter arrived by way of the staircase following on a great Valkyrie cry from below. Her name was Hilda, and on being told who Felicity was, and having demanded how many children she had, announced the names of her four and sat back beaming, her English exhausted.

Felicity paraded her story of the Elizabeth Stuart film script, and explained that she was bound for Heidelberg to view the Schloss.

Herr Frühling promptly burrowed among books in vast glass-fronted cases against one wall to produce two worn volumes. One, with a twenty-six-word title beginning *"Beschreibung der Reise . . . ,"* was a modern copy of a 1613 document about Elizabeth's honeymoon journey; the other, Steinberg's factual and statistical horror on the Thirty Years War, which Felicity had already skimmed through and fought shy of in London. "Are you a historian, Herr Frühling?" she asked.

He had in fact been a dealer in secondhand books, but he insisted on penning a short note to the very professor of history at Heidelberg to whom she already had an introduction. "We were in Goering's Luftwaffe together," he explained, "and that is worth more than a recommendation from a post-war graduate any day."

He smiled at her. "Perhaps you think we should have refused to fight in our country's war? There were long enough queues for martyrdom without us, and it took a little time for us expertly deceived young people to discover what kind of folk hero was our leader. By then we were committed, and many of us dead. It is only now we can afford the luxury of saying 'Thank God the Nazi Reich did not win.' "

Yes, the shared compulsion to offer your life for a cause you abhorred might well solder men's friendships, she thought. "I find such a war hard to imagine," she told him.

"It was a crazy business," Hilda said, with a woman's sweeping scorn for all warfare. Probably she was a Green, had all the answers. But at least the Kümmelkuchen was comfortably old-fashioned. When she had reloaded the tray into the lift and taken herself off, Felicity rose to go.

"Did my father stay long in Frankfurt?" she asked. "And do you know where he went next?"

Herr Frühling sucked in his cheeks. "He was here a single night and left next day by train for Cheb. I understood he was waiting for someone to come out from Czechoslovakia. After that he would return and pick up his belongings. As he did not do so, I shall now get them for you. It is only a small package."

She touched his arm as he rose to go. "You understood he intended coming back?"

"Understood?" It was like a groan. "I understood nothing. He *said* he would return, but I did not know what to think. I could not read him."

"How was he?"

"I do not know." The old man shook his head.

She tried to picture them together. "But you were friends. What did you feel . . . ?"

Herr Frühling sank back on his chair. He seemed to shiver. "I felt—*afraid*. It seemed he was once again the young officer who had interrogated me as a prisoner. He had such alarming stillness. It was as if at any moment he could disappear into his own silence and you would be left quite alone. After a time you wanted to cry out, just to hear the sound of a human voice. For me, such things belong to the past, not"—he gestured to include his book-strewn table, the room with its lingering scent of coffee and Kümmelkuchen—"not this."

The evil past returned, she thought, like a childhood nightmare stealing out of the buried subconscious to terrify the sleeping adult. She knew such terrors herself. But for him how much worse, having lived through the physical horrors of war, the conflict of loyalties, shared guilt for crimes against humanity. How many more thousands, millions perhaps, still suffered in the same way, the permanently disabled of so many nationalities? "Perhaps," she offered, "my father was afraid too. He had sorrows of his own which he kept silent about. That could be what you felt then."

"I was disturbed by him. *For* him. I even, God forgive me, did not care to give house space to what he left behind. I feared it might somehow incriminate me." His voice died away. Then, shamefaced, he admitted, "Or even blow us all up."

Because, intuitively, he had sensed the avenger in her father, although he was not the object of the other man's quest. She let him limp from the room this time, to fetch the package, and while he was gone she examined the chessboard again, unable immediately to see the strategy of her father's moves. On an impulse she pulled the mini-camera from her shoulder bag and photographed the table-top lit by watery afternoon sunshine. When Herr Frühling came back she was seated again on the shiny brocade of the stiff sofa.

She looked at the flat package in the old man's hands. "What shall I do with it?" she asked him.

"That is up to you. I have held it for him since he came. What is certain is that your father cannot come and retrieve it himself. Please take care of it now."

Herr Frühling had clearly communicated with his daughter since leaving the room, for now he suddenly pressed Felicity to stay overnight with them. There was always a guest bedroom available. He would be honoured, and for Hilda what an opportunity to use her very neglected English.

Felicity thanked him and declined, using as excuse a fictitious early morning engagement in Heidelberg for next day.

"And after Heidelberg?" he demanded. He scanned her eyes with a troubled frown. "But I think you are determined to follow your father's trail to Cheb and beyond. Isn't that it?"

"Or the Princess Elizabeth Stuart's trail, when she became Queen of Bohemia."

"I trust the enterprise will not end so disastrously for you. Indeed, I should be relieved if you would send me a postcard from London on your return. I must worry for you until then, even pray for you, if you do not find that presumptuous."

"Thank you. I have been offered every assistance by the authorities in Prague. It could bring useful sterling to them if the film is eventually made there on location."

"Ah yes, the film. I wish you well with that also."

She left him leaning on his stick outside the upstairs room as she went down with her father's small package and the two books which the old man had given her tucked under one arm. At the bottom she waved up to him as he bent over the handrail to call goodbye. Hilda materialized with two of her small ones clinging to her skirt. They were rosy and flaxen. Grandchildren were something Felicity hadn't repaid her own father with. The reminder saddened her and made her final leave-taking more abrupt.

Back at Central Station there was a train almost due to leave for Heidelberg. She recovered her luggage and a porter helped her aboard. Within two hours she was in the foyer of her hotel, silently rehearsing the German sentences needed to claim her room.

Its windows faced south and if she craned out she could see, floating high above the mellow, tiled rooftops of mediaeval brown and cream houses, Elizabeth Stuart's Palatinate castle, dull red against its rich forest setting. From here the windows were dark as though the rooms behind were whole. Tomorrow was soon enough for disillusion. Tonight she would eat out somewhere with a discreet view of it, and lose herself in the part she was to play.

On the table beside her bed were the two books from Herr Frühling and her father's package bound around with sticky tape. She shone the bed-head light full on it to examine the seals and found what she was looking for: a tiny hair trapped crosswise where the two ends overlapped.

If he had taken such precautions to check against interference she would do well not to open the package herself until she'd found a stationer's and bought tape to reseal it equally securely. Curiosity must wait until then. It was not, after all, as though she could do him any good by discovering what the contents were. He was dead, and no amount of haste would bring him back. She had all the time in the world to discover what he had intended in the six weeks he'd wrongly believed were left to him.

She laid the package back beside the books, wondering how Superintendent Yeadings—Mike, as he expected her to call him— was getting on with the surprise packet she'd told him of in her final phone call. How long would he put off going to collect the disc? Perhaps it would have been better to leave that to Paula who already had the keys. But there had been so little time, because she had only found the disc just as the taxi came to take her to the airport. Still, it was done now. She had told Mike, and he wasn't the sort to let it slip his mind. Was he?

7

Still keeping all inquiries concerning Swaffham at a strictly unofficial level, Yeadings denied himself the advice of the force's own electronics men, taking the disc into a software shop in Maidenhead and being given a comprehensive list of machines on which it might possibly be used. But even when a compatible system was found, he was told, he could first need a start-of-day disc similarly formatted in order to read it. In fact, one needed to determine in advance which computer language was the key to it. He declined their offer of help in checking this.

Here again, he thought, Paula might be useful. According to Angus, she was *au fait* with present office aids and competent to use several systems. That must all wait until evening. Meanwhile crime within Thames Valley required his immediate attention.

The blue Mercedes from which the number-plate had been transferred to the beaten-up tan Cortina with the girl's body in the boot, had still not turned up. The man Whittle had twice phoned the Met for information and been told that since it had not been found abandoned with an empty tank, joy-riders were less likely than professional car thieves to have been involved. In which case the Merc would no longer be blue nor in the same locality. Some-where, possibly on the continent, it could already have been re-sold with forged papers and the registration of some written-off wreck—unless it had been required for a specific criminal pur-pose, after which it would also have been abandoned. He was advised to consult with his insurance company and resign himself to a replacement.

Nor was there great hope of tracing the history of the murder car itself.

Details of missing girls from the continent had now swelled the UK Missing Persons register, and the Incident Room was con-stantly in touch with relatives and other local forces trying to match descriptions.

A separate file had been opened to deal with house visits check-ing on the Afghan hound population in the Home Counties and Greater London area. As a result of this last quest a phone call from West End Central reported that one Kabul Florissante III, registered at an address in Eaton Square, was presently at the family house, Pollards, near Henley, where its owner, the Hon. Celia Manton-Jones, spent the summer months.

The DS detailed to check on this establishment as well as on seven others in the southern divisions of Thames Valley, sug-gested the "blankety arsacrockery" might fit in a round of servant-strangling between polo on Smith's Lawn and Royal Ascot. "A chukka-out the attic window, like?" he put to DI Angus Mott.

"On your way, joker," Angus ordered him. "Remember the title Honourable is not to be taken literally until proved so. Anyway, it could be the under-gardener who dunnit. It's the house and surrounds you're looking at, first time round."

"Then, if it tallies, pluckings of the aforesaid Kabul Florissante III and a sample of newly tarred ground under high windows," the DS breezily offered.

"With as much past history as possible on old cars of family and staff. Full list of residents and anyone visiting daily. That goes for all the addresses. Don't take the whole day. Arrange regular phone-ins with Incident Room desk." Angus nodded him off and went back to his ordnance map.

The Serious Crime Squad now had a diversion to the case of the warehouse break-in. The injured night-watchman had recovered consciousness, and a phone call from Wexham Park Hospital informed them that minimal interviewing would be permitted at the Intensive Therapy Unit. Yeadings took this on himself, appreciating the delicate balance between his own requirements and that of the houseman hovering to ensure the patient wasn't harassed.

A conscientious, taut-featured man with a close-shaven head showing between heavy bandages, he was barely capable of speech, yet he had a tale to tell and there was no rest for him until he'd got it across to authority. It took some little time, the doctor intervening and the injured man—Brock by name—feverishly eager to complete.

He'd stood no chance at all. There had been five of them, two with pump-action shotguns, so he'd done just what they told him. All the same, one of the other three was a psycho, had to leave his mark. He'd gone for the guard with a pickaxe handle. Sheer gut-aggression. Last thing, as he blacked out, Brock had caught the man's name. Someone shouting, "For Godsake, Mel! Lay off, you bleeding effer!"

Mel. Not a common name; and so violent, bound to have a record. Yeadings nodded, gently touched the man's shoulder in reassurance, started to rise.

"More. *Saw* one! One with gun, in passage, fixing mask. Know—him again."

"Can you describe him?"

Brock tried to nod, had to get by with blinking hard.

"Tomorrow," the houseman insisted.

"Just one more question," Yeadings said quietly. "You mentioned masks."

There was a pause, a fresh effort. "Monkey-faces." The injured man grinned feebly through his dressings, his eyes closing heavily. He sank back into sleep, unburdened.

"He needed to get that out," Yeadings said shortly to the young doctor.

"I guess so. Still, he could relax too far, now that it's off his chest. He isn't out of the wood yet."

Yeadings eyed the houseman evenly; a cautious lad, erring on the pessimistic. Not a bad way to be with so much responsibility. Underpaid, unsung, likely to take the blame whenever overpunished human tissue finally succumbed against violent odds. Must take a lot of guts, patience and devotion. "What keeps you ticking?" he asked on impulse.

The young man in the white coat looked sheepish, dangling his stethoscope. "Same as you, I guess. Just habit."

Yeadings drove into Slough and phoned instructions from the divisional inspector's office there: tomorrow, medical staff permitting, a police artist to sit by Brock, and photo-fit facilities on standby.

There were no new developments with the girl-in-the-car case. Routine inquiries were continuing. Deadly phrase, sounding so negative, covering such painstaking, niggly turning of stones and sifting of straws. At the end, nothing or something. A statistic either way. He left the pot to boil, turned off towards the M4, making again for London. Sneaking time for a personal inquiry on the Swaffham front.

He could have rung Danny Norman, but that wasn't like having him there in front of you. Actor or no, his face had to show something. Even a total blank told some story, had a function, as in dominoes.

The single-fronted, brick terrace house he pulled up opposite was noncommittal, the ground-floor window primly masked with white net, the two floors above having lined curtains pushed roughly open as if by an indifferent male paw.

Rented apartments. Three cards set in a brass frame beside the open front door gave the tenants' names. No entry phone. Yeadings pressed the bell button opposite the middle one advertising D. Norman and waited hopefully.

He was in luck. Through the coloured glass panels of the inner door he saw movement, and the lock clicked. The door opened inwards to reveal a tall young man in jeans and sweater, with neatly trimmed fair hair, long features and a wide, humorous mouth. "Yes?" he questioned, giving Yeadings a cool glance from top to toe.

"Mr. Norman? Danny Norman?" Yeadings asked pleasantly.

The young man inclined his head, giving nothing away.

"I'm a friend of Felicity Marlowe's. She said you might help me."

"Ah." He surveyed Yeadings again, head tilted, and then he smiled, hopefully. "You're not casting director for an all-star production of *King Lear on Ice,* by any chance? One can get a little tired of resting, you know."

"You wouldn't admit that, if you really thought I had stage connections."

"True. But I still believe in angels. Do come up. And mind the third stair-rod, it's loose." His voice was light, with an underlying timbre as if he used only a part of it. Climbing the stairs behind him, Yeadings could well believe that astride some caparisoned war-horse, Danny Norman could do more than justice to *"God for Harry! England and Saint George!"*

Shades of Freud!—there was the name Harry again, leaping out of his subconscious. But the one Swaffham had reputedly "never got over" wasn't Henry V.

The room they went into overlooked the road. It was comfortably but unremarkably furnished in colours that reminded Yeadings of old tapestry, and it was comfortably untidy too, with books and magazines left about. On the folded gateleg table under the window was a half-eaten apple and a well-tended evergreen hibiscus with four scarlet flowers fully open, their tasselled tongues hanging out as if panting.

"Rather fine, isn't it?" Danny Norman invited, observing his visitor's interest.

"Magnificent."

"One needs company. Women can be so possessive, dogs need walking and even cats are a nuisance when you want to go away at a moment's notice. Anyway I can't stand their smell. Cassandra and I get along well enough and I pass her downstairs when I have to travel. She comes back just sufficiently wilted to flatter me that she pines a little." He made a throwaway gesture with the fingers of both hands. "I think it's actually the blank verse she misses."

Yeadings, who had on occasion caught himself mumbling to various cherished items in his own garden, didn't find this necessarily affected. "I talk to my plants sometimes," he admitted. "Curse the weeds mostly."

"Is it gardening that you . . . ?" Danny probed. "I am, as Felicity probably told you, a man of many parts. How is she, anyway?"

"Very well when I last saw her. Off abroad for a week or so at the moment."

"I heard on the grapevine—and it sounded pretty authentic—that she's being considered for the title role in a new TV historical by Rex Fielding. It could outdo *The Jewel in the Crown* by all accounts. I'm hoping, like half London's board-treaders, for a few crumbs to fall from her table."

Yeadings grunted, dropping into the chair Norman waved him towards. "It's early days yet, but I'm sure she'll use what influence she has. She's looking for locations in Germany while the film-script takes shape. It's not even certain they'll make it, but Granada seem very keen on the outline."

"So—nothing doing before October," Danny calculated. "It should be safe enough to fill in until then. In what way do you want my help?"

Yeadings took a deep breath and went hot between the shoulder blades at the thought of how Nan might take his off-the-cuff proposition. "I believe you do interior decorating . . . ?"

Afterwards he was to ask himself why he'd chickened out of asking a direct question about the Swaffham job and leaving it at that. Something in the air? Something about the young actor's breezy acceptance of him as a potential client recommended by a friend? Surely not sympathy because the lad hadn't any work at present? Maybe his enforced "resting" meant he was a pretty hammy actor, could even be a messy decorator too.

Nan was going to raise the roof at having anyone working inside the house, with young Luke just cutting his first premature tooth and Sally entering one of her temperamental phases. If he'd had any sense he would have demanded an estimate for painting the exterior. At least then the chatty young actor wouldn't be under the family's feet, except when he expected cups of tea. And which rooms could he be put to work on, when Nan already had the colour schemes just the way she wanted them? Trouble, Yeadings promised himself; and he'd walked wide-eyed into it.

"I have to ring him tonight and say when it's convenient to start," Mike ended his confession that evening. Nan was patching a pair of green corduroy dungarees for Sally. After the first hard stare when he mentioned interior decorating, she hadn't looked up. Now she did, but it was to reach for more thread, cut off a length and rethread her needle. "So you'd better do that," she commented.

"Well," said Mike, figuratively standing on one leg, "when can he come?"

She had only to say, "Never," for him to be snookered. Instead she smiled wickedly and offered, "What's wrong with tomorrow? We need the information at once, don't we? I suppose you've cast me as chief interrogator?"

"Um. I thought that, chatting with him, perhaps . . ." His voice trailed off. "Tomorrow would be great. But what can we give him to do?"

"Plenty of little jobs I've been promised," murmured Nan, head bent again over her sewing, "which somehow never get done. Whitewash the larder for a start. Then I'll make a list." She looked up, her eyes bright with teasing. "Mind, it'll cost you."

"I knew I should have third-degreed him on the spot," Mike groaned. "Okay then, I'll ring him now. You know, you only had to *say* you needed those things done."

"I did. Several times. Like most husbands, you have selective hearing, love." She snipped off the end of the cotton and patted the mend flat. "There, another job jobbed, as Gran used to say."

And me put properly in my box, Mike admitted silently, on his way to contact Danny Norman.

"Tell him to bring his toothbrush," Nan called after him. "He can have the little room over the hall. It'll save all that commuting."

Mike stopped in his tracks. "You're joking! You haven't even met the man."

"*You* have. If he gets your okay, he gets mine. I know you wouldn't let him into the house if you weren't sure he's all right."

How do I end up feeling worse than if she'd blocked me? Mike asked himself. That's twice today I've had an attack of conscience over Nan. Getting old and soft, that's what. He plodded to the hall phone, rang through to Danny Norman and was assured he'd be there by two next afternoon.

As he replaced the receiver it cooed at him twice. He detested this new Telecom noise, more like a sick parrot than a phone ringing. "Yeadings," he told it.

Angus was on the other end. "We could have found the right Afghan hound," he reported. "Beaumont visited Pollards, the Manton-Jones house near Henley. There's a strip of newish macadam at the rear alongside a jutting kitchen extension. What's more, eight slates had recently been renewed on its roof, directly below a second-floor window of the original building. This suggested the right scenario to Beaumont but he didn't take anyone up on it, just checked on the dog with reference to some local sheep-worrying. The Hon. Celia M.-J. remarked sweetly it must be the only animal in the Home Counties to have an unbroken licence from puppyhood, particularly since all the official havering over cancelling the need."

"How did Beaumont take that?"

"Said he was sure such a law-abiding family would never let an animal stray wittingly. Left it open that there could have been an accidental escape."

"Mm. Too late to follow it up tonight. Go down in the morning. I'd like to come along, Angus. Pick me up at eight. We'll catch them at breakfast."

In the event, Yeadings was thwarted in that part of his purpose, because the Hon. Mrs. Manton-Jones was an early riser. When Mott had shown their cards to the uniformed maid, they were led into a small ante-room off the square hall. From the next room an amplified voice could be heard reading continuous prose. After a few minutes of waiting they were joined by a middle-aged woman in a severely cut brown linen suit. She introduced herself as Mrs. Cutler, housekeeper-companion to the lady they wished to speak with.

"I must warn you," she said, "that my employer does not enjoy robust health and should not be alarmed. Furthermore, she lives somewhat withdrawn from the—er, *cruder* aspects of modern society—"

"—being, perhaps, blind?" Yeadings suggested.

The woman raised her eyebrows.

"I recognized the Talking Book machine," he explained. "Its resonance is quite unlike any radio or conventional tape-player."

"Mrs. Manton-Jones is not blind," he was corrected, "merely partially-sighted. I will inform her that you are here, Superintendent."

"Guarded by a dragon," Angus observed when the woman had left.

"Perhaps that's why madam has her machine so loud, keeping her at bay." Yeadings was listening, head cocked, to sounds from the next room. The volume was not turned any lower and the women's voices were a mere added susurration. There was a short pause before the housekeeper returned.

"Will you come this way, please." It was a command. This time she opened double doors set in the wall opposite the window and they entered a morning-room bright with early sunshine, flowers and soft colours. A fine-featured woman lay back in a chintzy armchair facing open French windows, her eyes closed. As they approached she reached out and switched off the machine in mid-sentence. Then she opened her eyes and proffered the same hand to each man in turn, smiling. "Visitors so early in the day. How delightful."

"Detective-Superintendent Yeadings and Inspector Mott of Thames Valley Police," the housekeeper reminded her grimly.

"Of course. You said so before. Don't be tiresome, Nancy. There's no need to hover, dear." She waited until the woman had withdrawn, then turned to Mike. "Did she pronounce your name correctly, rhyming it with 'kneadings'?" A smile lurked at the corners of her mouth.

"Not quite," Mike allowed. "It really rhymes with 'beddings.' "

The lady gave a little gasp of laughter. "Perhaps that's why

Nancy bowdlerized it. She's rather governessy, you know. Now do find somewhere comfortable to seat yourselves, Superintendent, Inspector, and tell me how I can be of service to you."

Mott, who had never before seen a Talking Book, had been discreetly examining the clumsy-looking contraption boxed in two-tone grey metal on the table beside her. Now he turned to its owner and was immediately reminded of Virginia Woolf. She had the same narrow, high-bridged nose, the large, liquid eyes and finely sculpted lips, but instead of the sexless, headmistressy swathing of indeterminate hair, this woman's face was framed with a springing mass of lightly faded gold threaded with white. She had once been very beautiful, was striking still and, visually handicapped or not, kept a lively grip on life, belying the housekeeper's warning.

"I must apologize for interrupting your reading. You had a long journey back," Yeadings told her, smiling.

"From *The Land of the Blue Poppy*. Ah yes, you recognized the passage. A delightful book. I do so miss books. I'd be quite lost without my machine. It's a lifeline." She patted the jumbo cassette. "Dear old RNIB."

She cocked her head and raised one of the fine, gold eyebrows. "I hope you haven't come to sell me tickets for the Police Ball. That's rather beyond me, I fear, though the children might attend if they're down from London that weekend."

"Not the Police Ball," Yeadings admitted. "We're making inquiries in the neighbourhood about an old tan Ford Cortina found in suspicious circumstances, but perhaps you can't help us with that."

"I can distinguish colours perfectly," she claimed, "and I see quite well over a narrowly defined area. I have tunnel vision, you know, so I can distinguish a make of car once I centre on it. In any case, they all sound so different, don't they? Fords are quite distinctive, I find."

"So do you know of any such car as I described?"

"Old, tan and a Cortina," she considered. "I can't think of one. What were the suspicious circumstances, Superintendent?— Oh!" She put up a long-fingered hand to cover her mouth. "It would be something to do with that murdered girl in the gravel pit. I heard about it on my talking newspaper, the local one. Poor child, have you discovered who she was?"

"Not yet, I'm afraid. There were no identification marks on the car or her clothing."

"But surely the licence number . . ."

"It had a false number-plate. And even that had been altered." Yeadings stopped himself almost on the verge of apologizing, and quickly took over the initiative. "But you still might be able to help us, if you will."

"Tell me how, Superintendent."

"In cases of serious crime the victim's clothing is subjected to microscopic examination by our forensic branch—"

"—at Aldermaston," she interrupted cheerfully. "Yes, I've read about that in the chief constable's annual report. Or rather, I've had it read to me."

"So you know how the minutest clues can sometimes lead to the solution of complicated crimes?"

"Yes, it's most impressive. And in this case?"

"A number of animal hairs were found. On examination they proved to have come from a long-coated dog, such as an Afghan hound."

The woman was clearly startled, but not dismayed. "So, of course, you must check among the owners of such dogs. I have one, as no doubt you have discovered. She's a two-year-old bitch we call Florrie. Just a moment and you shall meet her."

She put out a hand and felt along the edges of the Talking Book until her fingers encountered a slim silver whistle. She placed it between her lips and blew it inaudibly.

Yeadings and Mott followed her concentrated gaze towards the open French windows. Through it they saw a sloping lawn, bordered on the right by a deep band of colourful herbaceous plants and shrubs. To the left, beyond a stone-flagged terrace with a low balustrade, rose a distant spinney of young birches interspersed with clumps of rhododendrons. From that direction came bounding a flurry of golden-brown fur and flying legs to land skiddingly before the doorway.

"Kabul Florissante III," said Mott admiringly, hunkering to offer a hand to be sniffed. "Hallo, girl."

She stretched out nervy nostrils, showed the whites of her eyes, came warily closer, then moved in on the group, wagging her whole posterior beyond the waist.

"Florrie, you're too nice-natured for a good housedog," sighed her owner. "But you're lovely, and naturally enough you know it. Irresistible, isn't she, Superintendent?"

"Completely." Yeadings was thinking of a young girl—lonely for certain, since she'd never been missed—burying her face in the creature's soft coat, pulling it close, the loose hairs brushing against her clothing. So, if this beautiful Afghan was the source of the hairs examined by Forensic, who had the girl been? Where had she come from?

"Does Florrie run free in the grounds?" he asked, remembering the open gates between driveway and public road.

It appeared that she did, in a limited way, for an hour after breakfast, as now, and again after she was fed in the evening.

"And has she ever run away?" Mott pursued, seeing where Yeadings was leading.

"Never. She answers to the whistle immediately. In London, naturally, she has less freedom. My son or daughter, or the chauffeur, takes her out for exercise on a lead. Naturally she much prefers being down here in the country."

"How do you transport her? Is she good in a car?"

"An angel. She sits beside me on the back seat, very regal. I sometimes expect her to wave to the populace as we go past." Mrs. Manton-Jones turned her wide, vague eyes on Yeadings and demanded, "Do you really think that somewhere Florrie could have brushed against that poor dead girl? She was strangled, I seem to remember. Thank heavens—for whatever dog's sake—she hadn't been mauled."

"Well, what do you think, sir?" Angus asked, steering the Rover out again into the traffic flow bound for the river.

"I think we might get some coffee somewhere in the town, then we'll mull it over."

Although the jigsaw pieces seemed to be fitting together, they didn't amount to much. The Hon. Mrs. Manton-Jones had had no knowledge of the new slates on the kitchen extension roof. Why should she have? Her upstairs sitting-room and bedroom were at the front of the building. She had little occasion to go round to the yard. She knew about the new strip of tarmac because she had smelled it on arrival five days ago when the pitch was still fairly fresh. It had replaced a straggly strip of herb garden which had grown unsightly. A soak-away had been added to take water from hosing down the cars. Cars plural, because both her son and daughter had their own. The housekeeper travelled with her employer or used the local buses. No one here owned, or had ever owned, an old tan Ford Cortina.

Nor could the housekeeper, Mrs. Cutler, be of much help. The first she had known of the damaged roof was when the rain came in the second night they were here. She had rung the builder next morning and the men came to fix it the same afternoon. She had never thought to ask them what ideas they had on the cause of the damage.

Yeadings and Mott were agreed that Pollards might well be the scene of the girl's accident. They had asked to see the room from which she would have fallen or been thrown, but it was a perfectly normal spare bedroom with the blankets and pillows neatly folded on a bare mattress on the single wood-frame bed.

Before Mrs. Manton-Jones's return from London the house had been unoccupied for a month, although the gardener's wife came in twice a week to open the windows and redirect any post. Once or twice "the children" had spent a night there. Her son and daughter, Sam and Hilary, lived and worked mainly in London, at the Eaton Square address, so it was unlikely they knew of anything untowards happening in the neighbourhood. The gardener and his wife, the most likely to be of help, had gone on holiday to Ibiza two days before the house was reopened.

"Get on to the repairs people," Yeadings decided. "See if they've any idea how and when the damage occurred to the kitchen roof. Saturate Henley and surrounds with the artist's impression of the dead girl. Maybe someone will recognize her better that way." It wasn't easy, after all, to picture the young girl's features before strangulation, when looking at photographs of her after the event.

"And maybe someone will have seen the Afghan on the loose or in other company," Mott suggested.

"That too. Meanwhile"—Yeadings patted the envelope holding

scrapings taken from the tarmac—"see if Forensic can come up with something on this."

Mott suddenly opened his mouth as a new thought struck him, then subsided gloomily.

"Come on, then. Give," Yeadings invited, having observed the change of expression. "You've just discovered a big BUT."

"Well, if we tie in the dead girl with the damaged roof and the fresh macadam at Manton-Jones's—"

"Yes?"

"—how could she come in contact with the dog, which was still at the London house?"

8

It was a question of timing, they decided. On arrival back at Pollards from London, the Hon. Mrs. M.-J. had smelled fresh pitch from the new strip of tarmac, an improvement ordered earlier by her son. Mrs. Cutler then found that the roof of the kitchen extension was apparently damaged, letting in rain on their second night. By then the unknown girl had been dead for several days, according to the pathologist's findings. So far it all matched up; the incident could have occurred while the house was supposedly unoccupied, and any unauthorized lights showing at the windows would not have been observed since the gardener's family were already away on holiday.

The alien factor, as Angus Mott discovered, was in connection with the dog hairs clinging to the girl's clothing—the very clue which had led them to this house in the first place. If Kabul Florissante III had not yet put in an appearance there, how could the girl have picked up her loose fur?

"Either," Yeadings surmised, squinting into his coffee as he slowly stirred it, "she was with the animal elsewhere before coming to the house, or else there were brushings off its coat already at Pollards where she could easily pick them up. Suppose she had handled a blanket from the dog's box used on a previous visit? Or, having already been killed, her body was concealed under some such cover while being driven to the gravel pit?"

"But there was nothing like a blanket found in or near the old Cortina, though it could have been removed after the car was dumped. Dragging the gravel pit hasn't produced anything useful. Should we organize a search of the house and grounds?"

Yeadings grunted. "Ruddy manpower shortage. I'll get Allocation to see if uniform branch can spare us six more men. Chances are that if dog hairs got on the girl in that way, some trace off her would also show up on the fabric, especially in view of her injuries. The principle's well enough known to the general public, so it's odds on that the thing's either destroyed or laundered by now."

"Which would have been noticed by whoever's responsible for the dog's comfort."

"You mean that they'd find it was missing, or ask who'd washed it? Anyway, this is all supposition. We can't be totally certain it happened at Pollards. The circumstances could be coincidental, and the girl be a kennel-maid or working for a vet who'd had a new driveway laid. Let's keep an open mind on it, Angus, at least until the tar analysis comes through."

They sat in silence a few minutes, then Angus queried, "Anything fresh on the Swaffham front?"

Yeadings fumbled in his jacket pocket. "This," he offered, producing the floppy disc. "Paula lent me the keys to Felicity's flat, which incidentally you might return for me, Angus. I looked through the box of books Felicity had removed from her father's place, and there was this foreign body in it. I've yet to break into it. In case it contains something of a confidential nature, I haven't asked our computer people to help. Do you think Paula would oblige again? We really ought to take her on the strength at this rate."

"She'd probably be glad to try. She's very keen on all this personal computer lark." He turned the disc in his hand. "I suppose it won't self-destruct like those tapes on TV?"

Yeadings treated his inspector to a contemptuous grunt. "Oh, there's the Danny Norman business too." Briefly, and with a degree of self-mockery that had Angus hard pushed not to grin at his discomfiture, the superintendent explained about Felicity's last-minute mention of the actor, and his own follow-up the previous day.

"Nan has dived in at the deep end," Yeadings ended the account, "setting him to work this very afternoon, repainting the larder. Which is why I'm keen to get back when he arrives and lead the talk round to what it was he did for Swaffham just before he went off to Frankfurt."

"Could it be significant?"

"He was a devious man, Swaffham. The girl too, I feel. I have the distinct impression of being paid out details like a climber's rope. Just so much permitted until I'm lodged on a sure patch of ground, then a little nudge and they're at it again."

"Both? The girl continuing where her father left off?"

"In some form of pre-planned collusion. But she may not know much, could be just a move or two ahead of me. It's like a treasure hunt with no rules on how to use the clues when they surface."

Angus jangled the keyring. "I was going back to Maidenhead, but I could as easily check in there by phone. If there's nothing pressing, I've a theory I'd like to test."

Yeadings raised one bristly, black eyebrow.

"These keys. Rather a lot for one young girl, but there's nothing resembling a safe vault key. There are two distinctly different door keys, though."

"I noticed that. I thought—maybe a boyfriend's flat."

"I doubt it. According to Paula she's a detached individual, her own woman. It doesn't preclude her from a connection of that kind, but I think that if she had something going it would be with someone she could trust with her secrets. He'd be the one pulled in for what we're trying to do. Paula and I discussed this earlier. We both get the feeling Felicity doesn't have a love-life."

"So—?"

"How about Daddy leaving his own key with her?"

"I was afraid that was what you were heading for. You don't need me to tell you the drawbacks of trying to gain an entry, however openly and with whoever's legitimate key, to the lair of anyone from that department."

" 'Twould ring the bells of heaven," Angus suggested. "Only, he isn't in the department any longer. What's more, he's dead and buried. (I meant to tell you: the funeral took place while you were tied up with the Earley siege.) The spooks wouldn't overlook tooth-combing Swaffham's place the minute he died and giving it a certificate of sanitization. Any equipment they had there will have been removed and all alarms disconnected. Otherwise it should be just as Swaffham left it, unless Felicity was in a hurry to sell off the furniture."

"So you want to take a look?"

"Purely as a 'friend of the family'—who happens to have a warrant card if anyone objects. No one will connect you with what I'm there for."

"No," Yeadings said heavily. "It's not on, Angus. Nice try, but this is something I have to do myself. As I said, he was a devious man. I'll have those keys back after all."

So it was that Mike got no nearer Danny Norman that afternoon than a phone call to Nan to ascertain that the actor had arrived, was setting up his things and almost ready to start. "As a matter of fact, he's here in the kitchen now," Nan assured him, "having a cup of tea. Was there any special message I can pass—? Oh, all right. See you then, love. 'Bye."

Trust Nan. She knew what it was he needed to find out, but she'd talk of everything else under the sun for fear of sending Danny into his shell, forewarned for when Mike made his own casual-seeming inquiry. Such a simple question to ask: "What job did Howard Swaffham want you for, the day before he went abroad for the last time?" Already Mike had put off asking it when he first met the man. Now he was permitting interruptions that meant putting it off again. There was a block of some kind, some subconscious worry getting to him, warning him off.

The white-fronted Regency house, like Swaffham himself, had an impeccable exterior, conventional, blandly noncommittal. If the parallel went further the place would have hidden secrets inside. There was only the one bell, no name-plate beside it, but level with the keyhole was a small rectangle of smoked glass like a minute TV screen. The second door key on Felicity's ring turned easily in the lock with a faint click followed by a hum.

Yeadings pushed at the door which remained firmly closed. The glass panel lit up with the words "Right Thumb." Without great expectations, he placed his thumb where invited.

Since this was the girl's key, presumably it was meant to match her individual print. What kind of raspberry would he get for having attempted a fraud? There followed a second, duller click. He removed his hand and warily stepped to one side. The hum was repeated as a hidden computer decided how to deal with him. And the lock slid back.

The heavy door, released, opened a mere half inch and dared him to go farther. *Heads,* he reckoned, he'd earned himself an intruder's reception; and *tails,* with remarkable foresight Swaffham had somehow obtained Mike's own prints, fed them to his computer, and now was offering him the freedom of his private lair. The former possibility was the more likely, but Mike wouldn't put either past the quiet man on whose shoulders so much responsibility for the nation's security had once rested.

Mike looked up and down the street, saw no one watching, then pressed the door fully open with the sole of one size-eleven brown brogue, again stepping smartly to one side before the movement was complete. Nothing happened. The broad, loftily arched hall-way decorated in stark white had a chequerboard floor of black and white tiles, unrelieved by any rug.

"The old bugger!" Mike said aloud. Hadn't Swaffham been a chess fanatic? Wasn't this just the test he would set for anyone coming in unannounced? One or more of these squares, once trodden on, could activate the overwarm reception. It was no coincidence, surely, that there were eight tiles to each rank, the first in the right corner being white. So what was the opening move?

He felt sweat inside his collar and it angered him. Dammit, the man couldn't deliberately arrange GBH for an intruder. That would be going too far for any department answerable to the Cabinet committee. At most it would be a sudden shock, a scare-off, or some means of holding him until someone arrived to sort him and his motives out. Which could be embarrassing for a member of a provincial police force operating unofficially on the Met's patch.

But he wasn't an intruder; he had a key, entrusted to him at second hand by the dead man's own daughter.

His mouth set in a grim line as he selected the tile to put his first foot on. Okay, so it was a chessboard. Act bold, be the strongest piece there. He stepped decisively forward, on to the queen's square.

Ahead, from behind the claret velvet curtain half-masking the corridor below the staircase, came a low chuckle. "Come in, Mr. Yeadings. I've been expecting you."

There was no mistaking the quiet, measured voice with its hint of wryness. Despite his being prepared for the unexpected, it made a cold shiver run down Mike's spine. A voice from the dead. Howard Swaffham's.

In the Incident Room Inspector Angus Mott enclosed the specimen of tar macadam together with a note in a second envelope, sealed it, added his initials and the date, and addressed it to Forensic at Aldermaston. "By despatch rider," he ordered the young WPC who was hovering as though it was a longed-for birthday present.

The first batch of prints from the artist's impression lay before him on the desk. Angus looked at the young face, puppy-pretty with its blunt, unformed features. He hadn't waited to see them tidy up the body at the morgue. That attention had come later.

The artist had portrayed the girl with her hair brushed back to fall in loose natural waves on her shoulders. The Path people would have advised him about that. Habitual partings took time to grow out. You could be virtually one hundred percent sure in which direction the hairs had been dressed, from the behaviour of the first quarter-inch after it left the follicle. But that still left plenty of leeway. Below the full-face portrait were three side-views with different hair styles. In one she wore a squaw headband, in the next a pony-tail, and the third had a topknot.

Taken all round, it was a very impressive piece of work. Angus removed the first two copies for his own and the Guv's use. After his instant reaction of pity for the young life brutally wasted, came a strong urge to get to work. But he'd have to get the Guv's approval. There was no reason why he shouldn't make a move himself, but there was a lot at stake and Mike Yeadings had involved himself personally in the case. Only right to consult him.

He asked for an outside line and then instantly cancelled the request, checked out, retrieved his car from the yard and drove to a public phone-box. Chances were that the Guv hadn't been able to get in at Swaffham's or, if able, had already left. In which case there would be no answer. If he was still there, they would need to keep their references anonymous and vague. Angus shoved in his phone card and dialled the number taken from Felicity's address book.

He heard the phone ring eight times, then the receiver was lifted at the other end. "Yes?"

"It's me. Got some rather nice photos. Thought I'd go up-stream and show them to auntie at the dogs' home."

There was no reply as Yeadings considered this.

"You there, Gu—Gustav?"

"I am. Heard you okay. Why don't you do that?"

"Right." Angus hesitated, aware of some unfamiliar tone to Yeadings's deep voice. "You all right? You sound a bit odd."

"Just had a surprise, that's all. Nothing to bother you. Mind how you go."

This time Mrs. Cutler came out on the portico when she sighted the car drawing up outside. She looked distinctly annoyed. "A *second* visit in one day, Inspector?"

He wanted to retort that he too could count that far. Her gover-nessy manner provoked a childish reaction. "I should like to see Mrs. Manton-Jones if she is at home," he said firmly.

The woman sighed, pursing her lips. "I'll go and see." She showed him into the same small ante-room but left the door ajar, perhaps to hear if he started loading the Ming vases in a swag bag?

When her footsteps had died away Angus went out into the hall. A wide central passageway led back to glass doors which were open, and framed in them he saw the distant figures of two women in conversation. He walked out uninvited into the bright sunshine of the garden and the scent of lime trees in blossom.

Although his footfalls were softened by the grass, he saw the taller woman stiffen and turn towards him, her head tilted as she listened. The Afghan bitch, engrossed in some complicated sniff-ing ritual several yards off, was only just slower to locate him and came bounding over, eager for recognition. Angus put a hand to her nostrils before fondling her ears. She fell in happily behind him as he strode on towards the dog's mistress.

"Mr. Mott. Inspector," said the Hon. Celia, sounding sincerely pleased. "How good of you to call." She turned her head. "Thank you, Nancy. Mr. Mott will see me back indoors."

They waited in silence until the woman was out of earshot, then Mrs. Manton-Jones put a hand gently on Mott's arm. In the other she carried a short bâton which she shook out sharply and it became a slim white wand. She used it to sweep the way before her, like a mine detector, but infinitely more graceful, as Angus appreciated.

"This is not a purely social visit, Inspector, is it?"

He looked at the grave, still-beautiful face and almost hoped his inquiry would be fruitless. "I'm afraid I have come in an official capacity again."

"I knew you would be back. I couldn't understand. Nancy Cutler said you were so interested in one of the upstairs rooms. I know I agreed she should let you see over the house, but— It had nothing at all to do with Florrie, you see. There's something else you haven't told me, isn't there? It's connected with that awful murder. I don't want to believe it, but however much I cudgel my poor brain there's no escaping what it is you seem to think."

"What do we seem to think, Mrs. Manton-Jones?"

She appeared to draw herself taller as she summoned her resources to admit the unspeakable. "That—something quite horrible happened here while we were away."

"We have to examine the possibility." Dammit, he was nearly apologizing now for his profession. "When we reach the house I have something to show you. And I hope that you will be able to make out what it is."

He waited until she had collapsed the jointed cane and was seated in the chintzy chair where they had first found her that morning, and he watched her steel herself for some revolting sight. When he put the enlarged photograph in her hands she looked hard at him first, then moved it close to her face and passed it from one side to the other. He saw the moment of horrified recognition and the way her fingers tensed on the paper. A small sound, midway between moan and sigh, escaped her and she lowered her head.

After a few seconds she looked up blindly, her eyes moist and her face blanched. "That poor child. There's no doubt at all. Bonnie Hall. She came to us in February, just sixteen. Oh, how am I going to tell her mother, Inspector?"

"Sixteen," he repeated, "and nobody has yet missed her? How could that happen, Mrs. Manton-Jones?"

"It doesn't make sense! There was no reason why she should be here. She was Cook's help in the Eaton Square house. I don't understand, Inspector. She would have gone on holiday when we left, at the same time as Cook, because my daughter takes over the kitchen when there's only herself and my son there. Oh dear, I think I'd better ring my son right away. He should be at home today. Would you have any objection, Inspector? I mean, how much may I say?"

"Everything is going to come out now," Mott said warningly. "Can I dial the number for you?"

"It's all right. I'm used to it; my fingers go on the right buttons from habit. But stay close, please. I'd like you to speak to my son when I've told him."

He moved away to give her some vestige of privacy, but he stayed alert, picking up the gist of all she said.

"Sam, darling. This is some quite awful news I have to break. What? He is? Well, yes then. All right." She waited a moment, the receiver laid against her breast as she stared into the pattern of the chintz, a haunted expression in the partially sighted eyes.

What was she seeing then, in the centre of her tunnel vision? The face of a young girl, flushed from the heat of an oven, since February as familiar about her town house as any member of her family?

A metallic voice sounded in the earpiece and she started speaking again. "Darling, listen. Little Bonnie Hall. She's not there by any chance? No, I thought . . . yes. When did she go? *Before* we left? I see. Oh dear. No, of course I wouldn't object, but as it happens it would have been better if . . . Well, this is the terrible part, darling. We think—the police think, that is, and I'm terribly afraid they're right—that the poor child is dead. You must have seen it in the papers. That car in the disused quarry. Yes, murdered. Isn't it unthinkable? I can't imagine how she came to—

Listen, darling, I have a detective-inspector with me now. I think he'd like to have a word. Shall I hand you over?"

There was no call to go into gruesome details or make arrangements then and there for identifying the body. Mott kept it brief, merely asking for and obtaining an appointment to interview the man next morning at ten-thirty. It would be a Met job with himself or Yeadings alongside, but he was certain Scotland Yard would okay the fixture. If not, the hour could be altered by a later phone call.

He liked the sound of Manton-Jones. There was no reason to think he'd been anything other than shocked at the news, but he had good control of himself. As indeed had his mother now, valiant old doll.

It was left to Nancy Cutler, governess-in-charge, to throw a fit of the vapours. When it was her turn to examine the photographed artist's impression she first exhibited tight-lipped disapproval. Then, when Mott indicated that this was the likeness of the murdered girl in the quarry car, she gave a strangled gasp and crumpled to the floor.

Yeadings wasn't at Maidenhead when Mott went back to report. He wasn't at home either. Nan answered the phone in the middle of putting Sally to bed and she hadn't heard from Mike since breakfast.

In view of the rather odd way he had sounded when Angus rang him at Swaffham's earlier, he ventured a wild guess and rang him there again. The phone went on ringing unanswered.

So, one reported in at the Incident Room, notified the Action Allocation officer, knocked off for the night and went home. If Mike wanted to make contact he knew his number well enough. Once he heard that Mott had a probable identification on the girl he would get in touch straight away. The acting investigation officer would meanwhile contact the girl's family in Chippenham to arrange a morgue visit for identification.

At a little short of eleven, when Angus was watching a resurrected Western, Mike came through, sounding grimly cheerful. "How did you get on at Swaffham's?" his DI asked him. "Anything tricky?"

"Uh, I got an electronic welcome. Swaffham greeting me by

name. Gave me quite a turn, but it was recording gadgetry tied in with a thumb-print identification at the street door—obviously a personal refinement of Swaffham's, or the department would have removed it. Whatever way their men effected an entrance, it can't have activated this programme."

"So he had expected you to turn up there?"

"Yes. It's beginning to weary me a trifle, this beating-me-to-base game, but I did find his personal computer. It was left out in the open. Of course, breaking into the floppy disc isn't so simple. I shall have to call on Paula again, as I thought."

"So it's been a bit of a no-go day then?" Mott sounded cheerful even to himself, relishing the news he had to pass on about his own progress of that afternoon.

"Not exactly. I've just been out drinking with Danny. You remember I spoke of Danny Norman, friend of Felicity Marlowe?"

"Interior decorator by appointment to the House of Yeadings?"

"That one, yes. Caught him going out for a jar as I was coming home, so we made an evening of it."

"To some purpose?"

"He told me what Swaffham had hired him for, that last evening before he went abroad."

"I'm listening."

"Yes, well, so is the phone. I think actually I'll leave it till morning. Would drive across and see you, but I must be well over the limit."

"Message received. I'll be parked two lamp-posts down from your front gate in twenty minutes. I've some progress to report myself."

When Mott drew up at the kerb, Mike Yeadings was waiting under a laburnum. He stepped forward, swung open the door and eased into the passenger seat. "Sorry about the peppermint," he muttered. "Reminds me of old Fry and his deskbound dyspepsia. I couldn't go home stinking like a brewery."

There was nothing wrong with his enunciation, Angus noted, although "deskbound dyspepsia" had perhaps come out with unusual care and deliberation. "So Danny delivered?" he prompted. "What kind of job had Swaffham given him?"

"An acting role. He wanted Danny to be his chauffeur."

Mott had to admit that was disappointing. Unless— "Driving him where?"

"Not just driving, as it happened. He had a speaking part, lines to learn. It went like this. Hire of an immaculate Roller; arrival in uniform at a given house in Mayfair; entry on cue, hat under arm, ready to drive an unnamed lady away from a meeting with an unnamed other person and Swaffham."

"So where did he take her?"

"To the cab rank at Paddington station."

"And that's all?"

"No. Now comes the interesting part. If later that evening he was questioned as to the lady's destination he was to inform the inquirer that he'd overheard the address she gave the cab driver."

"And did anyone inquire?"

"The other gentleman present with Swaffham at the earlier meeting. He hung around afterwards on the off-chance of finding out. So Danny, as chauffeur, supplied the information, was duly rewarded, and the gentleman who made the request made off in his blue Mercedes, highly delighted."

"You want me to believe that Swaffham was actively pimping, or alternatively setting up the lady for more than she was willing to give?"

"Leave that open for the present. The story continues, with Danny collecting Swaffham from the house and driving him— guess where?"

"I pass."

"To the same address which Swaffham had Danny pass to the man interested in the unnamed lady."

Angus frowned. "If I hadn't your word for the man's character, I'd have said they had set up a version of the old Badger Game. Character who may or may not be the husband walks in on torrid sex scene with wifey and fall guy, who gets choice of violence or cheque-book athletics."

Yeadings's chin had sunk on his chest and he looked half asleep, but Mott wasn't fooled. The Guv was never more mentally engaged than when he appeared on the verge of torpor. He gave a neutral grunt now and turned his eyes on the DI. "Would you get the same impression of his game, I wonder, if you knew what the address actually was that they were all converging on?"

"Try me," Angus invited, certain he was waiting for the crunch line.

"It was a house called Pollards, near Henley in the county of Berkshire."

Angus was caught with his mouth open. Not only did Swaffham's venue come under Thames Valley Police authority, but their official case of the murdered girl was now suddenly interfaced with Yeadings's personal inquiry regarding Swaffham. Each case could be a part of the other.

After such a blow between the eyes, his own report would seem a damp squib. However, he delivered it.

"It looks as though the murdered girl was a domestic called Bonnie Hall," he said shortly. "I'm booked to interview Manton-Jones at Eaton Square about her tomorrow morning at ten-thirty."

9

They sat side by side in hunched concentration, brooding over the new development.

"The good news," Mott volunteered, "is that we can now tackle the Swaffham riddle in official time."

"Well, can we? There's nothing from the murder-case side that leads towards Swaffham. Without the posthumous clues which he's been feeding us there would be no connection at all."

"But we know now he was there, at Pollards, on or about the day the girl died. So has he been pointing us towards the murderer?"

"It isn't possible. There wasn't time. He already had his 'three-core lead' set up, and he may well have been laying a trail towards Pollards, but I think the girl's death was accidental—*inci*dental, anyway. You saw the window she went out of. No one could hope to kill her outright with that short fall to the kitchen roof. Instead they'd have taken her to an attic overlooking the concrete courtyard. I see her trying to scramble out, possibly in the dark, falling awkwardly on the roof slates, then—unable to hold on—sliding to the edge and falling the rest of the way to the yard. We know what her injuries were: a badly torn left leg and dislocated ankle. She would have been in agony, but undoubtedly still conscious, able to cry out. Someone else there panicked. She was strangled to keep her quiet."

"Which means there were *two* people at Pollards then who didn't want their presence known."

"While Swaffham, on the other hand, arrived openly, as if invited, by Roller, up the front drive. Invited by whom? we ask ourselves."

"Which presumably is what I ask Manton-Jones tomorrow."

"Not as starters." Yeadings sounded grim. "Do we know what his job is? When we begin questioning the man, are we going to get a thumbs down from Special Branch if we drag Swaffham's name in? It would be just our luck, after all the publicity there's been over the murder, if Pollards turns out to be an MI6 safe house."

"He's in insurance. Lloyd's underwriter and so on. The Hon. Celia gave me the 'my son in the City' line. Apparently she inherited Pollards from her father, and the town house was bought by her husband eighteen years ago. He was a financier, been dead over seven years."

"You sound like a family friend already."

"I liked the old doll. She's gutsy. Young Sam sounded all right to me too, on the phone. A touch urbane, but his reaction to the news about Bonnie Hall seemed genuine enough. Controlled shock."

"Instant psychological assessment via Telecom," Yeadings commented sardonically. "You could advertise in *Psychic News*. The idea could take off: get the judiciary to try cases that way. Empanel juries like a radio audience."

Angus allowed a grin to escape him. "What about your Danny Norman? Did he stay on at Pollards himself, keeping up the chauffeur act?"

"According to his version of the events, he delivered Swaffham to the door, carried in his bags, then departed. Swaffham had settled up with him in advance, including hire of the Rolls, which Danny was to return at nine next morning."

"And in between—?"

"He had seven hours of undisputed possession left. What would you have done?"

"Peeled off the chauffeur's uniform, opened up the engine and burned up the nearest stretch of motorway."

"There speaks the happily betrothed man. You overlook a basic need. He first drove into Henley to check on the night life, which isn't excessive. He managed to pick up a little lady who'd lost her escort to the gaming tables. *Then* they hit the motorway, circled back through the leafy lanes and ended up down by the river."

"So he has an alibi for almost the whole of that night?"

"We'll get it checked, but that's how it looks at the moment. He tells a good tale, but one has to remember he's an actor; persuasion is the name of his game. However, taking it all round—and until I've proof otherwise—I tend to accept the story at face value."

"Which leaves us still completely in the dark about who was with Bonnie Hall at Pollards when she climbed out of the window."

"And we don't yet know *when* it happened. That should become clearer when we interview your man tomorrow. At least the cook must know which day the girl went off duty."

Mott had been listening absently to this last, slumped over the steering-wheel. Now he lifted his face off his arms and sat up straight. "Just had a fantastic idea. Swaffham went to *Prague,* didn't he? I was never hot on history, but isn't that the place famous for defenestrations?"

"It was an accident," Yeadings stated flatly. "The girl was simply trying to get out and fell. Which is what I'll do, flat on my face, if I don't soon get to bed. See you in the morning, lad. Nine sharp at the shop. I'll have to stay warming my seat there for a day or two. The brass isn't keen on my getting out among the nitty-gritty when there's paper to be shuffled. I got addressed as 'Inspector' yesterday by the ACC. He apologized, but *if* it was a slip it was a Freudian one."

Mott wasn't entirely sorry to be left carrying the investigation, much though he enjoyed working in harness with the Guv. The forthcoming interview with the Manton-Jones household in London promised to be a vital one. Driving back to his flat, his mind still held the picture of the young, puppy-faced kitchen-maid climbing out over the sill. In a desperate hurry, so she was clumsy.

Why such haste? And why hadn't she simply used the door? Perhaps because there was someone downstairs who mustn't see her?—because she wasn't supposed to go out?—or because she wasn't supposed to be inside? Was she, in fact, running from, or running to, the person who had stopped her agonized cries by tightening his hands round her throat until she was silenced for ever?

And who at that time was at Pollards who mustn't be allowed to hear such sounds? The more Mott pondered the scenario, the greater the cast threatened to grow. He seemed to see shadowy figures all over the house, but they had no faces. With any luck, once he'd asked a few questions at the Eaton Square house tomorrow, those faces would have grown features, and would answer to names.

The Met man allocated to share the questioning with him was a cheerful, freckled DS called Rook who looked barely old enough for the rank nor big enough to be in the job. He was, however, sharp as a honed razor, as Angus quickly appreciated, even without the recommendation that came with him.

They arranged that after introduction Angus should be left to put the obvious opening questions with a minimum of follow-through. Then, when the subjects were starting to relax and Angus stolidly checking through his notebook, Rook would fill the silences with inconsequential chatter and slip in the catch questions.

Not only was Manton-Jones himself waiting for them at Eaton Square but he had recalled Cook from her holiday. There were, besides, an ancient with a perpetual, uncertain smile, who was introduced as "Nanny," and the one remaining member of staff, a schoolmasterly-looking manservant referred to as "Starling." The dead girl had been given general duties which extended beyond the kitchen, and was known to family and staff simply as Bonnie. Only Starling, Cook, and the Hon. Celia who interviewed her for the post, had ever known her surname.

At Manton-Jones's suggestion the two policemen went downstairs and began the interviews with Cook and the manservant. From a locked desk in his domain, Starling produced correspondence between Mrs. Manton-Jones and the girl's headmistress who had evidently been a country acquaintance of the lady of the house and was anxious to get the girl settled in a respectable position, since there was no turning her from the determination to seek her fortune in London. That this Mrs. Alison was a conscientious and kindly soul came across well from her writing, and Angus made a note of her address in Chippenham as being the most likely person to fill in background on the dead girl.

At school, the testimonial claimed, Bonnie was popular, punctual, well-intentioned and honest. Although of slightly above average intelligence, she had expressed some scorn for academic work, preferring to turn her skills to cooking and homecraft generally. During the holidays, although under age, she had worked at a local licensed hotel and had learned the basic duties of kitchen help and chambermaid.

Her family was respectable, and the girl's sudden intention to leave both school and home was partly inspired by her widowed mother's need to take under their roof her eighty-year-old father who was both eccentric and a martinet.

If the Hon. Mrs. Manton-Jones could see her way to offer the girl a position in her own household she would gain a loyal, cheerful and energetic young woman willing to turn a hand to whatever task was required of her. It would also considerably relieve the mind of the writer who feared the outcome of such a trusting young country girl becoming employed in a city hotel where she had neither friends nor reputation.

"Sounds an old-fashioned, innocent girl," commented the Met DS wistfully. "Just the sort I've been looking for."

"She certainly was," Cook said emphatically, giving Starling a hard look. "As nice a girl as I've ever had to help me in the kitchen." She sat on a straight-backed settle in the staff's basement sitting-room, still wearing her outdoor clothes, an enormous handbag hanging by its strap from clasped hands in her lap.

"Popular at school," Rook again read aloud from the recommendation. (He thought he'd heard the man sniff, and he didn't appear to have a cold.) "Brought a real ray of sunshine into the house, I guess?"

Starling's mouth straightened into a hard line. "A little free, I thought myself," he offered.

Cook grunted disagreement. "Mr. Starling is rather hard on young people."

"They don't know their place these days," he complained.

"Ah. Too much one of the family, was she, Mr. Starling?"

"Might have been, if I hadn't kept an eye on things," he said disapprovingly. "Not that Mr. Manton-Jones would ever have taken advantage of any unsophisticated young person, especially under his own roof."

"And, of course, his mother has a great deal of experience in dealing with—er, staff," Rook tempted him blandly, stumbling only in avoiding the word "servants," as being possibly offensive to present company.

"She has common sense," declared Cook, as if bestowing the accolade. "And if you're referring to the young mistress, Mr. Starling, with your innuendoes, I happen to know that Bonnie didn't want to take that dress she was offered, because she said it was too good for her to wear. Only Miss Manton-Jones insisted, it having got too tight."

"Where *is* Miss Manton-Jones?" Angus put in, to stem the threatened bickering. "I didn't see her upstairs with her brother."

"In Canada, sir," Starling told him, grateful for the reprieve. "She has gone for six weeks, first to her cousin in Toronto and then touring."

Mott extracted from him her *poste restante* address, entering it on a new page of his notebook.

"While we're on the matter of departures, let's get clear," he demanded, "just when everybody who's away actually left."

There was no disputing this because it was all clearly marked up on the trade calendar on the staff notice-board.

"I was due to go to my sister's at Balham on the Sunday," Cook explained, "and Bonnie had the same holidays, but I let her go two days early, seeing that Saturday was May Day and there was something special she wanted to go home for, some dance or other. She was going to wear that dress I was telling Mr. Starling about. She'd altered the bodice and it looked really nice on her. Not so smart, but prettier somehow."

"Got a feller she was sweet on, back in Chippenham, I'll bet," Rock suggested.

"I don't think so, or over all this time she'd have mentioned him. Besides, I think she'd come across someone who took her fancy just recently, up here. She hadn't got around to admitting she was interested or who he was, but I think I know the signs. It wouldn't surprise me if she was taking him down to meet her mother, though she never said as much. Some girls are like that; don't like to mention the new boy in case it's unlucky and he gets scared off before she's sure of him."

"So you've no idea at all who he was, or where she would have met him?"

Cook shook her head. "None at all, more's the pity. London's a big place, but I know some of the places she used to go on her day off. She liked exploring on her own, she said. Museums and art galleries and the parks. I'll make you a list of places she mentioned, if you like."

"Thank you. I believe she had been down to Pollards before?"

"That's right. For Easter. We went by taxi with all the linen and some groceries, just the two of us. Madam arrived on the evening of the next day, with the chauffeur and Mr. Starling; then the children turned up together early on Good Friday morning."

" 'The children' being Mr. Manton-Jones and his sister?"

"Yes. Sam's twenty-nine and Hilary's eighteen months older, but I still think of them that way, I'm afraid. I haven't been with the family anything as long as Nanny has, but I do remember them both being away at boarding-school, when the Master was alive."

"So, returning to Pollards, Bonnie was familiar with the house and grounds at Henley? Did she make any friends down there? Can you think of any reason why she should break her journey to go there this time instead of straight home to Chippenham? Would she have wanted to see someone, or to pick up something she'd left there from last time?"

But it seemed that, however friendly and open the girl had been, she had not confided her plans. It was not even certain that she had informed her mother she was returning for a holiday. In view of her grandfather's unwelcome presence at home, perhaps she had left open how long she meant to stay there. Or perhaps she'd had no intention of going there at all. They would only get information on all this when they had the opportunity to interview the dead girl's mother.

Cook explained the domestic arrangements at Pollards. Over Easter when the whole family, plus guests, had been present, she had run the kitchen with Bonnie's help. Mrs. Cutler had taken her own holiday then, which left Mr. Starling to cover the dining-room service with a waitress coming in daily from Henley.

All staff had been housed on the top, attic floor. The family had slept on the first floor, as had their guests. The ground floor of the main building was given over entirely to reception rooms, and the domestic offices were in the single-storey extension beyond the one-time kitchen, now the family dining-room.

The present arrangement there, now that only Mrs. Manton-Jones herself was in residence, was much simpler. A general maid came in daily from Henley, and Mrs. Cutler would see to their shared requirements, doing such cooking as was needed for the three of them, the chauffeur having moved into his own cottage. (Without actually voicing criticism, Cook managed to sound doubtful of such a gastronomic risk.) Back at Eaton Square, with only Mr. Manton-Jones to be looked after at present, the kitchen staff were able to take time off, since Mr. Starling could cater for such snacks as the master chose not to eat out.

"Thank you, Cook. You've made it quite clear. I'm sorry we had to interrupt your well-earned rest," Mott told her. "Can I arrange transport for you back to your sister at Balham?"

"Thank you, sir, but it's not necessary. Madam sent a taxi for me, though I would have gone by the underground myself. And Madam's ordered the car to take me back, after it gets here with Bonnie's poor mother."

This last was news to both policemen, but Manton-Jones explained when they had returned to the morning-room. "Mother couldn't leave it to the police to break the news about Bonnie," he told them. "So she was driven down last night to Chippenham and called on Mrs. Hall with the headmistress who recommended Bonnie. Then they were coming directly here this morning, are due about now, because we knew you would be anxious to see Mrs. Hall."

As a source of information, Nanny was a non-starter. She had drifted in and out of the room while Angus was speaking to Cook and Starling. As he and Rook left to return upstairs she was half-way up, lost in vague thought. She looked sideways as the police-men passed by, but did not move in either direction. "I trust," she said falteringly, "that you don't suspect the children. They have been properly brought up. And Sam is away in Canada."

Rook grinned cheerfully at her. "That's right, Nanny." She had been in the same room with the young man not twenty minutes earlier, so any information they could extract from her would be worthless.

While they waited for the car's arrival, coffee was served to them, and the two policemen were able to question Manton-Jones on his own last appearance at Pollards, which had been in the week preceding his mother's return there. He had found the house in good order and had turned on the heating, set at a background level of 62° F. "It can get damp in just a couple of weeks at this season," he said, "and Easter was early this year. It was getting on for midnight by the time I'd looked around and checked every-thing, so I stayed overnight, left about eight next morning." He added this in a throw-away manner, but Angus, wise now to the fact that Swaffham had also made a call there on his final night in England, was aware of a shade of unease, just a hint of tenseness in the otherwise urbane young man.

Manton-Jones was tall, very correct, and unusually good-look-ing. Despite the dark colouring of his eyebrows, trimmed mous-tache and hair, his eyes were blue and his complexion as creamy as his mother's, but he was no milksop. His hands were large and well-formed, his shoulders almost as broad as Angus's own, devel-oped by swimming and water-polo.

"What's your sport?" Angus asked on an impulse.

Manton-Jones smiled widely. "I used to row quite a bit, stroke for Jesus, then for Cambridge nine years ago. Since then I keep fit in summer with single sculling. In winter I play squash and ski. What's yours?"

Angus told him. Neither asked what sport the spindlier Rook favoured. Going by appearances, it might have been snooker or darts.

All the while Angus pondered how to spring the name Swaffham on Manton-Jones. The longer he waited the more sure he was that he should hold his fire until he had consulted Yeadings. He led the conversation round to the arts, specifically the theatre. He mentioned shows he had enjoyed. The other man too was keen on drama. "My fiancée is friendly with quite a gifted actress," Angus confided. "Lovely girl, called Felicity Marlowe. Have you ever seen her?"

"Not to my knowledge. What was she in?" His disclaimer sounded genuine but there had been a brief hesitation before it. Mott couldn't tell if it was because the young man's mind was on something else or because he'd opted for the more expedient answer. If he'd known Swaffham well, would he necessarily have recognized the name as being his daughter's?

The car's arrival with Manton-Jones's mother and the distraught Mrs. Hall cut short further attempts to skate round the Swaffham connection. It was a full-time job coping with the shocked woman, even with the sympathetic support she was getting from the family Bonnie had worked for. And they felt a certain guilt, Mott recognized, because the girl had been entrusted to them in preference to her taking a hotel job among strangers. It was ironic that if she had gone to the seamiest house in London she might still have been alive today.

But Mrs. Hall blamed no one. It was beyond her. She wanted only to close her eyes to the truth, open them and find it had all been a nightmare dispersed at the dawn. Mrs. Manton-Jones, no stranger to bereavement, was at hand to help, and Mott was glad she would go with the other woman to the morgue for the terrible task of identification.

For himself, with enough information to mull over for the present, he took his leave with the Yard man, falling in with his suggestion of a couple of pints to assist the digestion of facts. There would be a better chance of getting what he needed from the dead girl's mother when she was less in shock.

He sounded Rook out about his reactions to the case as it stood officially, suppressing all reference to the other lead which had drawn them to Pollards from Swaffham's end. The Met man had no suggestions to offer that weren't already self-evident. It was Yeadings Angus was eager to get back to, and he found him at Maidenhead, in his shirt-sleeves, bending over the shoulder of a WPC who operated a computer. He stood up as Angus came in and gave him a swift interrogative glance.

"What are you on to?" Angus beat him to the question.

"It looks as though we may have pin-pointed the car. There's a scrap-yard just outside High Wycombe. A potential customer for wheels has had his eye on an old tan Cortina for a couple of weeks; been playing casual in order to beat the price down. He went to take another look today and the car had gone. No record of any sale, and the dealer was hopping mad, didn't realize the thing could roll. Anyway, you've arrived just in time to take the would-be customer over to Forensic to view the murder car. You can leave your notes with me. I'll take a look at them before they get logged."

"You do that, Guv," Angus encouraged him. "I think we've got some interesting dates to compare."

"Which fit in with the pathologist's findings?"

"And with your friend Danny's chauffeuring activities."

Yeadings hummed and stroked his chin. "I had a nasty feeling it would all come together. Which leaves me in a bit of a dilemma."

Well, he could say that again, Angus thought, giving him a meaning nod and handing over his notebook with the Eaton Square interviews. The dilemma, of course, concerned how far Yeadings now felt compelled to feed the Swaffham story into the murder log. He gave him a sardonic salute. "I'll pick up another notebook on the way out. See you later when I get back from Aldermaston."

He wasted valuable minutes at the Action Allocation desk fielding an objection that he was covering a task which a DC could deal with adequately. "It could well lead to something," he said significantly. "It's an idea the Guv's got."

He got away with it, ruefully admitting to himself that the only idea the Guv had at present was the need to compare the date-and-time lists he'd obtained from Eaton Square with similar ones he'd already made for the Swaffham business. Yeadings was a stickler for entering everything into the book, even if he didn't always act according to same book. Sending Mott on a minor inquiry would buy him the time to make up his mind on whether everything he'd learned from Felicity Marlowe on a confidential basis had to become official knowledge.

1 0

There wasn't a wax cat in hell's chance that the man Angus was accompanying to view the tan Cortina had played any part in the case they were investigating. If he wasn't actually a tinker he was a first-generation house-dweller. In the short journey to the forensic examination centre Mott had to hear at least seven times over a rapturous description of the beaten-up old car and the uses to which it would be put and the transformation it would undergo before being launched on the market as (presumably) a "low-mileage, one-careful-lady-owner, economic-to-run bargain."

"Look, Buster, it's scrap," he protested finally. "It was scrap before it went into sludge up to the dashboard, and it's scrap-plus now that it's been dragged out. You may get women to take mud baths for beauty, but if the used-car trade goes for that, it's taking sex-equality too far!"

His passenger looked affronted and settled lower in his seat. "It's a nice liddle car all de same, sor. A nice liddle t'ing." From then on he sulked in silence, only balefully offering Mott "t'ree t'ousand, cash," for his MG as he climbed out on arrival.

"Let's just do what we came for," the DI offered curtly, firmly keeping his hands in his pockets.

"What, back again?" observed the forensic examiner brightly. "D'you fancy the Cortina, Inspector?"

Mott fixed his eyes six inches above the joker's head and announced, "This gentleman thinks he knows the car. He will describe in some detail its finer points. Shall we just check them over?"

There could be no doubt that it was the same car the ex-tinker had shown an interest in at the scrap-yard—such a close interest that he had been into the engine and deposited identical dabs to the ones he was now smearily bestowing on its bodywork.

"It's in a turrible state!" the man objected. "Oi'll need compensation, mister. Oi spent hours getting the flaming thing to go!"

"It isn't your car," Mott reminded him. "You were only supposed to be looking at it in the scrap-yard. Maybe you'll get it at a better price now it's extra mucky. On the other hand, when the dealer knows it actually works, *he* should get the better price."

The point went home. The man had lost interest enough to take out his spite on the tyres, walking round the machine and kicking each in turn as if the car had played him false.

"We'll just get those fingerprints photographed," Mott suggested innocently, "then I'll give you a lift home."

"What fingerprints, mister?"

Mott pointed. "Yours. Under the bonnet too. See? That's the powder we blow on to—"

"Listen, mister, I don't need no lift. I got friends I can phone to. And I ain't having nothun to do with that beat-up old car."

"Suit yourself."

In the end they compromised. The man agreed to call in at Division and sign a statement identifying the Cortina as the one he'd inspected in the scrap-yard on condition nothing more was said about fingerprints.

"Couldn't the dealer have come and done it?" the forensic assistant asked, staring after the figure stomping into the distance, hands safe in pockets.

"Not really. To him it was just junk. This character's a specialist, like his grand-dad would have been with horses. They really study what they covet."

"Well?" Yeadings demanded as Angus looked into his office.

"We have a positive identification on the Cortina."

"Mm. The trouble is that we haven't a definite date for its disappearance from the scrap-yard. The place was closed for a fortnight from May 10th while the owner had an operation on his big toe. He'd fired his assistant at Easter and hadn't taken on anyone else. Too mean, his wife says.

"As he's been hobbling on a stick for some time I doubt if he went the rounds properly at all. Your friend of this afternoon only missed the car last Tuesday when the place reopened, and he went to make an offer. Caused quite a stink, apparently, when the dealer denied he'd got rid of it."

"I should think he would. Over a period of visiting the thing, he'd tinkered it into working, just as the scrap-yard closed. I suppose when he eventually went to collect the car he took a tow-rope to keep up appearances."

Yeadings grinned grimly. "Life's rich tapestry! I suppose it's progress that he did offer to *buy* it. And we actually have an address to find him at when we need him. Any chance he's the one we're after?"

"He might well panic and strangle to get out of a sticky situation, though by nature I'd say he's more of a punch-thrower. But if the girl was the sensible country kid she sounds, she'd have recognized what he was and avoided him like the plague. Anyway, he'd never have kicked up such a fuss about the car going missing if he'd been involved in anything so serious. His kind are great at fading into the distance. Have you any detail there on the scrapyard end? If they discovered the Cortina was missing last Tuesday, why the delay in reporting the theft?"

"Half a dozen reasons. What's scrap, after all, when your damn toe's still aching? And what do the police care about stolen cars anyway? But mainly, I guess, it was mutual suspicion kept both of them simmering. Then they had a second barney over it and each persuaded the other he was on the level. By then it seems the dealer's grouch reached wifey's ears, and as soon as she knew the disputed car was a tan Cortina she remembered there'd been a policeman round asking about one, a week after her man had his op. She'd fobbed him off, being in a hurry to get to Wycombe Hospital at the start of visiting hours."

Angus dropped on to a chair. "As they say, it's easy when you know how. But it's galling how things like that hold everything up."

"Time," Yeadings said ponderously, "is the enemy all right. I've been trying to work things out in your absence. Pull your chair up and have a look at this."

He had set out a calendar of events in two columns. The left one referred to the case of the strangled girl; the right one to all he knew about the Swaffham affair. On the degree of correlation,

Angus knew, rested the decision whether or not to make official Swaffham's approach to him.

The calendar began on Friday, April 30th, exactly a month ago, with Bonnie Hall going supposedly home on holiday from Eaton Square, and Felicity Marlowe calling on her father for the box of books as Swaffham left the Pimlico house by taxi, presumably for his office.

"No connection there," Yeadings pointed out. "There's none until we get to the early hours of May 1st. Then we get Swaffham arriving at Pollards, where the girl Bonnie sometimes worked. Pollards is the link. I've photocopied this list for your use. Take it home and brood over it; in the bath, while you eat, on the throne, every moment and everywhere. By tomorrow I must decide whether to throw Swaffham to the computers."

Angus stood up, sliding the folded pages into his jacket. The Guv was looking jaded, as well he might, having had no break since the siege at Earley. The backwash on that single case, with the Police Authority questioning every aspect, was enormous. He didn't need a hostile inquest on this case's outcome, hampered as well by Special Branch putting out a closed lips order.

"I'll do what I can, Guv."

He picked up some fried chicken on his way home, and let himself in to find Paula leaning in the doorway of the kitchen, smiling at him over a glass of wine. "Welcome back. I've been given tomorrow off. Old Wheatman's gone to see a sick colleague down at Hereford. How do you fancy a live-in lover for one night?"

What he needed, to top up her offer—he explained when he had properly reacted and they'd celebrated the occasion—was added brainpower on Mike Yeadings's behalf. He presented her with the dilemma and the calendar of events while he went to put supper together. When he came back to light the single candle on their low table and carried in the plates, she handed the papers back. He saw that three names on it were now ringed in pencil.

"What's this, then?"

"The people I'd want to know a lot more about."

"Swaffham, Felicity, and Manton-Jones," Angus considered. "Well, the first is dead and the second's abroad, so we'll have to concentrate on the third for the present. But why him especially?"

"Because Pollards is the link," she echoed Yeadings's words. "M.-J.'s mother is disabled, so he's the virtual owner, visits to check on the property, etcetera, probably pays the bills, must have ordered the work done on the new tarmac which conveniently marked Bonnie's clothes. I'd want to know just where he was on the night Swaffham turned up, freshly retired from one of the skulduggery services."

Yeadings had suggested quite a few occasions to concentrate on his problem, but not bed. Angus recalled this, grinning contentedly as he cradled Paula's dark head on his arm. But he had reckoned without her stimulated curiosity.

"I keep thinking about Felicity," she murmured. "The way she kept the funeral so dark, never invited anyone. Of course, Mike was held up just then in that hostage business at Earley, but she could have rung Nan. Nan would have gone to support her. It just came up in conversation the night before she left. I didn't even know the body had been flown over.

"And then suddenly she had to be off abroad. Nothing could stand in her way. She really worked like stink over that script idea. If she'd put half as much effort into her career earlier, her name would be in lights all over London by now. I can't help thinking she knows something she hasn't told us. By now she'll have had her two days in Heidelberg and be moving on. Just what do you think she's up to now in Prague?"

"Nothing anywhere as interesting as what we have in mind," Angus reminded her. "What do I have to do to get your attention —cry 'Order, order'?"

It appeared not.

Tuesday, once Mike's free time, was just another workday. While a murder inquiry continued and the Incident Room remained active there was no leave for the Serious Crime personnel. Briefing was timed for 9 A.M. At 8:55 Mike Yeadings stood at Chief Superintendent Faraday's office window and stared unseeing into the precinct. Pollards was now confirmed as the place where Bonnie Hall had fallen from a height, and very probably the place where she had met her end. The tar scrapings taken from the yard there had matched the marks on her skirt and blouse. As a result, scene of crime experts had been let loose on the house and had picked up her dabs on the window-frame of the room from which she'd fallen and, more significantly, from the sill where she'd clung momentarily before dropping away.

Nor could there be any doubt that it was to Pollards that Swaffham had been drawing his attention, through Felicity, who in turn had pointed him towards Danny Norman as eye-witness, with her useful exit line. The awareness of having been manipulated galled him, even though he trusted its source. At the same time he drew back instinctively from passing such knowledge to a superior officer and permitting the two areas of inquiry to lock in. Perhaps this was from lack of confidence in the senior uniform man seated behind him now, almost certainly taking some further dose of settler tablets before facing up to the morning's briefing.

Yeadings turned round, ready to go, and Faraday rose slowly to his feet, six feet two of yellowed oatmeal flesh hanging loose on its frame, the tunic even looser. "Sure you feel up to it, sir?" Yeadings risked asking.

Faraday's folded face tightened. "Just the old constipation. Self-inflicted wound: insufficient exercise. Tried every remedy. Taken enough bran to win the Derby. I'll be stamping my hooves and peeing in the gutters next."

Not today, Yeadings told his problem, and shelved it. The chief super wasn't up to taking on the added load with its shadowy threat of crossing the security services. But what danger did delay invite? He must get right into the connection himself, shake the damn case together.

"Shall we go down, then?" Faraday muttered, hugging a sheaf of notes to his medal ribbons. "Let's set the ferrets to their task."

The lecture room was full of chattering men and women, uniform and plain clothes. About a dozen late-comers were leaning against the wall behind the ranks of filled chairs. There was a scraping of shoe soles, a rush of short, final remarks and then a settling silence.

"Windows," the chief super commanded like a schoolmaster, and three constables sprang to open more.

"Right, then. All names provided in your reports have been checked with Criminal Records. Apart from the colourful would-be purchaser of the tan Cortina—with a list of minor convictions as long as my two arms—there's only one notable offender: the

Hon. Celia Manton-Jones. I refer to two charges of driving without due care and attention, and one of dangerous driving which led to a successful civil case for damages of tens of thousands. Missed a manslaughter charge by a whisker and the surgeon's skill. No alcohol taken, but the lady was registered partially-sighted shortly after she lost her licence."

He paused, and Yeadings at a nod poured water from the carafe on their table and pushed the tumbler along. Faraday drank, grimaced and continued. "Time of the crime: post-mortem findings confirm that death occurred soon after the girl's fall. Cause of death, as everyone knows, manual strangulation, the killer being right-handed and almost certainly kneeling over the prostrate body. (For those with vocabulary difficulties, I will remind you that prostrate means lying face down; supine, face up.) The intention was evidently to silence—even permanently—the injured girl who would have been in considerable pain. Any questions so far?

"No? On then, continuing Time of crime: stomach contents indicated a meal taken some five hours before death and including raw apple, dark chocolate and some form of pastry cooked with chicken. When the girl left her place of work a little after 2 P.M. on April 30th the cook gave her a packed supper in case she stayed on in town and caught a late train home. The meal consisted of a large Cox's orange pippin and two homemade chicken pasties. Either the girl already had the chocolate with her, or she bought or was given some. Following that up may lead us to witnesses.

"As Bonnie had consumed a hearty lunch before leaving the house in Eaton Square, it's possible that she didn't eat supper much before her normal hour which was roughly nine o'clock, after the family had dined. (Apparently she was supposed to eat first, but the cook was indulgent, allowing her longer free time in the afternoon provided the girl was willing to stay up late clearing up on her own. No doubt she also enjoyed the best leftovers in that way.)

"Assuming then that she kept to habit and ate about nine, it would bring her death to somewhere near two on the morning of Saturday, May 1st. We must give or take an hour or two for medical reasons, and to allow for her eating earlier or later than estimated. It still leaves her killing to have occurred during the hours of darkness between April 30th and May 1st—unless you prefer to believe she carried her supper around with her for a matter of days."

There were grins and shuffles. The chief superintendent drank again, gave Yeadings an agonized stare and passed his papers along the table to Angus. "Carry on, Inspector. Superintendent Yeadings, a word if you please."

He rose and made for the door, Mike on his heels. Outside, he leaned against the wall, pulling at his collar with shaking hands. His face, grey now rather than yellowed, had two sharp bars of crimson under the eyes. He was sweating profusely.

"Sorry, Mike. Hospital, I guess."

"Can you get to my car?"

They made it, by the yard exit, Yeadings removing Faraday's tunic and throwing his own jacket over him laid out on the rear seat. No need to excite outside comment when they reached Casualty. A dark blue uniform as a stretcher case always attracted press photographers, and this one had a lot of decoration on the epaulettes.

There was one good result of this disaster, Mike considered grimly, waiting while nurses stripped off Faraday's clothing in a curtained cubicle: there was no one left in the squad for Mike to report to. It rested with him officially now whether to feed in the Swaffham facts or go it alone. The assistant chief constable was interested only in *faits accomplis*.

First thing I'll do, he promised himself, is to pin down young Manton-Jones. He seems a damn sight too smooth for my liking. If his alibi holds, he must still have some idea who was at Pollards that night. According to Danny Norman the house was open, lights on and all that. M.-J. has to know more than he's admitted. Best thing, face him out with it; demand to know if he's another spook.

Casualty Sister whizzed up. "Mr. Yeadings? Your friend insists you don't stay. We're sending him to a ward when doctor's finished here. I can't say which one, because we have to search for a bed that's free. Phone in after eleven and ask Admissions. Oh, and he said to tell you, 'Carry on,' whatever that implies. So don't wait. Visiting hours today from six to eight." She whizzed off again, still talking over her shoulder.

Mike stuck his head through the curtains, gave a grin and a wave towards the apprehensive face beyond the heaped blanket, reclaimed his jacket, and was off to do battle. He'd made up his mind. When he'd dealt with M.-J. he was going to feed the Swaffham case in by one corner—the witness Danny Norman—and watch carefully that it didn't blow up in anyone's face.

Back at the briefing Inspector Angus Mott worked through Alibis to Subsequent Action, which he translated into "Follow-up," omitting asides and digs because he still felt he belonged on the other side of the table. There were a number of quite sensible questions which he dealt with succinctly. "Right," he said at the end, "let's get stuck into it, then." He went back to Yeadings's office, where about twenty minutes later the superintendent returned with news of Faraday's removal from the action.

"Poor old bugger. What is it, d'you think—appendix?"

"He's had it out. Ulcer of some kind, perhaps. Perforated, I should think. I dropped in to tell his wife. She's in a tizzy, so I've had WDS Potter sent round. She's a motherly soul, even if she is half the other woman's age."

"So what's next on our agenda, Guv?"

Yeadings looked grim. "Notify the Met and bring in Manton-Jones. I want him *here,* for questioning. And leave me all you've got on alibis."

Angus went off to arrange things and Yeadings settled to his reading. It soon became obvious that Manton-Jones was perfectly covered for the night in question, vouched for at a dinner-party at a country house near Tetbury. He had arrived early, at about six, to talk business with his host, a Tory Member of Parliament. The guests had included a stipendiary magistrate and a famous transplant surgeon. M.-J. had stayed on talking till midnight and, thinking better of driving back to London, had gone only a couple of miles then put up for the night at a nearby pub. The local police had been contacted to check on all this and phoned back confirming the registration. The alibi looked sound enough, but Yeadings wasn't taking anything at face value, especially where anything connected with Swaffham was concerned.

The interview was fixed for two-thirty. From an upstairs window Yeadings, lighting his pipe, watched the young man park his

Porsche and walk across to the building. In due course he was announced by a WPC and came in, amiable but wary.

"Superintendent." He offered his hand and Yeadings touched it with his own. Seconds out of the ring, he thought wryly.

They went through the alibi, detail by detail. Manton-Jones was able to recall some of the table-talk and items of the menu. His booking in at the pub had been on the spur of the moment. Not that his alcohol consumption had been all that high, but it was coming on to rain again and he had thought better of motorway driving if his reactions were at all slowed down. In any case, he had had a heavy week and welcomed a break. Did he, Yeadings asked himself, protest too much?

"What was the pub like?" he inquired.

Manton-Jones was able to satisfy his curiosity. It all sounded genuine enough, including a thumb-nail sketch of the ancient who had brought his morning tea.

There was nothing to guarantee that the young man hadn't stayed at that pub on some previous occasion and his recollections were from that time. It would be worth running a glance back through the register, if they kept a proper one. "Ever stayed there before?" Yeadings asked casually, as though running out of ideas.

"That was the first time. And the last." Ruefully.

"Mm." Yeadings stretched out his long legs under the desk, leaning back in relaxation. His eyes were half closed, his voice took on an after-lunch drone. "Suppose we level with each other, Mr. Manton-Jones. This is, after all, a murder case. Just tell me two things: when did you first meet Howard Swaffham; and just how well did you know him?"

There was a marked silence. Momentarily something flickered in the younger man's eyes, then the easy confidence returned. "I can't think what this has to do with Bonnie Hall."

Yeadings was looking grim now, all signs of lethargy gone. "The connection is Pollards, on the night of April 30th to May 1st. Swaffham and Bonnie were both there then, and now they're both dead, one of them by violence. I should like for two reasons to keep Howard Swaffham's name out of this inquiry, but if it is germane to the case then I shall not hesitate to follow wherever suspicion leads. Now answer my questions, please."

Manton-Jones nodded gravely. "I understand, Superintendent." He took a deeper breath. "I met Howard five years ago, when my sister brought him home to dinner. And I got to know him as well as a man does his twin's fiancé."

It shook Yeadings. Swaffham getting engaged, five years back? But there was something wrong with the story. Yes, Mott's notes had stated that Manton-Jones and his sister were eighteen months apart in age. He'd have to tread carefully here.

"You said 'fiancé.' Didn't they marry?"

"Sadly, no. She was killed in a shipping disaster a few months later."

"I'm sorry." Yeadings looked at him impassively. "You did say *'twin* sister'?"

"Yes. There were three of us. Samantha the youngest, in Canada at present, and us two—Hilary and Harriet."

"Harriet?" Of course, that was the answer. Harriet, familiarly called Harry! And according to his old colleague Maybury, Swaffham had "never got over young Harry."

And, dammit, Manton-Jones had said his own name was Hilary. Yeadings was sure that somewhere in Mott's notes he had called him Sam. A pox on these androgynous names. The official statements would have all his names in full—not a part the busy plod would read through too carefully in any case. So Mott had blundered, skimming the long rigamarole, usually referring to the man as M.-J. and passing on his wrong assumption to Mike. Correction now: Sam—female, Harry too; Hilary—male.

"Am *I* allowed to ask a question?" Manton-Jones inquired. "If so, what were your two reasons for wishing to keep Howard's name out of this investigation?"

Yeadings eyed him evenly. "You may ask. I'll even give you the answers, because the second one leads naturally to my next question to you. First, then—because he was a man I admired. Second —because of his profession. So now I need to know: are you in the same business that he was?"

As he watched Manton-Jones the young man seemed to age visibly. "No. I am what I claim to be and no more. I never was; but you see, Harry was. For years she was one of Howard's best operatives. He recruited her straight out of Oxford."

11

"Tea, I think," Yeadings said, and Angus put his head out of the door to make the right noises. He glanced quickly at Manton-Jones as he took up his place again. The man's normally smooth face was tense and set. Seeming unaware that he'd been granted a few moments' reprieve, he went on talking.

"Her death was a terrible blow to us all, especially to Mother. The most painful part was that Howard always blamed himself for it. It was because of him that she was on that ship which was blown up.

"If it hadn't happened, Harry would have retired from field-work and married Howard, and I would probably never have had an inkling what work they'd been engaged on. Till then I thought Howard was some terribly senior think-tank merchant for the Cabinet."

"I see. And did you continue your relationship with Swaffham after your sister's death?"

"He'd become an extension to the family, yes. But as you probably know, he wasn't one for intimate circles. He came occasionally among Mother's other guests, and he in his turn would entertain us at various hotels in London or the country."

"So he knew Pollards quite well?"

Manton-Jones hesitated. "That is where Harry brought him, the first time, but after that he always came to the Eaton Square house. No, I wouldn't say he was familiar with Pollards."

Yeadings smiled, watching closely. "You knew he was there that weekend, didn't you? Perhaps even lent him your key?"

Manton-Jones drew a deeper breath. "There was no need. I was there to let him in."

They stared levelly at each other. "And your alibi?" Yeadings asked quietly.

"Not a complete fabrication. The first part, until midnight, was quite correct."

The pause this time was a little longer, then: "And the hotel you supposedly stayed at on your way back from Tetbury?"

"I had a stand-in, by previous arrangement, who said he was me."

"So your statement will have to be amended. Now who else was at Pollards besides yourself, Swaffham and Bonnie Hall?"

"Bonnie wasn't in the house," he said hurriedly. "Or if she was, she had no right to be, and I certainly never saw her. I looked after everything for Howard myself, preparing a light supper, airing a room for him and so on. He was staying over the single night, before flying to Germany for a retirement holiday."

"He was dying, not just retiring. Didn't you know that?"

"Not at the time. I knew he was ill, perhaps very ill. Anyone could see that. But I expected him back in a couple of weeks or so, possibly refreshed."

"And since he had already retired, at midnight of April 30th, what need for this secret meeting requiring your assistance, as a private citizen?"

"Official secrets," Manton-Jones said vaguely. "The understanding carries on indefinitely. I covered myself with the false alibi because he'd insisted on complete discretion. Look, Superintendent, I know no more than I've told you. Howard asked me if he might spend the last night there before he left the country. I wasn't to mention it, and to be there myself. That's God's truth."

Yeadings continued to stare flat-eyed at him. For a short while he had thought Manton-Jones might be the third core of the lead which Swaffham had promised him, but he wasn't. He really didn't know any more than he'd said, because he appeared to be as baffled by it all as Yeadings was himself. So what had Swaffham been up to at Pollards, and where was the still missing part of the cable?

"There was one other person there, wasn't there, Mr. Manton-Jones?"

Had Yeadings not been so intently watching the other's face he might have missed that lightning flicker in the eyes. "Because I believe you when you claim you never knew Bonnie was there. And Swaffham didn't kill her. Between you both, you would have seen to her injuries and got her to Casualty in no time. So tell me: who else was creeping round that house at dead of night not wishing to be discovered?"

"There was one other man there," Manton-Jones admitted after a tense silence. "But I've no idea who he was. He didn't give me his name, and Howard had warned me not to ask. He drove up at a little after one-fifteen and waited in the dining-room until Howard arrived."

"To see Swaffham. So you had set up an assignation, and Swaffham was no longer a member of any government agency. What did you think the man was, a newspaper editor paying Swaffham to do a Peter Wright?" Yeadings's voice was a whiplash.

"I fervently hoped not. They—"

"Yes, go on."

"They both signed a document, and I witnessed it. Howard covered the man's name when it was my turn to sign. I trusted him implicitly. It's only since then, when I knew he was dead, that I wondered. He seemed so—"

"So what?"

"Full of some almost-satisfied emotion."

"And the other man, the nameless one?"

"Completely negative. He might have been the plumber changing a washer. He only stayed about forty minutes after Howard arrived, then he said good night, picked up his car, which he'd driven round to the old stable yard, and went off."

"The car. Description, please."

"Dark and large, probably a Volvo."

"And you didn't notice the licence number, of course?"

"I didn't want to know."

Yeadings changed the position of his legs, recrossing his ankles the other way. "The old stable yard is that part by the kitchen extension, I believe, where the new macadam strip is?"

"That's right. Where your inspector thought the girl had fallen."

"And how long did this mystery man take to fetch his car?"

"I don't know. Two or three minutes, perhaps. I would have

gone with him, but I was getting Howard's supper out of the fridge."

Yeadings sighed, dragged a pad of paper across the desk-top towards him. "Describe him."

"Five eleven, or maybe a little less. Greying hair, had been dark, receding at the temples. Dark brown eyes. Otherwise nothing distinctive. No facial moles or scars. Neither fat nor thin, no unusual way of walking."

"Left-handed?"

The man considered this. "He can't have been, or I'd have noticed when he signed."

"There's something more, isn't there? You just remembered something then. A ring perhaps?"

"No. Nothing." Manton-Jones stared back unshaken. "That's all I remember." He was willing his mind to blank out the vital detail, the latex gloves which the *incognito* had worn from the moment of entering the house. "I suppose he could have come across Bonnie, but why should he want to hurt her? In any case, he didn't seem the violent type."

"Psychopaths seldom do," Yeadings said sourly, "most of the time." He rose and nodded. "I shall probably ask you to help us again. Please inform this division if you need to leave London and the Home Counties, and give us a phone number."

"I'm spending the next two weeks at Pollards, working from there. My mother isn't the nervous kind, but I wanted to be sure she's not disturbed further." He made it sound a rebuke: crude constabulary, fragile lady of the manor.

"Well?" Yeadings demanded when Angus returned from seeing him out.

"We're getting nearer. A new scenario at Pollards. Cool customer, isn't he? Can't quite make my mind up about him. An innocent doing a favour for a lover of his dead twin? Possible. Or a conspirator more involved in some hanky-panky than he cares to admit? I shouldn't like to put money on it."

"Swaffham meant to lead me to him," Yeadings pursued. "He laid a trail, via Felicity and Danny Norman, to Pollards. At Pollards, after the alibi fell through, we're offered M.-J. and the mystery man. Why? Is one of them the villain Swaffham wanted me to finger? But not young M.-J., I think. Swaffham wouldn't drop his dead fiancé's twin down the pan through my agency. If it needed doing he could have done it himself a dozen ways. No, I have to opt for the other one, the nameless one whose signature M.-J. was prevented from seeing."

"Look, Mike, that signing business, the whole Pollards scene, was set up in advance, and we're agreed that the girl's killing was a spur-of-the-moment job, so probably it had nothing to do with Swaffham. Suppose there was an intruder already in the house, or someone there with the girl for a dirty weekend, wouldn't that make silencing her more credible? Wouldn't she have been desperately trying to get out of the house without being discovered? The Swaffham/M.-J. business could be totally coincidental."

"Don't I know it? But I'm feeding all Swaffham's information into the computer just the same, and a hell of a lot of detail from other cases on our patch. Tell traffic to toss in all they've got. Then get the VDU wizards to pick out random aspects of the Bonnie Hall case for connections across the board.

"Start with anything at all we have on cars. There must have been one that transported Bonnie's body from the scene of the crime. That was May 1st. The tan Cortina wasn't available until May 11th at the earliest, when the scrap-yard closed. It's confirmed that the padlock there was fiddled, but we don't know when. And the car wasn't missed until your tinker friend went to claim it on the twenty-fifth. Whenever the switch was made, the body must have been stashed elsewhere until then. The path report insists on a cramped, comparatively airless place and specifically suggests a car boot for the whole time. So find another car, from which the tan Cortina took over."

"In fact the killer's own, with the gruesome memento travelling round with him in the intervening days, or secretly garaged, until its presence began to make itself evident? Then a scout round for a substitute cache, and a clean-up of the family saloon?"

"Wherever it is, there must still be microscopic evidence which couldn't be completely removed."

"I'd have dumped it, myself." Mott nodded.

"So look at everything we have on cars reported missing, cars in pounds. It wouldn't be the first time the car we were looking for was already in our own hands. Extend that beyond Thames Valley, to neighbouring counties and the Met." Yeadings made scooping motions with his hands which included his inspector and the door. Angus accepted his dismissal.

He found that there was already an ample file on transport for the case, which covered all the Manton-Jones vehicles, the tan Cortina and—since that morning—Swaffham's hired Rolls. There were also all the possible rearrangements of the letters and figures of the false licence plate attached to the Cortina when found. Which led Mott's memory back to the interview at Highgate with the owner of the lost blue Mercedes.

Blue Mercedes. That rang a bell. Somewhere in all this bumf there had been another mention—"Use the 'Find' function," he told the computer operator. "Put in 'Blue Mercedes' and see what comes out."

Of course! It was in Danny Norman's account of the night of April 30th–May 1st. The car had been driven by the unnamed man who inquired where Danny had dropped the unnamed lady, after they'd both been with Swaffham at the Mayfair apartment. Danny had told him Paddington cab rank and—true or false—added he'd heard her ask to be driven to Pollards.

So was that unnamed man the same one who had again met Swaffham there, and signed a document which M.-J. witnessed? Had he run into Bonnie when he went to retrieve his car (large and dark; might have been a Volvo) from the yard where Bonnie had fallen? And then killed her? Could it be because she'd seen him, and somehow knew who he was?

Then had he bundled her body into his car boot, and driven around with that damning evidence for days until he'd happened on an untended scrap-yard, had broken in to dump it, discovered a wreck that actually rolled, then devised a more complicated disposal plan to confuse the hunt?

He could have passed near the gravel pit between Pollards and the scrap-yard. So he had returned that way with the loaded Cortina, had run it round to the far side which wasn't visible from the road, and pushed the thing in.

But he was a stranger to the district, didn't know the pit was shallow. He must have been furious that the car didn't disappear entirely. And either he'd been obliged to walk back from the gravel pit to the scrap-yard to reclaim his own car, or else he'd had an accomplice who'd driven it out to pick him up. The last act of his far-from-perfect crime had to be getting rid of his own, marked car. As he'd since asked for police help in tracing it, he must be pretty sure it was gone for good.

With these ideas surging in his mind, Angus Mott strode back to his super's room and plunged in. "How's this?" he demanded, spilling out his reconstruction of events with all its variables.

Yeadings seized on it. "The killer found it was impossible to clean the Merc sufficiently to fool Forensic, so *then* he changed the licence plates, with the letters and figures of his own rearranged. It's the only way he dared to bring his own car into the story. So where's the Merc now? Would he be likely to offer it for respray when the bloodstained condition of the boot might leave him open to blackmail? Or did he have to drown it somewhere really deep this time?"

"It doesn't matter for the moment," Angus interrupted. "The point is that we've got a name for the blue Merc's owner. I interviewed him, the bloke at Highgate. Fellow with bulgy green eyes. White, wasn't it? No; *Whittle!*"

"And you believe this Whittle was with Swaffham at the first signing, drove down to Pollards to follow up the woman—presumably to an unfamiliar address—got there before Swaffham, waited for him to arrive, then quietly sat down and signed a second document Swaffham produced? Finally, going out to pick up his car, finished off a youngster with a dislocated ankle he just happened to find lying in his way?

"No, lad. That sounds far too busy an evening for one man. Besides, your man Whittle had green eyes. In the dark, Danny didn't get a good look at his man, but the one M.-J. described as signing the document had dark brown."

"I'll give you that. But a *prowler outside* could still be Whittle, coming on the girl, panicking when she got a clear view of him, and silencing her so she didn't bring everyone running. Shall we pull him in, sir?"

"Get me a line to the Met sergeant you interviewed him with. Tell him to take Whittle in for questioning and I'll go up myself. He can cool off till I get there."

They had almost two hours to wait, and then the call came back. Adrian Whittle was out of the country, left on the twenty-ninth, taking an early holiday in France, touring the wine regions.

Mott swore under his breath. "Are you certain? Could he be lying low? It is a murder case, Sergeant."

"Checked it myself with the travel firm and his minicab to the airport. BA are still going through their arrivals lists, but they're eighty percent sure he boarded."

"Thanks." Angus subsided. "I interviewed him on the twenty-second. During the following week he rang twice to ask if the car had been traced. Then scarpered on the twenty-ninth. Scared, would you say? Do we go after him?"

"We haven't enough yet to hold him. If we went across to question him, he might run for good. No harm in asking the Sûreté to check on his movements, though."

"I'll see to it. Meanwhile how does that leave us?"

"Not smelling of violets, I'm afraid. We still have no idea what Bonnie Hall was doing down at Pollards. I wish we could dig up a boyfriend for her. What direction do you intend casting in, Angus?"

"Any that offers. I'm a bit stumped at present." He lifted his shoulders and grimaced. "Did I tell you Paula turned up last night? She went on and on about Felicity; what we thought she was up to in Prague now."

"Well," said Yeadings reflectively, "what *do* we think she's up to?"

12

It was purely accidental, Felicity thought, that she should be crossing the frontier into Czechoslovakia on the last day of May, just a month after she had said goodbye to her father. If he had lived as long as the specialist had predicted he would still have had a week or so left.

When the three German immigration officials had left after

casually looking through the train at their customs post, the train clanked on a few hundred feet and again slowed. Felicity looked out at the hard-faced group in uniform lining up to board when the wheels stopped turning. There were twenty-seven. Perhaps it was one way of solving an unemployment problem.

Four of them came in and loomed over her; three uniformed men she took to be soldiers because they carried rifles and had hand-guns in their holsters. The other was a middle-aged woman, squat, square and authoritative, in civilian dress and smelling of stale nicotine. She sat, thighs spread, on the seat beside the girl and balanced a tin of oddments on the tight grey material of her skirt. "Money," she ordered, and Felicity gave a rundown of what currencies she carried.

"And travel cheques."

Felicity handed them over for examination. She was treated to a hard stare. Assessing her for truthfulness? Hell, why should she want to lie about money?

The woman muttered to herself, the only recognizable word being "*vizum.*" She flattened the open pages with her heavy palm before perusing each word of the splendid green and red full-sheet stamp placed there by the London Embassy. Finally—with reluctance, it seemed—the ink-pad's lid was lifted, the oblong rubber stamp pressed on its surface and then scrupulously applied in the bottom right-hand corner, in green ink matching that of the left-hand side of the visa. She made a note on her clipboard of Felicity's name and passport number, with the amounts of currency held. The soldiers' mien became less aggressive, but there was no welcome. The woman handed back the passport, rose and waddled to the door. Then one of the uniformed men wanted Felicity's cases opened. When he had glanced through the contents they all moved on to the next compartment. After twenty minutes the train gave a little jerk and continued on its way.

She was conscious of being at some considerable height although they hadn't felt to be travelling uphill. The panorama now was one of open, rolling plain, vividly green and broken by dark forests. She seemed to hear the music of Smetana somewhere in the background, flowing with the rhythm of the train. Then the line was enclosed by grassy hills and cliff faces interrupted by irregular cave openings. And after that the industrial outskirts of a city began. They began to slow and drew up at a platform that announced *"Praha."*

At Prague Central Station she had to grapple in German with securing a taxi. The driver was cheerful and shiny-faced, threw in her two cases and understood her request for the hotel she'd been allocated. "Alcron Hotel, *ano. Ano, ano!"* he shouted, swivelling to grin at her over his shoulder and jab his thumb up in the air, several times threatening traffic disaster on their short journey. Perhaps he took her for an American and expected a fat tip.

They ended in a narrow, grey street, and the hotel interior they entered from it astounded her with its Victorian vastness and opulence.

Her bedroom displayed the same voluptuous magnificence. She threw herself back on the wide, plumped bed, staring up at the huge hanging chandelier of Bohemian glass, intricate with crystal branches and multi-faceted droplets.

Which, she wondered, hid the microphone?

She unpacked and hung her clothes in the walk-in wardrobe, changing for the evening into a sheath of dark blue silk with a single strand of brilliants in the scooped neckline.

The corridors and wide staircase by which she went down were those of an empty palace. She felt totally alone, unwanted queen-presumptive in a land where royalty was as outdated as the outrageous building itself.

The vast dining-hall sparkled with silver and glassware, and was equally empty. On a dais at one end, chairs and music-stands were arranged. As she selected a table and seated herself facing the little stage, five elderly men in dinner jackets emerged from behind a curtain and silently took their places. Stolidly and without acknowledging her presence, they began to play; a string quintet, she thought, by Brahms. There were actually potted palms leaning in on either side, framing the musicians like a Victorian daguerreotype.

An immaculate *maître d'hôtel* was suddenly at her elbow, Jeeves incarnate. She let him bow her into the menu—French cuisine, of course. Czech dishes weren't upmarket enough for the Western myth, and they hadn't learned yet to eat Chinese or even Italian.

On cue a man entered left, hesitated, smiled charmingly and took the next table. He was thirtyish, tall, with fine fair hair which waved smoothly above the temples, and his eyes were a frank blue. Male Lead, Felicity dubbed him, thinly spreading butter on her Melba toast and managing to ignore him throughout the meal. The approach would probably be made later, when she went through to the lounge for coffee.

She teased him by taking her cup and saucer upstairs to her room. As she turned the angle of the grand staircase she looked down and caught his affronted expression. When she came down some twenty minutes later wrapped in a light overcoat several tables were occupied and the quintet were giving a thin rendering of Tchaikovsky's *Nutcracker Suite.*

Felicity passed the Male Lead flirting with the girl at the reception desk. He had his back turned, and the girl gave him a sudden stab with one finger so that he looked back startled to see his prey escaping.

It was dark now, and after the brightly lit hotel the narrow street was slightly sinister, but if she turned right it should bring her into Wenceslas Square. She stood at the junction a moment and stared, total tourist, unable to reconcile the scene with old film clips she'd seen with Russian tanks drawn up here against a surly populace.

It wasn't really a square at all, but more of a very wide avenue that led up towards an imposing building at right angles. A museum, she thought, trying to recall the street plan.

If she went downhill it must bring her to the river, and eventually it did. Over a low stone wall the Vltava lay wide and flat under a half moon that kept mysteriously sliding between clouds. Two long, wooded islands in midstream seemed grounded in the shallows.

She looked again at the water and saw that it was not still but rapidly swirling. She was aware of a quickening of her heart, without quite knowing the reason. There was a hidden element of danger, and an uplift because the Elizabeth Stuart thing was once more taking physical shape, but also she felt herself drawn to the beauty of the place.

Farther along the embankment a still figure caught her eye, watchful and waiting. She moved away, drawing her coat about her as if she felt the cold, and as she walked the footfalls matched her own, his steps the longer because of his height. By the edge of the Karlov Bridge he would catch up with her if she didn't break into a run. She let him come on, then suddenly turned with a startled catching of her breath.

"I had no intention of alarming you, Fräulein," he apologized. "Please forgive me, but there are dangers in being out alone at night. If you are returning to our hotel, may I perhaps escort you?"

His smile was all charm and reassurance. Tentatively she smiled back.

She had a choice now: accept his company and return to the Alcron, or claim she intended crossing to the Mala Strana and so risk his insisting on coming too. That would prolong their time together and might afterwards seem to him like encouragement.

He had already assumed she would return with him, taking her elbow and steering her towards the road-crossing. Really, the Male Lead was too smooth to be true. He was introducing himself now as a West German industrialist in Prague on a business trip. But in the hotel foyer her sharp ear had caught him speaking to the reception clerk fluently in some Slav-sounding tongue.

It was easier to fall in with his intentions and give him something satisfactory to log in his report. Now he was asking her whether she had been in Prague before, and this opened the way to confide that she was here to do a little historical research. She mentioned the projected TV film, omitting that she was interested in playing the title rôle. Let it seem that she was cautious and modest. Overstating her status as an actress might even make it seem suspect to the opposition.

"I had rather hoped," she admitted, accepting the offer of drinks in the lounge on their return, "that Cedok would have provided a guide, since I want something a little more specialized than the average tourist. I shall go for all the advertised tours, of course, but a lot of that will be irrelevant. And I've only three full days here to find out so much."

"Do as I've done, and prolong your visit," he suggested, having claimed to be looking for glassware and his orders already made up ready for dispatch. "Perhaps I can be of some help to you? I happen to know quite well a professor at the Strahov Palace. He is responsible for the Napoleonic library items, but I am sure he has some trustworthy colleague whose interest is the seventeenth century. May I mention you to him?"

She let him do this and thanked him. They had progressed to the stage where they were Felicity and Dieter, although she was sure he was really something more like František or Ivan.

"Felicity—that is happiness. I shall think of you as Miss Happiness," he said, squeezing her hand as they said good night. He made no attempt to extend his company into her bedroom. Perhaps his masters had declared a ban on overtime.

As expected, he appeared when she was half-way through breakfast next morning, slapping his thigh with a German newspaper and smugly boasting that his friend Professor Hranaček was free for lunch if she would make a trio with them. They could hire a car and spend the afternoon up at White Mountain, site of the great defeat after which Elizabeth and her husband's court fled into exile.

Felicity had already booked at the hotel for the morning coach tour of the city, starting from the Cedok office in the Staré Mesto. Dieter clearly thought this would keep her fully occupied but she had a free hour between its end and her meeting with the two men. She planned to make good use of it, going on foot to see the street her father had been staying in when he died.

The tour was cleverly arranged to end in front of the mediaeval astronomical clock in the Old Town Hall tower, on the south side of which, on the hour, bells rang like mad and the twelve apostles processed round the gallery, followed by a crowing cock and Death the Reaper. Felicity moved back into the shade of the arcade, more interested in the other spectators than the mechanism itself. Everyone seemed enchanted, momentarily the frowns had lifted and they smiled like children.

Suddenly her heart was beating in her throat and she moved into the shade of a pillar as a figure she knew turned, blinking in the sunlight, and headed in her direction. The man passed quite close, so that she could have reached out and touched him. There was no doubting who he was. She had last seen him only a fortnight before, standing under a tree as she left the graveside from her father's funeral. And although there was nothing else particularly memorable about him, she could not mistake his rather protuberant eyes which were the green of ripe gooseberries. She turned after him and started following.

The man who called himself Dieter kept looking anxiously at his watch. Professor Hranaček, under orders, sat patiently waiting until at last the younger man sprang up and almost ran to the glass doors as the girl came breathlessly in, full of apologies for being so late.

"Only twenty-three minutes," Dieter told her with a tight smile. I was anxious that you had become lost."

"Oh, I had," she said sunnily. "Prague is full of little alleys and passages, isn't it? I've no idea where I was, but suddenly after walking for ages I seemed to recognize some houses, and I came out behind the Tyn Church. I must remember to take my street plan with me next time."

The professor was a mere shadow of his counterparts in Heidelberg, but he knew his subject and was able to convey it in acceptable packets. What she must see, he told her, was the Hvezda summer-house of Archduke Ferdinand, where Elizabeth used to ride out when she was queen for a year. He drove her up to White Mountain and then they seemed to walk for miles before they reached the strange, star-pointed building. It was now a museum, and sitting there the old man seemed to become freer and to revel in his stories of the past.

Clearly Dieter had detailed him to take over the English girl for the afternoon, satisfied that so far she had seen nothing that she might report to the state's detriment. Now that she had passed her *viva* with the prof, would Dieter be satisfied that she was only interested in the seventeenth-century aspects of Prague and so leave her alone?

Every now and again the prof had brought in some later Habsburg element and she had had to remind him. It wasn't absent-mindedness, because he would regard her shrewdly and nod whenever she brought him back to base.

"You will find it is the same all over Prague," he excused himself. "The mediaeval has been protected well, but eighteenth-century baroque has tended to supplant the Renaissance world which would have been so familiar to your Elizabeth."

He made out for her a list of surviving buildings which she must not miss. One of them was in the same street where she had located her father's hotel before lunch. She would have gone in then and there, to ask for the man who had sent back Howard's things, but as she approached the door a heavily built officer had come striding out and nearly knocked her into the gutter. He had apologized gallantly in a stream of incomprehensible words, and when she had assured him, "I'm all right, really," had beamed and spoken to her in English.

"Are you going in?" he inquired, incredulous.

She decided suddenly against it. Such a place, the haunt of the military, was best approached less openly. "I just wanted to ask where I am," she explained. "I seem to have got lost."

It was that officer who led her out by the maze of alleys and pointed her towards Wenceslas Square, already late for her lunch with Dieter and the prof.

They returned from White Mountain in the prof's two-door Skoda which appeared springless, rattling over the cobbles of the older streets and threatening at times to bash her head on the car roof.

When he said goodbye the old man held her hand in both of his to shake it. "Take care of yourself," he urged her, "and get home safely. Oh, and if you happen to visit the Strahov Palace and ask for me, they will bring you someone else. It isn't my real name, but I am a historian, or was. You must understand, things are not always what they seem in our country." He shook his head sadly and made to go, but she held on and whispered fiercely, "You've been very kind, very helpful. I shan't forget."

She found herself quite tired after her walk in the fresh upland air and decided on an early night after dinner. All that remained to do first was post the picture cards she'd bought that morning and written while she sat over her coffee in the lounge. The text was innocent enough, but to her the key sentences indicating she had no news showed up like warning lights. She wouldn't trust them to the open post-box in the hotel, but walk until she found a public one.

She didn't trouble to fetch a coat, tucking her handbag under her arm and slipping out of the hotel door when the porter on duty was busy with an arrival's luggage.

She was still opposite the hotel's frontage when a taxi drew up ahead and the front passenger door opened. She felt a sudden shove from behind and she was being bundled into it. Someone followed her in behind and something hard pressed into her shoulder-blades.

"Sit back and keep quiet, then no harm will come to you." She froze.

The car turned down towards the river and crossed by the Karlov bridge. They seemed to be following the route she had gone that afternoon, and there was no attempt to prevent her seeing where they went. "Are we going to White Mountain?" she asked.

There was no answer, but the pressure increased between her shoulders and she subsided. Her guess was right, because she saw the bivouacs of soldiers rank on rank where the prof had pointed them out on their return journey, saying gloomily, "We have more military than we have roofs for. But at least these are not Russians."

Half a mile farther the car turned off the road into the forecourt of a country inn with coloured lights strung over tables occupied by cheerful troops and their families.

"We go inside," the man behind her said. She glanced across at the driver but there was no help for her there. The man stayed silent as he had been all the way. In answer to another hard nudge she opened the door and stepped out to face her captor. It was the heavily built officer who had nearly knocked her over that morning. He grinned widely and flung an arm round her shoulders compelling her forward through the scattered tables towards the inn door. She had no doubt he still had the gun trained on her and if she had made a break for it the man would have run her down, making some rough lovers' game of it for appearances' sake.

Hopelessly she went on, inside and upstairs, past doors to a second rear staircase and up again. Finally they stopped outside a low door, and the officer opened it with a key from his pocket, still keeping his left arm wrapped about her.

The room was larger than she had expected, with a sloping ceiling and a big, square window which was open to the sounds of the beer-garden below. Beside it a man was sitting in a deep, winged chair. He leaned forward and the light caught his face.

"Come on in," he invited. "What kept you?"

Felicity stumbled forward with her arms outstretched and fell beside him, burying her face in the rug on his knees.

13

"This is Jiri," Swaffham said, when she had overcome the sudden emotion at being with him again. "You can speak freely in front of him."

"Jiri." She offered him her hand uncertainly. "I must apologize. I thought I'd been abducted."

"No. *I* am sorry. I had to frighten you or you might have resisted, and then someone from the hotel could have come out and seen you. Even out here at this inn, where people are necessarily blind about some things, it is better if I seem to be forcing you a little. Otherwise *I* might be thought under *your* influence—a Westerner, ugh!—and there would be trouble for me." He rolled his eyes, Fozzy Bear in a blue-grey uniform. "When we leave, please seem more pleased with me, and I shall be arrogant about my conquest. And forgive, please, if I stay with you and your father now, but it must seem I am busy—" He faltered, lost for the word.

"Seducing me," Felicity supplied.

"Yes. But, please, I interrupt. You must spend every minute with your father. We have not long."

"I heard my death was in *The Times,*" Swaffham said mildly. "Was that your doing?"

"As soon as I had the news from Prague I rang the department and spoke to someone called Maybury. I expect he arranged for the notice. But I made the paper add 'Suddenly in Prague.' Mike Yeadings saw it and got in touch. He—seems a good man."

"How did he connect me with Felicity Marlowe?"

Somewhere inside, she winced. Even now it must be as it always had been: that fearful distancing between them, as if coming closer and admitting love might overstep some forbidden boundary. So she must go on playing it his way, provide the information he required, observe a seemly discipline. "As it was a police inquiry, *The Times* released my name as next of kin. At the time we believed you really were dead. It was only at the undertaker's, when I ordered the coffin to be opened—"

"My poor love!" At last the iron seemed to break, then the recovery was swift. "What had you expected to find?"

"Some message from you as well as—as the body. That man— he was rather like you, as it happens—how did he die?"

He glanced away. "That is a closed subject. It was Howard Swaffham in that coffin, and he died of leukaemia as was expected."

"I see." If she had been frank she would have told him that he looked worse—older, greyer, more ill—than the man they had buried in his name.

He turned his head slowly to explain. "The notice about Swaffham in *The Times* must also have been seen by the Czech Embassy in London, and was news to them. A connection was then made with the death of a British citizen named Maskell in Prague on the same day. The coffin had not by then been released from the airport, so it was searched for hidden compartments and the body X-rayed for unusual contents. The death certificate accompanying it had been issued by a bumbling old medico I consulted on arrival, who based his verdict on cause of death on specimens he'd taken from me three days before. There was no proper postmortem, only crude surgery at the airport to ascertain if the body had been improperly—er, stuffed. Everything was found to be in order. No one who had ever met me in London actually came to view the body. It was passed as mine, together with a photocopy of the Maskell passport."

"But *why* all this charade? Why come here at all?"

He looked sadly at her, playing with her fingers as though unaware what he did. "You didn't ask me that when I set out."

"I thought you were going on holiday, up the Rhine. I expected you back. I've always tried not to intrude on your privacy."

"But now—?"

"There's—so little time. And now I'm here with you."

"I might ask why *you*'ve come, Felicity. To take me back?" He smiled wryly. "Arranging that would be a little beyond your skills, I think. Officially I am already home."

"To spend more time with you."

"To be with me at the end?" Now his teasing was almost too much for her. "I shall need to hurry then, since I understand you've only two days here after today."

"Do you have to stay here? Couldn't we somehow get over the border into Germany? You seem to have friends—"

"I do have friends, yes. And I owe them something. I've work to do, Felicity, and you mustn't obstruct it. Tonight I think we've covered your tracks, but I'm afraid you mustn't see me again. Don't try coming here because in an hour I move on. We just have now, and it's a poor, short sort of now to say everything in."

She was crying in his arms, silently. "I want you home. It isn't fair."

He knew what she meant by that childish protest: dying twice. Two bereavements. It was too much to take.

She lifted her head to look full at him. "You were saying good-bye to me that last morning, weren't you—when I came to take the books away? You said, 'Mind how you go,' just like when you saw me off to school."

"That's exactly what I meant. The future's yours. Make it a good one."

"I love you. I never dared tell you before, but I do. I do so much."

"That—is very—important to me."

She sat up abruptly, facing him. "You're hating this. I know it. Look, I'll go. Do what you have to. I'm sure you're right, whatever it is."

His eyes were tight closed and she kissed the lids, the centre of his forehead. Still unseeing, he reached for her hands, kissed the palm of each and folded her fingers over. "Thank you—for all the good years."

"I'll never forget you. I'll always remember," she promised. Then, almost savagely, "Jiri, I'm ready. Let's go now."

She clung to the man's grey-blue sleeve as they went down the stairs, through the passage full of drinkers, past the tables of soldiers with their women. She turned her head away from the lights and the laughter, barely able to keep up with Jiri's stride as he parted the crowd. Later she realized that her drying tears and her broken clinging would all have strengthened the impression he wanted to leave, and made their position safer.

This time he drove the car himself, with her alongside, shoulders covered by a coarse sweater he pulled from under the seat. It smelled of the outdoors and comfortably of Jiri himself.

They were going downhill past the army tents, in the general direction of the Lesser Town, when she called suddenly, "Jiri, I have to go back! There were things I had to ask him. Oh, I've wasted the chance I had!"

He scowled over the steering-wheel. "There is no going back."

"You don't understand—"

He took one big paw off the wheel and put it gently on her wrist. "You wasted nothing. You told each other all the important things. Leave the rest to him."

He was right, of course, "But there's something I should have told him. It could be important. Will you carry a message for me, Jiri?"

"Tell me, then."

"Say that I saw a man in the Old Town Hall Square today, and I recognized him. I'd seen him before. He'd been at my fa— He'd been at the funeral, and I hadn't invited anyone. Tell him that the man had green eyes. I don't know his name, but he had these prominent green eyes, like ripe gooseberries."

Jiri was laughing and it made her blood run cold. "Green eyes like gooseberries. Oh, he has a lot of names, that one. So he is back? Was he looking at the clock with its little procession of figures? And did he carry a plastic grip?"

"Yes. You know him, then?"

"I know his habits very well. He comes straight from the airport and keeps a—an assignation—with that old clock. It is a sort of superstition, to hear it strike twelve before he reports in at his office. Well, he has done it for the last time. It was his last trip, this one he made to London."

"You seem glad he's back."

"I am delighted. And your father will welcome your news. He has been waiting impatiently for this."

His voice chilled her. "What will happen to this man?"

"Has happened. He is certainly being held." Jiri's smile was wide and savage. "Ready for me to interrogate in the morning!"

She tried not to shrink away. He was a younger version of her father, then. They were colleagues. But surely on opposite sides of the Curtain. An official, something important in Military Intelligence, and she'd taken him for a mole on her own side.

Father hadn't gone across, hadn't been in the other camp all along, had he? That was what Maybury and those others at the funeral could have thought, because he had chosen to come here the minute he was free of the job. It couldn't be true, though. He'd spoken with such scorn of such traitors, men whose training in duplicity had penetrated too deeply, men who sold themselves for money. "I really don't understand," she said weakly.

"This man, gooseberry-eyes, is a Czech with an Irish mother. He belongs to no one, has no loyalties. A go-between, for whatever he can make out of it. It is better that you know nothing about him. Your father has been of service to us in obtaining information on him at an unofficial level. Now we officially cook the goose of gooseberry-eyes. I do not think you will be seeing him again in the UK."

She was going to be sick. Frantically she scrabbled for the window handle and instead found the door catch. Jiri's arm came lashing across and bound her into the seat. He was scowling horribly. "What do you do?"

"The window, please."

He pulled up at the kerb and wound the window down. "I drive too fast perhaps? I will go slow now."

They were down near the Vltava, by the narrow entrance to the Karlov bridge. The night air was cool and lightly scented with some unfamiliar blossom. Idiotically she remembered that it was June now. As on the previous night, she was aware of the slightly sinister beauty of the silent river and the scantily lit streets. The scene had the romance of the Middle Ages, and more than hinted at their dangers.

Jiri was looking at her doubtfully. "Is there anything you would like to ask me—which you could not ask your father?"

Her mind had gone blank, paralysed by the shock of realizing that Jiri was not the traitor to his uniform she'd taken him for when he seemed to be helping Howard.

"What will happen to him?" she asked in so small a voice that she had to repeat it for him. "My father, I mean."

"Surely you know that. He is going to die. Quite soon, I think. My friends will take good care of him and he will be as comfortable as he would be in his own home. And happier, because you will not be there watching him fail. He is getting regular transfusions. Tonight he will be taken into the country—loaded as a drunken sergeant into an ammo truck—to the farmhouse of a friend of mine, where the wife was a hospital sister. He will be her uncle, in delicate health." Jiri looked at her with a bitter twist to his lips. "If he can trust me, why don't you?"

"Because it's so complicated! No, no, I do trust you, but—"

"This is a complicated country. Remember that. I am a good Czech. Your father is a patriot too. But both of us can see things that should not be. That is all you need to understand. It is not always possible to approve of everything one's government does, but one must be loyal to the—Oh!" He threw his hands up in despair, impatient at her incomprehension and the depth of the thing to be explained. "Listen, little lady. You want your father to die in his own country. Well, he cannot. The government here says he is dead already. I can help in small ways and keep silent, but I will not aid an illegal entrant to make an illegal exit.

"When he goes, quite soon and in his own time, it will be a simple thing for the farmer. Your father has had his service of committal already. You understand? This is what he has chosen for himself. You cannot interfere."

"Jiri, I *am* trying to understand. I think I shall, in time. I'm all right now. Will you drive on?"

The car crossed the old bridge and turned right along the embankment, left again on its way towards Wenceslas Square, to pull up finally at the rear of the hotel. As they drew up, Felicity put one last question tentatively to him. "The man who was sent in the coffin to London—who was he?"

He turned a hard stare on her. "A traitor. That is all you can know. Now you must go in by that brown door there, cross the yard and go up the wooden stairs. Turn left at the top and take the fourth door on the right. It will bring you out in the first-floor service room. If you meet anyone, explain you have lost yourself. I shall say '*Na shledanou*' now, and '*Spěte dobře*.' "

"Shall I see you again, Jiri?"

"Not in Prague. And my name is not Jiri at all, so do not try to find me." He was suddenly distant and correct, stood beside the car and gave a formal salute.

"*Děkuji vám. Dobrou noc.*" She had worked on her few polite phrases and he deserved them. She went then without a backward glance, to a sleepless, troubled night.

A little before two in the morning she rang Room Service for a sandwich and brandy. When it came she tore the sandwich up and flushed it down the lavatory. She drank the brandy together with the headache powder thoughtfully provided by the hotel and tucked in the tooth mug.

She wondered if anyone had checked earlier whether she was in her room. If so, it didn't really matter. Even if she could be traced to that inn where she'd met her father, he would have left by now.

The draught was a powerful one. She slept on heavily until almost ten.

During the next two days she visited the Hradčany Castle and what had been the Winter Queen's apartments. With the friendly little lady guide sent to her by Cedok at the Male Lead's request, she was allowed to go through directly from the palace chambers into the Cathedral of St. Vitus and the austere gallery from which the royal party had observed the Reformed Church Service.

The cathedral was hugely gloomy and uncared for, listed now as a national museum with "impressive exterior architectural features." Inside, dust lay on scrolled ironwork, and the wood had never been polished, but some people sat silently here and there on the rush-bottomed chairs, staring forward to the great east window. They might have been tourists, or housewives glad to sit down after their shopping. They might even have been secretly praying.

There was yet more architecture to see, notably some lovely Renaissance decoration on façades near the castle and in the Old Town. She went dutifully through it all, expressing interest she could no longer whip up. Back at the hotel she continued to eat the rather pretentious meals in solitary splendour, the Male Lead often appearing afterwards to converse, and ending by drinking coffee and liqueurs with her. She had given up resisting his attentions. He was only doing his job as instructed. Like Jiri—she guessed—who would now be interrogating the uninvited spectator at her father's supposed funeral.

It worried her that she didn't know who he was, only that he was a Czech with an Irish mother and he would not have an easy time with Jiri. What had he been doing in England, and why should he come to the unpublicized funeral? Had he known who was really in the coffin they lowered into English soil with prayers for Howard Swaffham? Then there was that same dead man, mysteriously available to take her father's place. She had not been allowed to know his name or how he had died. The nausea returned whenever she thought of her father in this connection.

The lady guide took her to the Cedok shop, where foreign visitors could obtain home-produced goods at incredibly low prices, and she was reminded that she was not allowed to take out of the country any Czech currency at all. So after all she was compelled to buy the gifts she had originally intended for her friends, but which in the past two days had seemed of no possible importance. Choosing them was another way of using up the intervening hours before she could catch the plane for home.

On Friday, June 4th, she sorted her last coins and found that after tipping the downstairs staff she would barely have enough for the taxi to the airport, so she scribbled *"Děkuji vám"* on a page from her diary and pinned it to a sun-top she had worn only once. She hoped the pleasant, red-cheeked chambermaid would understand.

The weather had turned suddenly hot. Standing waiting to board the BA flight—the plane so tiny after the huge Ilyushins continuously landing and taking off—her head had begun to pound as the sun blazed down on the high, exposed plain. In her window-seat she tried to close her ears to loud North Country voices talking of fraternal greetings and Comrade Chairman. She had recourse again to brandy, reflected that she could be an alcoholic in no time, turned her back on the neighbouring seat and slept most of the way to Heathrow.

14

"What we need at this point," Yeadings had said to close that morning's briefing, "is a new perspective. I want the woman's angle. I'd like our WPCs in particular to put themselves in Bonnie's shoes. Imagine yourselves Bonnie at 2:30 P.M. on Friday, April 30th, with her packed supper in her shoulder bag, and her case in her hand, leaving the house in Eaton Square, making—it's thought—for Sloane Square underground.

"Just to remind you, she's wearing a blue, flared skirt; a blue and white striped taffeta blouse; medium-heeled black shoes; new shortie raincoat, cream or beige. She has told Cook there's a May Day celebration next day at her village and she wants to go. There is one, but Bonnie hasn't even told her mother she has a holiday due. Leaving her options open, wouldn't you say? Well, where is she off to first? And who is she likely to be running into?"

Angus felt bogged down by the lack of progress. "Are we going to close down the Incident Room, sir?" he asked as the briefing broke up.

"Ask me this evening. If we do, there will have to be a press statement first, or the public will think we're admitting defeat. Bonnie may have been killed nearly five weeks ago, but the body didn't surface until seventeen days later. Will you draft that, Angus? Mention the centre of the investigation's moved away from the gravel pit. Area of inquiries being widened in view of further information received, etcetera. Leave a copy on my desk. And hope to God we have something useful come in soon."

What did come in was far from useful: a report of a pensioner from an old people's bungalow found dead by a neighbour who noticed milk left out in the afternoon sun. Severe facial bruising and deep cuts to the hands. The poor old girl had tried to fight off her attacker, and he'd finished her with seventeen stab wounds with one of her own carving knives. There was blood splashed everywhere, heavily congealed, and the place had been ransacked. A Friday night mad special.

Angus went out to Chalfont St. Peter to look at it with the scene of crime experts, although one of the other superintendents would take charge while Yeadings still had the Bonnie Hall case. His absence left Yeadings minding the shop, so there to take a lunch-time telephone call intended for Angus.

"Paula? Nice to hear you. Anything wrong?"

"Not really, except that I'm at the flat today, ran out for a loaf and saw Felicity. She got back yesterday. Odd thing is, she didn't phone or call round. Sent only one of those coded messages too. All I had was a 'no-news' one from Prague and a view card of Heidelberg with a comment on the weather. She does seem terribly depressed. I thought you should know, Mike."

"Yes. Thanks, Paula. Did you make any arrangements with her?"

"I invited her round, thought she'd like to get it off her chest, but she wasn't having any. Said she needed a few days to herself. Maybe she's been turned down for the TV film part. I didn't care to probe, she was so miserable."

"Mm. I'll ask Nan to give her a ring. She can't keep putting people off indefinitely."

"Good idea. Nan will get through to her if anyone can. I suppose—there's little chance yet of Angus getting time off?"

"Not while serious crime flourishes as at present. Next week-end, maybe. I guess you know what he's busy with at present."

"Actually, no. He's horribly discreet. All I do know is that the last time he stood me up it was for some pesky lost dog! Did he ever find it?"

Yeadings chuckled. "And then some! Nan's been stood up for smaller things than that, and she manages to survive."

"Hasn't any choice, has she? A prisoner shackled by the small gold band. I must lend her some feminist literature."

"You do that," Yeadings threatened, "and I'll put you inside where even Angus can't get to you!"

She laughed, sent love to the family and rang off. Mike was left pondering Felicity Marlowe and taking another whirl on the Swaff-ham carousel.

Towards five-thirty he was knocking out his cold pipe, with his mind on making for home, when an internal call came through that DS Beaumont, working with the Met, had reported in by phone and was due back shortly with Bonnie Hall's original suit-case. He decided to stay on and hear what Beaumont had to say.

It was worth it. The old leather case had been abandoned in the ladies' room of a Sloane Street store, and its contents transferred to a newly purchased sausage-shaped zipped holdall with a broad shoulder strap. It was made of a shiny man-made toughened fabric and was cornflower blue edged with scarlet. Really snazzy, Beau-mont thought, and he had bought an identical one then and there for his wife's birthday. Yeadings sent him along to Photographic with it, and an order to get handbills made for circulation to the press and door-to-door.

"So she wanted to look her best. New shortie raincoat, smart shoes, matching blouse and skirt. Now even a matching, up-to-date holdall," Yeadings told himself. "She wanted to make a swinging impression. A case of *chercher le jeune homme,* unless I'm much mistaken."

When Angus came in soon after, he noticed the Guv was hum-ming. A little spasmodic perhaps because he had his pipe going again and firmly crammed in the corner of his mouth, but the tune was unmistakably "Thank Heaven for Little Girls."

"I've pulled out all the statements from the Pollards locals," Yeadings told him, after a description of Bonnie's last known purchase. "There's no hint of any romantic interest, and village women are sharp enough of eye and tongue. Which leaves me to think that they didn't see because the action wasn't outside Pol-lards to see."

"Guests of the family," Mott said slowly. "You think she took the eye of some man staying there over Easter. So we want a list of house guests. I'll get it for you, but it sounds unlikely. You're making her sound like a gold-digger."

"Not necessarily. It could be a kind of hero-worship mixed up with adolescent urges. You're the one that goes in for fancy psy-chological reasons, not me."

"If she went to Pollards the second time expecting to meet up again with some man, he must either be a local or he'd told her he was going to be there at that time. We know that the only people present were Swaffham, Manton-Jones and the third, unknown man. Are you saying it was one of them?"

"Not either of the first two certainly, because they had too much to concern them without any dalliance. As for the third man, I don't know. In the unlikely case of him being the one who followed up Danny Norman's information on the lady taken to the taxi rank, then he wouldn't have known in advance he'd be going to Pollards. So he couldn't have given Bonnie the impression he would be there. That definitely scores him out."

"Bonnie was inside the house and climbed out," Angus considered. "We're agreed on that, aren't we?"

"There's no other way to read the evidence. According to the finger-marks on the sill she actually hung there before dropping. So she wasn't thrown out."

"And she went out by the window in order not to be discovered. Because, presumably, she'd been there when the others, or one at least of them, arrived. We were told that Manton-Jones prepared the supper himself, and later he was astounded that Bonnie had been there at all. I agree, we have to look for someone outside that little group. We mustn't overlook either that Bonnie could have met some man in London on her days off and, untypically bold, arranged to meet him at Pollards, showing off her plushy background."

Yeadings grunted. "We keep saying 'man,' for the person Bonnie wanted to make an impression on. But she was only sixteen and apparently without sexual experience. I get the feeling she was too well brought up to encourage any passes made at her by house guests. And too cautious to bring in an adult outsider to her employer's house covertly. But somebody of her own age? An adolescent attraction? A boy equally romantic, or one she thought was so? A boy who thought he might educate himself a little at her expense? Are we getting any warmer, I wonder?"

"We're back to considering locals again. Or the son of one of the adult guests? Maybe I should drop in on the Hon. Celia tomorrow morning. God, it'll be Sunday again! I've almost forgotten what a free weekend's for."

"Which reminds me that Paula rang. Felicity Marlowe's back

from Prague, and miserable. I'll get Nan to ring her when I get back, see if she'll spend Sunday with us. Why don't you combine business with pleasure by taking Paula along when you go down to Henley?"

"I had it in mind, actually. Just making a token groan about the Pollards visit, though!"

"Superintendent McEvoy's taking on the new case. Nothing for us in it, I suppose?"

"I doubt it. The old woman took some awful punishment. It's a neighbourhood roughneck, I should think. Went in for her imagined savings, began bullying her, used his fists, then she riled him and he went berserk with a kitchen carver. They won't have far to look for someone with a violent background. It's a decent sort of district, so we should get local cooperation."

Yeadings nodded, rising stiffly and starting to gather his papers together. "We've pulled in an old lag for the warehouse break-in and he's named two others. Some way yet to go. I'll be busy with him part of next week, so you'll be carrying the Bonnie Hall case. I've made a list for Monday. I'm knocking off now, going back to sit in the garden and smoke a pipe, brood on the Swaffham angle."

He arrived in time to see Danny Norman off the premises, after following up the larder job by rolling a fresh coat of emulsion on the lounge and dining-room ceilings. He'd made a good job of it, too, without any splashings on furniture or carpets.

"Of course not," Nan snorted, having seen the young man off with a cheque and a pound of her home-made marmalade. "We've performed Olympics in furniture moving, and I covered the floors with dust sheets. That's what is spinning in the washing-machine at the moment."

Mike watched her pegging them out on a temporary line over the vegetable plot. Then he patted the cushion beside him on the garden divan. "Come and have a swing and a cuddle. I've made some fresh lemon squash. You must be tired."

She curled up beside him, sitting on one foot. "Tired? A little. Not too much so not to recognize you're about to make some demand."

"Am I so transparent?"

"I'm used to the approach, love. Ask on."

"Could you stand a guest tomorrow?"

"Guest singular? Not Angus and Paula?"

"Felicity Marlowe. She's back from Prague, and down in the dumps."

"Ah. Reaction, I suppose. She's done all she could, and now comes the time to grieve. I take it the trip wasn't a great success?"

"We'll find out if she comes. Can she?"

"Of course she can. It will probably cheer her up. And Sally's very taken with her. We had planned a picnic lunch at Burnham Beeches. Felicity would fit in very well. Shall I ring her?"

"Not now. Leave her to be miserable as long as possible. I'm not being cruel. I just want to be sure she'll welcome the distraction."

"And you're going to question her again. I'm not sure we should—"

"I'll be very careful. But there's a lot she hasn't told us. There was before she went away, and there's more by now. I'd like her to confide. If she doesn't, I'll have to prod, because Swaffham's activities overlap now with this murder case."

Nan sighed and put her head on his shoulder. "Isn't the last of the sun lovely? This afternoon was almost too hot. Holiday weather. You shouldn't have murder and violence on your mind. How does the case seem to be going?"

"Anything but fast. Right from the beginning," Mike reflected, "I've had this feeling that Bonnie's death was only a part of something bigger—almost incidental to the main action. It bugs me that I can't fix just what that bigger thing was. And I can't ignore that Swaffham was right close, making some kind of deal. He has to figure in it somehow. If I hadn't known the man, or if I'd lost faith in my own judgment, I'd have to admit that the whole thing hung on Swaffham's defection to the Reds."

"Suppose he did defect. Wouldn't that account for Felicity's depression now? Something she discovered in Prague could have opened her eyes to the truth. She was so keen to get out there and follow up her father's last days. Perhaps she found out that he'd changed sides, and taken something of value with him."

"A document," Mike said suddenly. "Let's try that idea for size. He took a document signed immediately on his retirement. An agreement with an unknown man, witnessed by young Manton-Jones, the nearest he seemed to have to a personal friend outside the service."

"An unusual relationship," Nan considered.

"How so?"

"You said—and I think you had this from Manton-Jones himself —that Swaffham blamed himself for his fiancée's death. Hilary's twin sister. I just wondered if we could believe everything M.-J. says. He's smooth, isn't he? He might have cherished a secret need to avenge his sister's death, make trouble when he got the chance. You didn't have any doubts about Swaffham until this connection with his dead fiancée's family. It's only this young man's version of that last evening that makes you feel Swaffham was involved in something underhand."

"I wonder if you're right. I ought to have looked up that shipping disaster five years back. An explosion at sea. I'll get Angus on to it. It may show how far Swaffham was responsible. He was her employer then, and possibly sent her into danger."

"Knowingly or otherwise."

"But it's part of the job. Risks have to be taken. I've lost good coppers myself before now."

"But Swaffham was *in love* with the girl, Mike."

"Which makes it more complex, more uncertain." Yeadings sighed. "My guess is that because he loved her, Swaffham felt more guilty than the family would have held him to be. But I'll keep my mind open about a vengeful twin brother. If there is malice there, it's damn well hidden."

"That document," Nan pursued. "Three signatories. It could simply have been a new will, with two witnesses to Swaffham's signing it. He had only a short time left to live, after all."

"There again, it depends on whether we believe Hilary M.-J.'s version. He appeared quite convinced himself that it was some secret form of agreement between the other two, with himself as sole witness. More and more it becomes necessary to pick up the unknown third man present."

"How about fingerprints?"

"I doubt if much attention was paid to the dining-room table and chairs. In any case, any dabs made that night would have been overlaid by the time we got on the trail. There are two women in residence, remember, and the formidable Mrs. Cutler probably insists on plenty of furniture polish. We'll have to rely on shaking a better description of the man out of Hilary M.-J., then put out feelers. God, this case has so many tentacles! If we follow them all we could lose sight of the centre."

"Which is?"

"Simply that Bonnie Hall was murdered, in or near the rear yard at Pollards, at approximately the time that Swaffham and Company were in the house."

"I'll leave it to the great brain," Nan said, and kissed him lightly. "I have to cook supper or my husband will complain."

"Selfish devil." He grinned, leaning back to savour the evening air, puffing out fragrant tobacco to keep it gnat-free.

It was after eleven when Nan rose hastily from watching television. "It's almost too late to ring Felicity now."

But she hadn't gone to bed. She was staring at the blank walls of her elegant sitting-room, projecting on them scenes from her visit abroad: the unfinished chess game; the little package Herr Frühling had given her, containing her father's legal passport.

She had repackaged it between the two slim books the old bibliophile had given her, sealed it and addressed the wrapping to herself in London, and left it at the Heidelberg hotel to be mailed when she wrote for it. That had seemed the only thing to do, because she couldn't risk smuggling it into Czechoslovakia, in case it was found in her luggage. If she had done so, could she have persuaded Howard to use it and slip back into Germany with her at some provincial border-crossing?

But then had he ever wanted to leave? He'd chosen to go there to die, hadn't he?

Now she had come face to face with the agonizing question. Whose man had he been? A double agent: how else that *entente* with Jiri? Or could his heart truly have remained in Britain while he chose to be buried in a farmer's field of the communist block?

If not, by all the tenets he had taught her, he was a traitor.

Traitor. She said the word aloud several times, and with each repetition it seemed farther removed from the quiet, watchful person she had known and loved. The face remained the same. It was the word that became meaningless.

She saw him again in that upstairs room at the inn on White Mountain at the moment of her departure, his eyes closed as she withdrew her hands. Undemonstrative to the last. Loyal to the end too. Surely.

Felicity wept until her eyes burned dry. She had never been so alone in all her twenty-three years.

At that moment the phone sounded. She let it go on, then was suddenly angry at the insensitive purring, snatched up the receiver. And it was Nan Yeadings, calm, unhurried, friendly, saying that since the weather was staying hot she was taking the children to Burnham Beeches tomorrow. They hoped she would join them and make a lazy day of it.

15

Nan heard Mike creep out of bed in the pitch dark and go downstairs. She looked across at the luminous dial of her bedside clock and it showed three-fifteen. There was no sound from the children's rooms. Nothing came up the staircase except the smell of fresh emulsion paint escaping through the closed doors of the lounge and dining-room. Mike would be in the kitchen making tea, but she hadn't heard the power switch go on, nor the sticky sound of the fridge door closing.

She thought she was still listening, but the strenuous work of the afternoon's furniture removals had tired her more than she knew. She awoke to daylight to find Mike asleep beside her and a half-drunk tumbler of squash on his bedside cabinet. Now it was her turn to creep off downstairs and set the day rolling.

Raising the blind in the kitchen she saw what he'd been up to. A note-pad lay on the formica-topped table, its top sheet covered with his small, spiderish writing, so at odds with his substantial frame.

Poor old Mike, his subconscious going on working all night so that it broke through sleep and he had to go back to the grind. What had he been pondering?

Sat. Apr. 30—she read—*3 persons at Mayfair address: Swaffham,*

*unknown man and unknown woman separately. Descript., Danny Norman
—man indistinguishable; woman mid-thirties, elegant, expensive dresser;
good-looking; five-eight or -nine . . .*

She had read so far when Mike materialized silently behind her
and took the pad out of her hand. "Sorry, love. Private."

She didn't argue the point. His cases were confidential material,
granted. What he chose to mention to her was privileged information. She had no right to it and it wouldn't go further. All the same
—"Pity," she said. "That woman's description, I mean. Otherwise
how tidy it would be if she'd been Bonnie, and Swaffham the man
she'd been dressing up for. Then she could have been the one to
lure the unknown man to Pollards and so get herself killed by him
there."

"Well, it wasn't and she didn't. Bonnie was four or five inches
too short and never the luring kind. Nan, I suppose I've had my
allowance of eggs this week?"

"You have. How about a well-drained bacon sandwich after a
bowl of bran flakes?"

Paula had come down to Reading the previous night by train.
Angus awoke to the smell of coffee perking and the drumming of
water in the shower. Paula stepped out, lean and gleaming, twist-
ing her long, dark hair in one hand and coiling it in a towel on the
top of her head. "Awake," she commanded, "for Morning in the
Bowl of Night has flung the stone that makes you look a fright."

Angus sat up, rasping a hand across his chin. "Some think my
stubble has a charm of its own."

"Well, screw on your false leg and pop your dentures in and—"

They rolled together on the bed, grappling like schoolboys.
Panting, Angus grinned down at her. "I hardly need a shower
myself, I'm so wet. I know, don't say it! Just be a good squaw and
get some breakfast together, masses of everything."

By ten they had a cool-box, packed with lunch and two bottles of
hock, locked in the car boot and were ready for the road. "Maybe
the lady you want to interview will have gone to church," Paula
suggested.

"Then we'll sit in the garden and wait, keep Florrie company."

"Who on earth is Florrie?"

"The lady I stood you up for last week. A hyperdish. Even you will agree."

Paula's caution was justified. Mrs. Cutler—less disapproving than before, because the DI's companion did make the call appear closer to the social occasions she was accustomed to—showed them through to the sun terrace where they sat on white garden furniture and were offered a selection of Sunday newspapers.

"I could grow to like the life," Paula murmured, shaking out the fashion pages. "I even—good heavens, what on earth—?"

Kabul Florissante III had silently materialized and thrust her nose between lap and newspaper. Angus, fondling her ears and Paula's knees indiscriminately, made the introductions.

Just before noon a dark green Bentley came up the drive and disappeared round the front of the house. The Hon. Celia came straight through to greet them still in her hat and gloves. "Mr. Mott, dare I assume your visit is a social one? Mrs. Cutler tells me your fiancée is with you."

"We are on our way to the river," Angus said, "and I had just one other question on my mind. I hoped you wouldn't object. This is Paula, Mrs. Manton-Jones."

"I wish I could see you properly, my dear. What I can see is so delightful. But I mustn't keep you children from your boating. Ask away, Inspector dear, and I'll see if I can supply the answer."

Angus helped her locate a chair and sink on to it. "We know Bonnie Hall was here at Easter when you were entertaining. She just might have been in contact with one of your guests, and we should like a list of them."

Mrs. Manton-Jones frowned delicately. "I shouldn't like any of them to be embarrassed by police interrogation, Inspector. Especially as it's so unlikely they even spoke to Bonnie, except passing on the stairs or when she helped serve at table."

"We appreciate that. We shall be very discreet, ask for their sympathetic help."

"Get round them, as you do me, is that it? Well, if you have your notebook ready I'll list them for you." She reeled off seven names and gave their addresses. Two of those were familiar to Angus, one as a power in the city and the other an eminent barrister.

"Were there any younger guests? Under twenty-two years of age, say?"

"None at all. I can see where your questions are leading, but I don't think you'll find anything of an attachment between Bonnie and anyone of her own age. There just isn't anyone, you see. Unless, of course . . ."

"Unless?"

"Well, I was wondering. I didn't catch sight of him myself, but I believe he was expected over Easter. The gardener's nephew. Peter, I think he's called. He comes sometimes to stay down at the lodge. If he was there, he might well have run into Bonnie going in and out by the driveway."

In Burnham Beeches Nan Yeadings had trundled the buggy with Luke in it as far as she thought its axles could stand the rough terrain and scattered branches blown down by earlier storms. There she set up camp, seated on a log with the baby jigging on her knee while the other three plunged on into wilder woodland.

Luke had been fed, changed and put down for an early nap when the others came trooping back, hot and thirsty. Mike poured chilled fruit juice all round and rested the opened hock bottle in a mossy cranny.

Felicity was looking better already. They had kept off difficult subjects, drawing attention to Luke's new skills in directing a rusk into, or roughly near, his mouth, and leaving it to Sally to reassure her that no assault was to be made on sensitive areas. So it was Felicity herself who first referred to her father's affairs. "Did you ever make anything of the disc?" she asked Mike as she helped clear up from the picnic.

He avoided looking directly at her. "Not personally. I didn't want to use police personnel, so I asked Paula to help. She found a compatible computer and got into the disc but there's nothing there in the open, just your father's private finances, a copy of his will and so on. But there are three limbo files. We can't get them out until we have the right code word for each. That means any arrangement of letters and figures up to eight in number, followed by anything up to three figures. If you like to work out the combinations possible, you'll realize that the prospect's pretty poor, unless we have access to the key words."

Felicity was frowning. "Did he use numbers elsewhere in file titles?"

"I don't think so. Only for numbering letters in the correspondence files."

"Then what we have to look for is probably a set of eight-letter words that belong together."

"Words of *up to* eight letters," Mike corrected. "It could be only one, like *F* for Felicity, and if you put in the whole word it won't bring up the file. As it happens, Paula has tried both of those, with no result. A little green notice comes up, 'Error in: recovery from Limbo. File does not exist. Cancel operation.' The same happened when we tried my name, Yeadings having eight letters too."

"Isn't there some way of displaying the names of limbo files?"

"Paula thought there ought to be, but if there ever was a facility it's been removed. I'm not a computer buff myself by any means, but Paula is quite experienced. Now you're back you may prefer to consult a professional."

"Not if it has my father's private affairs on the disc."

No, well, he would have counted on her reacting like that. But he had meant her to have the disc, so why hadn't he supplied a way of getting right into it?

"I'll have to think hard about it. Didn't he leave you any clue, Mike, in the letter he gave me for you?"

"You saw it. The main message was about the so-called three-core lead. I've taken that to mean three people, because he gave me a start by saying the earth wire was himself."

"Yes. I see now why you tried my name and your own. We're not the other two."

"So it seems. I'm stumped on that, Felicity. The only hope is if you come up with some significant connection. Didn't you find anything useful on your follow-up to Prague?"

She waited so long before speaking that he thought she was refusing to answer. Then she folded her legs under her and leaned forward with her hands in her lap. The sunlight filtering through the beeches overhead played on her pale hair and he was reminded of the woodland nymph of the Glynt advertisement. "I went to Frankfurt first," she said, "to call on an old friend of my father. He'd been there before me, and left a chess game half played. It seemed so sad. I took a photograph of it. It's still in my camera. Then I went on to Heidelberg and did the Elizabeth Stuart thing."

She had paused again, deep in memories. "It's a lovely place. So is Prague, in a different way, but it depressed me. I suppose I'm just beginning to feel the loss. It's delayed shock from Howard's— death." She bent lower and the heavy pale hair fell over her face, obscuring the features. She put her hands up for extra concealment and her shoulders were shaking as she wept quietly, then aloud.

Sally, who had been picking harebells nearby stayed crouched, stared fearfully then started to howl.

"Take Sally away, Mike," Nan ordered, and went to sit with her arms round the unhappy girl.

"I'm so—sorry," Felicity managed at last, "but I do feel better for that." She did, and she wished she could unload the rest of the truth, about her father still being alive, and Jiri and the way it was all intended to end. She blew her nose and wiped her face, then stood up and called Sally back, to show everything was really all right.

The little girl sat on her lap, and while she cuddled her Felicity tried to give a description of the Czech city and the things she had done there.

"Were there any restrictions on your movements?" Nan wanted to know, so she told them, humorously, about the Male Lead seeming always just two steps behind her. "Not that I was exactly shadowed, but he supplied the people I contacted. Maybe he did much the same for all foreign visitors at that hotel. There seemed to be hundreds of soldiers about, but for all I know they could have been like our TA." But she said nothing about getting abducted in a fake taxi and taken to a man who asked, "What kept you?" meaning it to be taken as a joke.

"What do you think of her?" Nan demanded of Mike when they were strapping Luke in, ready for going home.

Mike answered with his eyes on the two girls in the distance. "She's hiding something. I'm damned if I know what. When we get back I'll drop the Pollards business on her, see what result that has."

He left it until the children were in bed and the three of them sat sipping pre-supper drinks on the patio. Nan provided the lead-in by complaining how rushed he'd been with local crime.

"Have you?" said Felicity. "I'm afraid I've a lot to catch up with.

I haven't properly seen a newspaper for over a fortnight. What's been happening?"

Mike scowled. "Enough. There was a warehouse break-in with violence, a shotgun siege on a housing estate, the girl-in-car-boot, and the Pollards affair."

"I remember the car-boot case," Felicity offered. "It was run into a gravel pit, wasn't it? But who was Pollards?"

It sounded a perfectly innocent question and they both stared at her until she was disconcerted. "What's the matter? Should I really know?"

"It's not a who, it's a place," Mike said slowly, watching her. "A country house near Henley."

"So what happened there?"

"You really have no idea? And you've never heard of anyone called Manton-Jones?"

Felicity's hand shot out and her glass went down to shatter on the stone flags. *"Manton-Jones?* How did you find out? Who told you? Oh my God! What have I let myself in for?"

Mike went through to the lounge and poured her a fresh drink. He avoided the glass fragments and put the whisky on the table between them. "Who do you think told me?"

"It had to be Danny. But I thought I had him completely fooled."

Yeadings began to see light, but he wanted her to commit herself. "Suppose you tell us how it all came about, and why."

"That sounds too easy. It was part of some plan of Howard's. I did it because he assured me he needed it, and I wouldn't be breaking the law. He told me precisely how he wanted me to play it, and I did, even to using a handwriting that was out of this world."

Mike had a little secret smile. "Ah. And how to dress. The sable coat and so on."

"The sable coat was my idea. He just said 'elegant and definitely affluent,' which I was. All he supplied was the dark wig."

"And your precise instructions?"

"Arrive at the address at 11:40 P.M.; the front door would be unlocked; go upstairs and make myself at home until an unnamed man arrived with my father. They would sign an agreement which I was to witness, signing myself Hilary D. Manton-Jones, Secretary. Then I was to leave immediately after that, refusing any offers of a lift from the unnamed man. Danny, as chauffeur, would drive me to Paddington and I was to take a taxi immediately home."

"And you followed that exactly?"

"To the letter."

"And the other man—did you see his name under your father's?"

"No, because Howard held on to the document all the time, and there was a piece of blotting-paper over the top. All I could see was the space where I was to write."

"So you went out to where Danny was waiting, while the unnamed man remained with your father?"

"They stayed behind. But Danny came in to fetch me down to the car. He was driving a Rolls and I could see he was terribly pleased with it, but he never let on he'd seen through my disguise."

"Was there any other car parked in the street?"

"Several. The nearest was a big Mercedes, some dark colour, blue or green, I think. You can't be sure in the street lighting. It was just after midnight when I left. Howard was giving the man another brandy. Are you going to tell me who he was?"

Mike smiled, turning the tumbler in his hand. "Eventually, when you've described him to my satisfaction."

"He was a little taller than me. Five-nine or -ten, I should think. Sharp-boned with forward-thrusting shoulders, and he had a way of pushing his neck forward and tilting his head back. A flat, oval face with blunt features. It didn't seem to match his body. Palish complexion, hair neither dark nor light. He wore gold-rimmed glasses with thick lenses. They made his eyes look huge."

"And the colour?"

"Green, and they bulged rather."

"Like ripe green gooseberries?"

"Exactly."

Mike smiled benevolently. It was almost identical to the description Angus had given of the man at Highgate who lost his Mercedes.

"The man with your father," he told Felicity, "was known as Adrian Whittle, but since Howard was obviously setting him up, we can assume he'd have some other names as well.

"There are some other things I ought to tell you. Howard was quite right: you didn't do anything illegal by writing the name of someone you had never heard of in a hand that was also assumed. It merely made a nonsense of the document. And Danny neither recognized you, nor gave away any secret. I led you on to tell me yourself. Devious, I'm afraid, as Howard was. And lastly, there is a real Hilary D. Manton-Jones, who lives at Eaton Square and the house at Henley called Pollards. I think the two of you should meet."

1 6

Nan was thinking about getting their evening meal when the phone sounded and she took the call in the kitchen. "Angus, hullo. How did the boating go?"

She listened, nodding, and when Mike put his head inquiringly round the door, beckoned him over. "Angus and Paula. They've come up with something."

"From Pollards?"

"A possible boyfriend for Bonnie, he said. Here, take it. If he's phoning from the flat, make them come over and join us. Tell him I'm defrosting in readiness."

Mike reached for the receiver. "Is it a long story? . . . Um. Well, in that case, can you stand one of Nan's thrown-together meals? Lad, if you could only see the looks I'm getting, and I can't think what I've done! . . . Good, about twenty minutes, then? Right. Oh, and Felicity's here. She has a tale to tell as well."

He returned to the lounge to pass on the news.

"I'll be glad to see Paula," Felicity said. "I cut her off badly when we met at the food-store, but I was feeling so wretched. Now I can apologize."

"You won't need to. Paula's one of the calmest, least offence-taking people I know. By the way, Nan says she made up the spare bed after Danny left and she expects you to make use of it. With those two here it will be a late night before we break up."

Felicity stood up. "I don't know what to say. I wish I'd had a mother like Nan. Maybe she was. I don't remember. I'm not very domesticated, but there must be something I can do to help."

Between them they put another leaf in the dining-table and laid it for five. Mike put out glasses for wine, "In the firm belief the lad's been properly brought up to do the decent thing."

Angus had, bringing a two-litre bottle of Soave and a litre of Valpolicella from his store at the flat. Over their pizzas and tutti-frutti ice-cream, the two sides exchanged information.

"We called on the Hon. Celia first," Angus summarized, "and it was a no-no on younger guests over Easter, but she recalled that the gardener's nephew had been expected over the Easter week-end. Nan, this sauce is terrific. Do you buy it or—"

"Have some more. I make litres of it and freeze it. But do go on. Bonnie's man friend, did you actually catch up with him?"

"We merely discovered a possible, and I haven't interviewed him yet. We don't know that he ever met Bonnie, but as she went shopping once or twice on foot, he could have seen her when she passed the gate lodge. I thought you'd want him brought in to-morrow, Mike. You remember the gardener and his missus went off to Ibiza for a fortnight just before the weekend of the murder? They're back now and I had the bright idea of dropping in to ask if he'd left the key with anyone. He hadn't, then as I was leaving, he said his nephew had a spare one, though. It came in useful some-times when he came up to London by car. I asked the old chap to elaborate. He said Peter would stay in town late, drive to the cottage and let himself in without disturbing him and his wife who worked damn hard and needed their sleep. I asked where Peter lived, and he told me Dowdeswell. He's his brother's son, so the surname's the same."

"So where at the back of beyond is Dowdeswell?"

"I had to look it up myself. It's a small place near Cheltenham, just off the A40 trunk road. It makes sense to go back from Lon-don by that route, starting on the motorway. And the Pollards lodge is only a mile or two out of his way if he wants to break the journey."

Yeadings laid down his knife and fork with an appreciative sigh. "Marvellous, love. Give the lad another dollop, keep his strength up for his drive tomorrow, to interview this Peter down at Dowdeswell. I'll get on to the Gloucestershire force first thing."

"He isn't 'lad'; he's 'Angus' or 'Inspector,' " Nan sighed. "And you still let him 'Guv' you, even now he's a Guv himself." Yeadings threw up his hands in surrender.

"So what's new with you?" Angus asked, grinning and accepting the second helping. "Is it the Bonnie case or something else?"

"It's not unconnected with Pollards, although Felicity—whose tale it is—hadn't heard of the place before. It's more to do with the Manton-Jones family." He looked encouragingly at the girl.

"I didn't know there were any Manton-Joneses either," she explained, "but I'd heard the name because it was one I had used myself—Hilary Manton-Jones. Apparently the real one is a man. I'll explain how it all came about."

It was clear that her story of meeting, in disguise, with Swaffham and the unknown man to witness their written agreement was as intriguing to Angus as it had been to his chief. She told it well, leaving her description of the third party to the end, guaranteeing maximum effect.

"My man at Highgate," Angus claimed enthusiastically at the tale's end. "The one who made out he lost a newish blue Mercedes."

"With a licence plate which rearranged just happened to be the same as the one we found on a certain clapped-out tan Cortina," Yeadings completed.

"Guv, we're there, aren't we?"

"Under Nan's new ordinance you address me as 'sir' or 'Superintendent,' " Mike corrected with mock offence, then nodded. "We certainly have a good tally of circumstantial evidence. If we could only lay hands on the missing Merc we'd be better placed for proof."

"I'd like to be there when you question him." Angus sounded almost wistful.

"Even if we raise him tomorrow, it won't be a short affair. Your business in Dullsville shouldn't take long. Get off there early. Peter Durnside, you said. I'll run the name through Records first thing, phone the result through to Glos. police if it's positive."

"Thanks, Mike. Sir!"

"Sorry, ladies, talking so much shop."

"Chauvinist pig," said Nan amicably. "Shall we drag you back now to discussing disposable nappies and twopence-off detergent?"

They talked in fact about Felicity's rehearsals which would start again at mid-week, and her prospects for the Fielding work on Elizabeth Stuart.

"I don't suppose I shall know for ages what my chances really are," she told them. "It took off so fast that there are bound to be hang-ups at the next stage. And like any genius, Fielding can be quite unpredictable, write nine-tenths of the thing and then throw it all up. I shall work on him if that looks at all likely, but do keep your fingers crossed."

"That reminds me," Mike put in, "Danny Norman had heard about it on the grapevine and regarded your taking the title role as settled. He hoped to gather the crumbs from under your table."

"That sounds just like Danny. He seems to have got stuck at walking-on parts. I think he was born half a century too late. He'd have been marvellous, brightly asking 'Anyone for tennis?' "

"Is he a very close friend?" Paula inquired hopefully.

"You mean is he my kind of man? Anything but." Felicity grimaced. "Despite my earlier mistake, I think I must be conventionally monogamous. And it just couldn't be an actor. I'd want a man tô be solid, the same person all the way through and all the time."

Like her father had been, Yeadings thought sadly. Even now, in company he hadn't met, Howard Swaffham had a way of making his presence felt.

Monday morning was a time for clearing up leftovers. Mike Yeadings surveyed himself in the bathroom mirror and noted bags under his eyes. They tended to come back more frequently these days when he had prolonged periods under pressure. The time wasn't far distant when they'd dig in to stay. Maybe he should get some spectacles with plain glass uppers instead of the reading pair he occasionally used at present. Glasses-wearers had that advantage of hiding the worst first ravages of time.

"You're vain." Sally had come in behind him. It must be a phrase she'd picked up from someone teasing her.

"I'm not really. Just cleaning my teeth." He rinsed the brush and hung it up, then ran hot water in the basin until the mirror misted over.

"Up, up!" Sally knew the next part, as her father lifted her close to the glass. Carefully she drew a round face with two dot-eyes. Then she made him wait while she made up her mind what kind of day it would be.

"Smile," she said happily, and finished the face with a wide upward-turning curve. He hoped it was an accurate prediction.

Installed in his office, he hung up his light jacket, examined the thermometer—already in the eighties—and neatly rolled his sleeves above his elbows. Then he went out in the corridor and moved computerwards. He handed over the slip of paper on which he had written *Durnside, Peter, aged 19+ of Dowdeswell, Glos. Request CR with details if any.*

As he regained his own room the buzzer sounded. It was the assistant chief constable's secretary to warn him Himself was on his way. Mike reached out for his jacket just as the ACC entered.

"Mike, thought I'd save you a journey. Going to be a swelterer again. Oh, for godsake forget that jacket!"

He wanted a rundown on the Bonnie Hall case. It was all available in typescript, except the later events of the weekend, or he could pull it out of the computer at will, but of course he wanted to do it the old-fashioned way, paced to a senior copper's mind: talk it over, mull it, grunt, and end by advising, "Carry on."

Perhaps because of the increasing heat, which was clearly getting to him, he was tetchy. "Not much to show for it, have we? Girl's been dead over a month now. Trail gets colder all the time. I'd hoped this was one we'd clear up quickly."

"We didn't get it until the body was a fortnight old," Mike reminded him. "That's something the hostile press skates around. Still, we could have something more tangible to show by tonight. There are two lines of inquiry we're following up." He told him briefly about Peter Durnside and Adrian Whittle.

"What put you on to them?" The Old Man wasn't all that dozy.

Mike told him about Inspector Mott's lead through Mrs. Manton-Jones and her gardener. Predictably, after grunting approval, all the ACC said was, "Should have been on to that earlier. Slipped up there, Superintendent. So what's the next move?"

"Inspector Mott has gone down to Gloucestershire this morning and is questioning young Durnside with the local force. I'm phoning down CR if anything is found."

"Right. What about this other feller, White?"

"Whittle, sir. I'm—er, cogitating for the moment."

The ACC's mouth snapped open for some tart response, then he caught Mike's eye and thought better of it. "I suppose that's some longer-winded version of thinking."

"I shall try to keep the wind as short as possible, sir. Don't want to make a false move there. We could be on sensitive ground."

"How do you connect him with the girl?"

"Only by time and place. We have a witness that he intended going to Pollards on the night in question." *Possibly* intended, Yeadings reminded himself. And although Felicity had described Whittle so well, Danny hadn't seen him clearly enough to identify him at all. Guesswork, which might trip him up later when he tried to prepare a case for the courts.

"H'm. So it's possible that by tonight we could have two separate men 'helping the police with their inquiries'? That should keep the newshounds from baying too loudly on our doorstep."

"Or whet their appetites for more."

Immediate on a rap on the door a WPC slipped in with a slip of paper.

The ACC scowled. "What's this, then?"

"CR on Peter Durnside, sir." She hesitated between them, then handed it to Yeadings who read it. "Anything else, sir?"

"Eh? Oh, sorry. No, love. That's fine." He looked up at the ACC with lifted eyebrows. "I wasn't really expecting anything, and nothing's what we've got."

"A blank sheet, eh? Well, murder would be diving in at the deep end, I suppose. So we may be writing that one off as a suspect, unless you can prove a positive personal connection with the girl. Not a sex crime, after all."

"I think Inspector Mott is fit to sort that out. A lot will depend on what kind of alibi Durnside has for the time in question. If Mott's not satisfied with the lad's account of things he'll be inviting him to come and talk. I think too that he might find our top brass here quite impressive. Would you like to be in on it if and when he comes up, sir?"

"I can't imagine why you want to cast me as an ogre, Superintendent. No, each to his own dirty work. Just tell me what comes out of it." He rose, muttered something about Mike's office having the advantage of day-long shade and went back to his own sun parlour.

Mike also muttered, but under his breath, that they lived in a climate where it was nine months winter. Then he buzzed and asked to be connected with the Gloucestershire force.

When Angus's end of the case was officially covered, he turned to his own, poring over the reports on the body's disposal in parallel with the interview with Whittle at Highgate. Eventually, noting that a previous attempt to contact the man with reference to the missing car had been unsuccessful because he was out of the country, he rang through to the Met requesting updated information.

It was phoned through a little before midday. There had been no reply to repeated ringing and knocking at the front door. The house appeared to be uninhabited and the garage at the rear was empty. Neighbours had not seen either occupant for almost a week. The milkman reported Whittle's order cancelled until further notice.

Yeadings decided that that sounded a little too final for his liking, but since Swaffham had held a meeting with the man *before* the actual hour of his retirement, there remained a further possible source of information. Gloomily then, because he saw his investigation being buggered by an SIS request to play down Bonnie's death as an accidental one in the course of an operation, he set about again contacting Maybury at one of his lunch-time haunts, reflecting that the department's veto might not be valid, because the death had occurred *after* the midnight which concluded Swaffham's service. The mega-fly in the ointment would be if Whittle himself turned out to be a government agent.

This time his search was shorter. He found Maybury in the same Dover Street bar where they had met before, and it almost seemed that he was expecting the superintendent. He was quirky as ever but perhaps with a more acerbic expression.

"Whittle?" he repeated, as if he'd never come across the name.

"Adrian Whittle."

"Mm."

Yeadings took their glasses away for refills. When he came back Maybury was hunched like a vulture over his elbows at the table and appeared to have reconsidered his own ignorance. He drank as if it was the next thing to do and best done quickly. He spoke sadly. "Whittle. Yes. Not a very pleasant person at all, Mr. Yeadings. Unrecommended. I should avoid him if you can."

"I'd like to pull him in. For murder."

"Ah." He ran a dry tongue round parched lips. Mike took the heavy hint and went off for replenishment. His own second glass was untouched. He came back to find it empty and Maybury smiling bleakly.

"Can you present a watertight case against him?"

"No. I said I'd *like* to pull him in."

"My money's on you not doing that thing. Very wily beggar, your Mr. Whittle. In any case, we have reason to believe he isn't in the UK at present. But then you've discovered that yourself, and that's why we're having this pleasant little drink together." He held up his glass, gazing at it with his pathetic, lopsided smile.

Mike sat on, patient as a bullock in the rain, and eventually Maybury seemed mildly interested in his problem. "Who is it you can't quite prove he killed?"

"A young domestic servant called Bonnie Hall."

"Really?" At last Maybury appeared to come properly alive. "I thought from your inquiries that you were on quite a different line."

"Why? Has he killed someone else?"

Maybury looked affronted, thought a moment, then said, "Not to my certain knowledge, Mr. Yeadings."

"Well, lines do cross sometimes, you know." He contrived to look total unimaginative Plod.

"Do they indeed? Well, I shouldn't grieve to see Adrian Whittle behind British bars for life myself, though my attitude may not be universal in the corridors of Whitehall and Westminster."

Yeadings waited a moment, then quietly, hazarding a guess: "Swaffham would have liked it."

"Swaffham—would have wanted to do it himself," Maybury finished with more fire than Yeadings would have thought him capable of. "And that's all you'll bloody get out of me, Mr. Yeadings. We never had this conversation. Next time we meet, if ever, I shall buy for you." His blank face was suddenly drawn and old. But it was clear that Maybury was not quite the burnt-out relic he played at being.

"My pleasure," Yeadings told him. "Perhaps by then we'll have something to celebrate."

17

Yeadings brooded on the two signings of a document, either side of midnight; one made while Swaffham was a government official, and invalidated by a false witness.

But *was* it necessarily invalidated? The falsification was for Whittle's benefit (or more likely intended for his loss, because he'd be in trouble when the agreement was scrutinized by any knowledgeable third party). The fact that the real Hilary Manton-Jones was male would brand as fraudulent any claim Whittle made relating to the document.

Further thought on these lines was pointless while the nature of the document was unknown. Yeadings pushed himself away from his desk and went to stand at the window. He saw nothing of the activity with cars and men below as he concentrated totally on the new idea emerging.

Swaffham detested Whittle. (By implication Maybury had confirmed this, revealing his own hostility towards the man.) So we have Swaffham, at the end of his life and the end of his career, setting Whittle up, putting him in the wrong with his masters.

And who were these masters? Whitehall? The Cabinet? Outsiders?

Whittle had not disappeared, and Maybury knew it; knew too that Yeadings had been looking for the man. Someone in the Met had spilled that to SIS. Or else there had been an eyeball operation on the house at Highgate because they expected the man to return and the Met's officers had been recognized when they called.

He felt he was getting very near the truth now. But there was something in his recapitulation just a little out of true. Well, leave it at that point. Shove it in the freezer, go on to the second signing of the document, after midnight, when Swaffham was no longer a government official.

No; correction: not necessarily *the* document. Signing of *a second* document. With a change of personnel. The real Hilary for the fake; a fake Whittle for the real.

He pulled up short and repeated that in his head, checking it for accuracy. A fake, a stand-in or an alternative? Whichever, Hilary had described the third man and he'd been physically different from Whittle. Not just a difference in the colour of eyes, which could be effected by wearing tinted lenses, but different in build too.

So, if the third man hadn't been Whittle, where was Whittle at that time, having been given the address by chauffeur Danny, because Swaffham counted on him pursuing the attractive woman he'd just met at the Mayfair signing?

No; stop there. It wasn't necessarily her appearance that intrigued Whittle. Suppose he was out to get at Swaffham just as Swaffham was out to get at him. The woman might be seen by him as Swaffham's Achilles heel. If Whittle could get a hold over the woman he might find a chance to manipulate the man.

That had the right smell about it. In which case Whittle would have gone post-haste down to Henley, seeking Pollards, because he thought the woman, as yet unnamed, lived there.

But why should Swaffham have wanted him there? Not to sign any second document, because he had his third party for that already.

The question was a good one. Pity it didn't have any answer.

The blank in his mind at last permitted other matters to intrude. Yeadings leaned forward to watch the milling of figures in the yard below. He made out DS Beaumont grappling with an enormous woman in a navy anorak and brown trousers whose angry bawlings had penetrated even the double glazing of this eyrie. Five uniformed constables had two prisoners between them and no one was concerned with extricating Beaumont from the appalling Amazon.

Beaumont had gone out to bring in the last two suspects for the warehouse break-in. Yeadings decided to give his mind a break by going down to view the booking-in. In the ground-floor corridor he ran into Beaumont with split lower lip and a swollen eye already turning purple.

"Sergeant, been fighting again? Who gave you that?"

Beaumont glared, then broke into a ghastly grin. "Her," pointing down to the duty sergeant's desk. "Prisoner's woman. Followed us in his car. Anoraksia verbosa!"

Well, I asked for that, Yeadings told himself. On the day the world blows up, Beaumont will make a feeble pun about it.

He returned to his office to await his own interviewee from Dowdeswell. In the meantime he rang through to Pollards and asked to speak to the Honourable Mrs. Manton-Jones.

As ever, she appeared delighted to have her routine interrupted. Probably she was, alone in that huge house, widowed, her children grown away, with only the disgruntled Mrs. Cutler for company. Even Florrie's ebullient worship couldn't make up for the frustrations of failing sight.

There was a little pause after he raised the subject of Felicity Marlowe. Then Mrs. Manton-Jones sighed. "We knew of her, naturally. Howard was very concerned for her welfare, but we never met." She sounded subdued. "Felicity had made an unfortunate marriage herself, straight out of school, and quickly obtained a divorce. Consequently Howard felt a need to introduce his own engagement very gingerly. He had still not mentioned it to his daughter at the time Harry was killed. Afterwards he felt it was rather pointless. He was prickly about sympathy, as you can imagine."

"So it's possible she had never heard of your family?"

"Quite possible, Superintendent. Although on good terms, Felicity and her father normally moved in quite different circles. No doubt you know she is an actress? Poor child, she must be distressed now. We would have attended Howard's funeral if it had been made public, and that would have provided an opportunity to make her acquaintance. I understand from Hilary that she's a charmer."

"Hilary has met her?"

"No, no. He has seen her in small parts in West End plays. If he'd been the stage-door-johnny sort, I'd have made him bring her home."

Not quite what Hilary had said when questioned. However . . . "So if I suggested bringing her to see you—?"

"Oh, would you, Superintendent? Does she know anything about us?"

"Only that you live at Pollards, where her father spent his last night in this country, and that he was acquainted with your family."

"And I suppose she knows too of this awful thing about Bonnie? I feel everyone must feel contaminated when they pass by and see the house name on our gates. I even suggested to Hilary that we should change it from Pollards, but he didn't agree. He said continuity was more important than a passing scandal. He's probably right, but it did strike me as rather heartless, until he pointed out that the name meant nothing to poor Bonnie now, and we mustn't distort facts out of concern for our own reputation."

"I suppose Felicity must know about Bonnie, Mrs. Manton-Jones, but I'm almost certain it wouldn't put her off. What matters is that you knew her father as well as anyone she could get in touch with. Just now that is important to her."

"Of course. We shall give her a warm welcome, Mr. Yeadings. When would you like to bring her?"

"An evening would suit me best, and I think Felicity starts rehearsals again on Wednesday, which will make her hours unpredictable."

"Tonight then, or tomorrow? See how either suits her, and perhaps you would ring me back? About eight for the first time perhaps, after we've dined? Eating can so get in the way of talking when the subject's important to you. At least, that's how it is for me, now that I don't see my plate very well."

He thanked her and rang off. Next he contacted Felicity. "Mrs. Manton-Jones is keen to meet you," he persuaded. "She's gone down to the house at Henley for the summer and it must be dreary on her own. Her companion is dour, to say the least, which must damp her natural capacity for fun."

"I must admit I'm curious about the place, if not the family. Will the impersonated Hilary be there, and does he know what I did?"

"I'm pretty sure she was going to summon him for the occasion. He's seen you on the stage and is interested. As to knowing what you did at the signing, that depends on whether your father told him. You could try telling him yourself."

"This could be so embarrassing."

"And enlightening. They were fond of your father. They'll certainly like you. So, tonight or tomorrow, at eight? Come here and I'll drive you there."

"Let's get it over with. So tonight, if that suits everyone. And thanks, Mike. I'll make it to your house for half past seven."

During this second call Angus had slid into the room, raised his eyebrows and been given the thumbs up to stay. He was sitting now on the narrow ledge of the window, hands in trousers pockets. "I see they've got their full house for the break-in. Let's hope the case against them sticks. I wouldn't give much for the Bonnie Hall show taking to the courts yet."

"How about your man?"

"It won't do him any harm to cool off below. He's in Interview Room B with a Cornish pasty and coffee, stoking up for the onslaught. A country type with a touch of bluster."

"Will he give?"

"He thinks not, but he will. He hasn't seen the photographs of Bonnie as we found her. I thought I'd leave that to a later stage. Started out by denying he'd ever met the girl, but he was clearly lying. Which he might have done whether guilty or not, now that the newspapers have spread the fact of her murder. Once he'd admitted talking to her at Easter I persuaded him to come up and give us what help he could. Mind, by the time we were half-way here, for two pins he would have bolted. What's new at your end?"

"I'm bringing together the two Hilary characters of the signings; a confrontation, with each explaining the scene to the other. That way something new may come out of it. It may be my suspicious nature, but all along I've felt that both of them were holding something back, perhaps only a small detail in each case, but it could be the essential ingredient. That little drama's scheduled for tonight. So should anything else come up in the meantime, cover it la- —er, Inspector."

Yeadings reached over to silence a persistent telephone. "Hang on," he called, one hand over the mouthpiece. "Something coming through from the Yard." He listened, grunting from time to time and muttering a brief question. "Very grateful. We have someone here who might match up."

"Our case?" Angus queried.

"A youngster marched into the Yard with a photograph, thought it could be our Bonnie Hall. He's out of work and it appears he borrowed a professional camera, bought a book of cloakroom tickets and took up a pitch on Oxford Street, doing the seaside promenade touch. That was Batchelor at the Yard, and he thinks an enlargement this lad brought in could well be of Bonnie. The interesting point is that she's got a man walking alongside and they're laughing together. The man accepted the numbered ticket but never applied for a copy. The photographer hung on to the negative—about six weeks, he thinks—because it was a good action still. He's building up an album, to help him break into some studio. He's run off six enlarged prints for our use and someone's dropping them in at noon on the way down to pick up a prisoner from Marlborough."

"Any description of the man in the photo?"

"Five or six inches taller than the girl, lean-cheeked, dark hair and eyes, aged eighteen to twenty, dressed in trendy Yuppy style, whatever that means to a Yard man."

"That certainly sounds like Peter Durnside. If it's him in the camera shot, we could have cracked it."

"Mm. Let's take our time now he's here. Since he's not been arrested there's no call to count the minutes."

"So we ask him to stay overnight, give him a good breakfast, let him think he's set for home, and then drop it on him. Right? Will you sit in on this?"

"Not until you have an admission he knew the girl and had a date with her for the weekend April 30th to May 2nd at his uncle's cottage. Then we might line up the heavy artillery. Till then I have other fish to fry. I'm set on taking Felicity across to Pollards tonight and I don't want any distractions."

Felicity arrived at the house ten minutes late, pulling on the hand-brake savagely as she parked in the road outside. Yeadings, who had been watching through the window, went out to meet her by his car in the drive. She was looking elegant in an aquamarine silky number with her hair dressed on the top of her head; full make-up. Defensive, Yeadings decided.

She transferred quickly to his Rover, murmuring apologies and waving to Nan who had appeared at the front door. Then they were away, the girl snapping shut her seat-belt and sitting tensely, her knuckles showing white as her fingers hooked into the soft cream handbag on her lap.

"It isn't going to be such an ordeal," Mike offered.

"It isn't that. I—"

"Do you want to tell me what's the matter?"

She didn't but, for all that, she found herself explaining, tightly and briefly: how she'd slipped out to the library that afternoon and come back to find two men on her doorstep. Special Branch.

"Did they threaten you?"

"Not really threaten, but it felt like that. It was about Howard at first."

"You let them in?"

"Yes, when they'd shown me their cards. It seemed better than risking a spat there on the street. I thought I could get Paula to come round, with her legal mind, but I couldn't raise her by phone."

"She'd have been at work."

"At the time I didn't know what day of the week it was. I was so scared."

And she still was, he saw.

"I panicked. It was stupid. I couldn't tell them a lot anyway. They asked if my father had talked much about the communist countries, Czechoslovakia in particular, and I said not. Which was true. Then they threw at me a string of Slav-sounding names which meant nothing at all. I asked them why they were suddenly so interested, when Howard had been dead for a month, and they hedged. Then they started on my visit to Prague, and what they called my 'Elizabeth Stuart cover.' They expected me to give them every detail about who I'd met and where I'd been.

"I kept asking why they needed to know, and they gave me the usual excuses about Official Secrets and a man with sensitive knowledge putting me in a position where pressure could be applied. They didn't actually say that Howard's loyalty was in question, but it made me angry just the same.

"I told them how scathing he'd been about the *Spycatcher* scandals; how he'd said that the versions revealed having been inaccurate made no difference to the fact of a man breaking faith. He utterly condemned the sort of operative who cared nothing for the consequent dangers to others still in the service: a man whose training in duplicity had penetrated him to the core, and who surrendered the last of his integrity for money as a loud-mouth . . . but they said, 'Words, mere words. What we go by is deeds.' And I felt somehow that they weren't asking what they really wanted to know. They were holding something back."

Just as she was, Yeadings knew, watching her as closely as driving permitted.

"Perhaps they needed to know how much your father had said to you; whether you too should be brought under the Official Secrets oath."

She seemed not to hear him. "One of them had been at the funeral. I remembered his face, square and yellowish with little dark eyes. He was the one who did all the talking."

"And the other?"

With astonishing accuracy she described Maybury. And Maybury *wasn't* Special Branch. "Do you know them? Can you make them leave me alone?"

"Can a mere hyena persuade the lions to leave the kill? It's a question of pecking-order, Felicity. Frankly, no."

His metaphor startled her, deliberately reminding her that beyond his status as a friend he too was an investigator who had to be satisfied. Realism in the place of comfort.

She stared down at the backs of her hands, frowning, then slowly began to relax, accepting the truth along with his honesty. "Well, this evening will be something else. These people, you say, were Howard's friends."

"As fond of him as you were yourself." He put a large hand over her fine fingers and gently squeezed. "After tonight you too will have made two good friends." (Even if what he must do to them all would put him out in the cold himself!)

"If Hilary Manton-Jones is there with his mother—"

"He will be. When I rang confirming tonight she said so specifically."

"Then I shall have to tell him what I did, using his name. Can we start with that and get it over? He may be furious; at the least, embarrassed."

"If you like I'll introduce you and explain you have something you want to tell them. But go easy on yourself."

She looked up at him. "Hare or hound, Mike Yeadings?" she demanded ruefully. "Do I have to remind you you're a copper?"

18

By the time Felicity walked into the drawing-room at Pollards she had full control of her feelings, looking deliciously cool and elegant. Her first-night nerves had been surmounted, Yeadings decided as he moved forward to make the introductions. There was no doubt about the warmth of her reception.

While Mrs. Cutler dispensed coffee and marshmallows the conversation was general, but when the housekeeper-companion withdrew, Mike said, "Felicity has a rather curious little story to tell you both, which may be of particular interest to Mr. Manton-Jones in view of something he previously told me. Go ahead, my dear."

She kept it brief, explaining the roles she and Danny Norman had played in her father's charade. "Mine wasn't a speaking part, beyond 'Good evening, please' and 'thank you,' but I did it using your name—Hilary D. Manton-Jones, Secretary, which is how I witnessed the document. And I truly believed it was a fictitious name dreamed up by my father."

The man covered his astonishment civilly with a mere raising of his eyebrows, but the existence of this first document was clearly news to him. He smiled at the girl. "I don't suppose any damage has been done. Howard knew I could always prove I was somewhere else at that time. He also implied you had a second forename. I own no *D,* unless he meant 'that Damn Manton-Jones'! Thank you for telling us, Felicity, but you really don't have to worry about it."

He looked across at the superintendent, one corner of the dark moustache lifted sardonically. "I take it that Ms. Marlowe knows nothing about a later document signed here?"

At a silent nod he turned to Felicity. "Your father spent his last night here before catching the plane from Heathrow. I'd arranged to drive him there myself. He arrived here towards two in the morning, but an unknown man arrived before Howard with a document they were to sign. They did this as soon as Howard arrived, and I witnessed their signatures as Hilary Manton-Jones, Company Secretary, which I am. Almost the same scene as yours, in fact. Curious, isn't it?"

Felicity was taken aback. "This other man, what was he like?" She frowned slightly as Hilary described him. "It doesn't sound like anyone I know."

"Two documents Howard wanted to complete before he took off," Mrs. Manton-Jones summarized calmly. "Nothing so strange, really. There must have been a lot of things to settle in a short time."

Yeadings coughed politely. "Both occasions a little special, surely? Howard Swaffham had made unusual arrangements for each. Stage management. Set-ups. Here a witness who arranged a complicated alibi to prove he was elsewhere, and a signatory who gave no name. I think too there was something quite special about that third man that I haven't been told of. And for all her openness about her impersonation, Felicity is still holding back something she knows is important, because she doesn't trust me with it.

"I want to make a claim. Every one of us in this room felt affection and respect for Howard Swaffham. Let me remind you that he left me a letter, and with it a charge: to make sense of a riddle he had left behind. How about it, then? Take a few minutes, if you must, to think it over. If any of you has any secret left concerning Howard, isn't now the time for us to discuss it between us?"

The two younger people looked uncertainly at one another.

Hilary was the first to respond. "You're right, I'm afraid," he said. "There was something I kept back because it disturbed me. The man signing with Howard was special in a rather odd way. All the time, from his arrival to his leaving, he wore latex gloves."

"Hilary!" This was his mother. "It must have struck you that the man could have been a criminal."

"I suppose that was at the back of my mind, and probably why I suppressed that detail until now. But I trusted Howard not to send anyone here who would cause any harm. That's why I found it—curious, rather than sinister."

"Was there anything else unusual?" Yeadings pressed.

"There was. When he arrived—early, as I told you—he asked me to leave him alone in the dining-room with both doors locked. And I complied, because of Howard having asked me in advance to do whatever the man required. But I listened and among other noises I heard him using a power drill. I assumed he was putting in equipment of some kind. Whatever it was, he brought it all in a large grip and took it away, dismantled, at the end."

"You must have hazarded some guess as to what he was fixing?"

"I thought at first he was just preparing to bug our conversation, but when we all went in later I saw the difference at once. One end of the room was quite dark, and elsewhere there were spotlights. I couldn't see any camera, but I'm convinced there was one."

"The position of the lighting must have hinted at the camera's location."

"I assumed that if there was one it must be positioned behind the man who had installed it, giving a view over one shoulder, with a good profile of both Howard and myself. That really is all I can tell you. I had hoped Howard would explain everything before he left, but all he did was thank me for my help, and then he just went to bed as if it was a perfectly ordinary night."

"Well, there's plenty to fuel our curiosity in that," said Yeadings, more intrigued than flummoxed. "How about you, Felicity? Are you coming clean at last?"

"I can't. Really, I can't!" She sounded desperate.

"Because it could be dangerous, is that it? For your father—*who is still alive?*"

"How did you—?" She stopped, with indrawn breath. "No! No,

be quiet! I won't listen." She put her hands over her ears and turned her face away, like a horrified child. There was a silence while Hilary Manton-Jones rose and faced him sternly. "Mr. Yeadings, this has gone far enough. I cannot let you—"

"It's all right. Mike?" She lifted her face in appeal. "Will you swear not to tell a word? Can I really trust everyone here?"

"Look, love, you know I can't promise anything that goes against my duty as a policeman. But whatever the truth is, your father meant me to know it, didn't he? Isn't that what's behind the letter he left for you to bring me? Isn't this moment of revelation just what it was all leading up to?"

"I want to tell you, Mike. I've wanted to all along, but I'm scared of anyone else knowing. Has he been in touch with you again, Mike? Or did you guess?"

"Felicity, my dear—" Mrs. Manton-Jones put out both hands towards her. "Can we really believe that Howard is alive and well—"

"Not well, no! That's the awful part. Alive, but still dying. It all has to be gone through again."

"So when did you know?" Yeadings asked quietly.

She sat dejectedly and for a moment made no attempt to reply. "I asked to see my father's body. I had no suspicion, but I simply wanted to say goodbye. He hadn't let me, you see. At the undertaker's I insisted. Well, then I saw."

"No body? Something else in the coffin, you mean?" Hilary was kneeling beside her, holding on to her hands.

"There was a body all right. But it was—was somebody else's. I asked, when I saw him, who it—"

"You met him in Prague, then?"

"I did, but for so few minutes! I can't tell you how or where. It involves other people."

"You're not being asked about anyone else. But did your father send out a message of any kind at all?"

"Nothing. It was just him and me, as if nothing else mattered. Afterwards, I was angry with myself at all the opportunities I'd wasted—"

"It sounds as if you did make the most of your time, Felicity." Mrs. Manton-Jones's face was twisted with pain. "Howard was tragically deprived of love in his lifetime. Nothing could have mattered more than your going to him towards its end. There is something that Hilary and I want to tell you, something very important to us all—Oh, Superintendent, are you leaving us?" She lifted a hand to detain him.

"Going for a turn in the garden, if I may. I thought I caught sight of Florrie out there." He stepped out on to the terrace and moved away into the cool, scented twilight.

"How considerate. This is, after all, a purely family matter . . ."

Yeadings walked down the stone steps and across the grass. From the distant spinney came a joyous bark and the Afghan came bounding towards him, fur streaming and her pelt seeming to move independently of the bony framework within. "Hello, girl. Steady, then. Let's go walkies."

She brought him a sizeable twig to throw for her to retrieve, and he caught himself wondering if a dog wouldn't be good company for Sally. She was big enough to handle a medium-sized one. Perhaps a Jack Russell, or a Manchester terrier. But maybe they should wait until Luke was on his feet.

Lights were coming on all over the house now. Glancing back occasionally, he saw the brilliantly lit tableau in the drawing-room, at first unchanging, like a still photograph of a stage set, the older woman bending towards the girl. It looked as if she was holding both her hands. Some time later the woman rose and her son went with her towards the door. Then he returned to sit beside Felicity on the settee.

Yeadings nodded, and threw another stick for Florrie in the direction of the spinney.

Shortly afterwards Hilary came out alone on to the terrace. With a gruff bark of joy the Afghan shot towards him, Yeadings following more slowly.

"Superintendent, you've done us a great service and we should all like to thank you. Mother has asked to be excused and wished me to say good night for her."

"I'm afraid this has upset her, talking about Harriet."

"In the long run it will be a good thing, I'm sure. It was a shock for Felicity. She'd had no idea of her father's engagement, being involved at the time with getting her own divorce. She won't stay over tonight, so as I have to return to London myself I'll see her safely home later."

She had come out behind Hilary and ran forward to hug the big policeman. "Mike, thank you so much."

"There's a lot to clear up," he warned her. "I'll be unavoidably kept at Maidenhead for most of tomorrow, but could we meet in the evening? At your father's house in Pimlico? I still have your key to it. I can be there at eight to let you in."

"Can Hilary come too? That is if—" She turned to consult him.

"I'd like to," the younger man said quickly.

"I'd meant to include him, of course."

There was only one thing Mike required before leaving, and that was to take a look at the dining-room where Howard Swaffham had held the second signing. Hilary pointed out the minute marks on the walls where brackets had been temporarily fitted for spotlights. The dark wallpaper had been skinned back before the drilling and carefully replaced later. Cameras employed at that meeting could have been concealed in the foliage of a tall indoor vine which spread up the walls in one corner. In front of it was the chair which presumably the unknown man had chosen to sit on.

Yeadings surveyed the layout and furniture of the room, nodded, thanked Manton-Jones and took his leave of them.

Driving home, he allowed himself a little smug satisfaction. If he never discovered the key to Swaffham's riddle, and never found the murderer of poor little Bonnie Hall, at least he'd been instrumental in providing Felicity with a caring family. Not that he needed to be so very pessimistic on the other two counts: for the one he now had a much clearer idea of what Swaffham had intended; and for the other, he had a choice of two killers. Tomorrow, sitting in on Mott's questioning of Peter Durnside could well clarify which one he'd finally go for.

The interrogation began at 9:10 A.M., a uniformed sergeant taking shorthand notes. Angus had considered using a tape-recorder and finally decided that the trendy Peter would be less impressed by familiar gadgetry than by the more solid arm of the Law personified.

Durnside had been expecting some brief formality and then to be released. He had even prepared a protest against the liberties taken in holding him overnight.

Angus began by reminding him that failure to answer questions satisfactorily had resulted in him being detained pending further inquiries. If he was now prepared to discuss reasonably his connection with the girl—

He denied any follow-up of the chance meeting at Easter when he'd stayed with his uncle, and Bonnie had come down to Pollards with Mrs. Manton-Jones. He had caught sight of the girl as she came and went by the driveway. She seemed a nice little thing but a bit young for his taste. There'd been no point in striking up an acquaintance.

He was left alone with the sergeant and allowed to feel he'd made a good case. When Angus came back he had the gardener's wife with him.

Durnside was appalled. Acting a little surprised at his reaction, Angus explained that Mrs. Clarence Durnside was there to make formal identification that the man making the statement was indeed her husband's nephew Peter. Could she do that? he asked her.

"Oh, I know him right enough. None better. That's Peter Durnside, more's the pity."

"You might have got my uncle to come," the young man complained to Mott. "She's always had it in for me."

"Your uncle's got more to do with his time, earning an honest living," she retorted tartly. "Not visiting police stations when you get yourself in trouble."

"I'm not in trouble!"

"Yes you are, lad." Angus nodded to the sergeant, who offered the woman his chair. "You see, what you've told us, and what has gone down ready for you to sign, is a right lot of old cod's, isn't it? We are investigating a murder case, not playing silly buggers. Take a look at these." He laid two of the forensic photographs down in front of the young man who, despite himself, felt compelled to do as he was told. He cringed back in his chair as if struck. "She—I never—"

"Let's start again, with your aunt jogging your memory a bit now and then. Easter first, when you waylaid Bonnie on the way out for a walk and came back carrying her shopping."

"You were spying on me, you old—"

"Just happened to be making the bed in the front room. Glanced out the window, didn't I?"

"So shall we get that written down in your own words, Mr. Durnside? Was it your first meeting with the murdered girl?"

It went on in much the same way, with Peter denying he'd made any move to continue the relationship. Then they trotted out the damning photograph that showed him later with Bonnie in Oxford Street. The young man had been getting progressively paler. Now he went quite green.

"Just my bloody luck that street photographer snapped us. I happened to be up in town and ran into her, but I never saw her again after that. Look, I wasn't anywhere near Pollards the weekend you were talking about. I can prove it!"

Mrs. Durnside sniffed and sat even straighter. "You're a fool, Peter Durnside. Must have got it from your mother's side. Whatever you may say about Walter and my man, they're neither of them fools!"

"You just shut up, shit-bag!"

"Why don't you let her say what she has to say?" Angus asked mildly. "Mrs. Durnside, tell him what you told us," he invited.

"What—about the bed? Been lying on it, hadn't he? While he was waiting for her to turn up. I know how I leave things. That's a very good duvet in the front bedroom and I plump it up proper. Had to be him. He was the only one had a key to the place while we were away, because I'd left my pot plants with Ada at the Swan."

"Oh my God! You want to have me sent down for life, you old fool? They'll say if I was there I topped her. Well, I never! I got there after midnight, so I was an hour late, wasn't I? And when I went up the drive, there were lights on in the house. I thought she'd gone batty. Then I saw there was a car round the back, Manton-Jones's Porsche."

He stopped for breath and Angus put in quickly, "Was Bonnie supposed to be waiting in the house for you?"

Durnside looked defiant, then shrugged hopelessly. "Oh, what the hell, yes. I knew where my uncle kept the Pollards conservatory key and I'd had a copy made a couple of years back. I let Bonnie have it. She was going to meet me there, spend the night, and we'd drive down to Chippenham next morning. There was some do on for May Day and a disco Saturday night."

"So did you see Bonnie?"

"Not then. I reckoned either she'd given up the idea because she'd heard her boss was coming down, or else she was there with him and had stood me up for a better deal. I went back to the cottage and had a bit of a kip. When I woke up I thought I'd give her another chance. She might have been hiding in the house when her boss turned up, and too scared to creep out in case he caught her.

"Well, that's how it was, wasn't it? I went round the back again and blimey, there were two cars by now. Lights on in four or five rooms downstairs. I heard someone rapping quietly on a window and saw Bonnie upstairs with her face against the glass. It was just over the kitchen extension. She could have dropped out easily, crawled over the roof and I'd have helped her down into the yard."

"So what happened?"

"She couldn't get the bloody window open. It had stuck. I wasn't going to spend half my night crawling over the roof and breaking in, especially as they might have left the alarms on. I made signs to her to bloody well come out and meet me down the drive or I'd bugger off. Well, she still didn't make it, so I buggered."

"And when you left she was still in the house, in the first-floor room at the back, trying to open the window?"

"Too true. I never had anything more to do with that chick."

He glared defiantly round the small room, made smaller since a large senior plain-clothes man had slid in just after his aunt. "Tell you what, though. Just before I drove out from the yard behind the cottage, I saw another car, without headlights, turn in at the gates. It went half-way up to the house and then pulled in under the trees, off the gravel. I thought it was a bit sus, like, so I sat there watching and a man got out. He went up towards the house, keeping on the grass. Then I pulled out."

"What time was this?"

"No idea. My watch battery was out, and I haven't got a car clock yet."

"Would you know the man again?"

"Never saw his face, did I? Too far away and too dark. But he had a smasher of a car. A big Merc, dark blue or green."

19

There was no reason to believe that Peter Durnside's final statement contained inventions. Although he hadn't been able to describe Whittle as the night-time intruder in the grounds at Pollards, his description of the car could well link the man he saw shadowily to the one to whom Danny Norman had given the address.

Presumably he'd come to spy out the land, possibly tried to see into the lighted rooms.

Durnside had mentioned two cars at the rear. These would belong to Hilary Manton-Jones and the unknown man. If one of them had been a Rolls, the car-conscious Durnside would certainly have included that detail. So if Swaffham was in the house at that time, Danny had delivered him and already gone on his way. And it seemed most likely that Whittle would have arrived after Swaffham because of not knowing the exact location, although he'd left London first.

"So we accept that Whittle did turn up there, and Durnside caught sight of him," Mike told Angus. "But must we accept that Durnside was on the point of leaving? Or did he go back, find that Bonnie had coped with the stiff window-sash, and encourage her to climb down by the kitchen roof? Then did he, when she'd fallen and was in agony from her ankle and torn leg, stifle her groans for fear the prowling Whittle should overhear and discover them? He's willing enough to lie to save his own skin; would he be as likely to panic and kill?"

"I've ordered his car to be sent to Forensic," Angus said. "I wish to God we could lay hands on Whittle's Merc. The fact that it's disappeared makes it the likelier bet. One of those two must have loaded the body in his car and left it there for at least ten days, until the scrap-yard Cortina became available."

"Whittle or Durnside?" Yeadings repeated. "Or Manton-Jones or the unknown man? Both of the last two had transport on the spot. The only one without was Swaffham, and he could as easily have loaded her into someone else's boot all unbeknownst."

"You really do like to spread your net," Angus complained, only half humorous. "What would be the motives for the last three?"

"One for the lot: to silence a witness. They were all involved in some deception. Bonnie had been inside the house and could have seen too much."

"Oh God," moaned Angus, "you're bloody right!"

They chewed it over together and committed the results to paper for the rest of the working day.

The rendezvous at Pimlico was for 8 P.M. Yeadings let himself in at 7, using Felicity's key and his thumb-print on the panel as before. And as before was welcomed by name in Swaffham's recorded voice.

Yeadings stood there counting the days, calculating whether the man himself could still be alive, according to the doctor's prognosis. The chances must be fifty-fifty. At least Swaffham had removed himself for the pitiable end, leaving his daughter to remember him on his feet and in possession of his faculties.

But why Prague? Why go there, and then on to an anonymous peasant farm to be disposed of like some dead farmyard dog?

He went straight through to the computer, plugged it in, switched on, inserted the script disc to start up, then exchanged it for Swaffham's personal disc which he'd recovered from Paula with her instructions. Sitting over it for days, she had finally broken into the program by typing in the eight-letter code word SOLUTION. (Easy when you know how.) That was as far as she had thought proper to intrude, when it had brought up the message: MIKE I TOLD YOU TO LOOK FOR THE THREE-CORE LEAD.

Yeadings typed in SOLUTION now and read the message for himself. "And I'm doing it, man," he told the machine. He spread his large hands above the keys and pursed his lips. Then he pecked out 3CORELEA. Dammit, the eight-character space didn't permit the whole title. On the screen the familiar green message came up: FILE DOES NOT EXIST. He tried the same command less the last three letters; with the same negative result. He thought again, remembered Paula had said there was space for up to eight letters followed by three figures, and typed CORELEAD 003. This time the word remained on the screen plus the instruction PRESS ENTER TO RECOVER FILE.

Mike pressed the button marked "Enter," the screen blanked out and then three eight-letter words came up: SWAFFHAM HMANTONJ AWHITTLE. The three he had been trying for all along, but they'd been concealed inside a limbo code.

He discovered his hands were trembling. He looked at his watch. He had forty-two minutes before the others were due. He drew a deeper breath, moved the cursor to the first name and pressed the button marked "Edit."

The percolator was plopping in the kitchen when the front door-bell rang. Yeadings went to operate the mechanism which would let Felicity and Hilary in. "I hope you've both eaten," he greeted them. "I've taken the liberty of making coffee, but there's no food to go with it apart from shortbread biscuits."

As he'd expected, they had dined together and come on afterwards by taxi. They had been celebrating the girl's successful audition for the Elizabeth Stuart TV film, and it looked suspiciously to Mike as though they might soon be celebrating some more personal occasion.

"What are we here for?" Felicity asked when they were seated. "I've told you absolutely everything now, and Hilary's the same. What do you want from us?"

"Just to listen, and now and again correct me if I go wrong. Tonight it's my turn to be story-teller. But first, Hilary, did Howard ever tell you the name of the man who killed your sister?"

"Not his name, no. I understood only that his plan—Howard's set-up at Pollards just before he went away—was directed towards the man's destruction. At first I thought he would be the third man of our meeting, but once he'd arrived and started setting the scene, I knew the man was in with Howard on this. And then no one else arrived, so eventually I guessed that whatever Howard had done to ruin this man whom he detested must be in the document I'd witnessed between the other two. But I've still no idea what its contents were, nor why we should be photographed signing it."

Felicity leaned forward. "Mike, *you* know now, don't you?"

"Yes. I know what was in the first agreement and why Howard asked you to sign someone else's name. And I know what was in the second one and why the unknown man had to be there. I know what happened to each of those documents, and how they were used to get a man life-imprisonment. And I know the man's name. It's Whittle, and I'd have liked to put him away myself."

"How can you know all that? Did you find a message in this house? I should have thought the department had tooth-combed the very bricks once Howard went to Prague!"

"It was all on the disc he put in with your books, Felicity. The open parts dealt with his accounts and investments, a copy of his will and so on. But there were three files in limbo with a sub-codeword to get at them which your father left me in his letter. It took a while, and without Paula's help I'd still be looking."

"So are you going to show us, or is it restricted information?"

"You have a right to know something at least, since he used you both. Shall we settle for an outline of events?

"It all arose because Howard was disturbed by certain questionable dealings of his department, notably the use of double agents. He felt that some moves recently had left our country vulnerable, and no action more questionable than what was expected of him as his last commission. He knew it had come his way because he was on the point of retirement. If things went awry, someone no longer in the department could take the blame. Doubly safe for them in his case, because he would soon be dead and not able to deny anything. So he took precautions."

"What was this commission, Mike?"

"To effect a secret agreement between the British and the Russians, with the dubious Adrian Whittle as independent go-between, to permit re-entry of a 'retired' British defector then in Czechoslovakia. Howard knew the defector in question, didn't trust him, and considered the permit to return absolute folly. But he was appointed the signatory for the British, and for reasons of his own accepted the commission.

"He decided to make such a nonsense of the signing that anything Whittle reported back about it would make him suspect. As soon as the document was received the background of the signatories would be looked into. Once Hilary was known to be male, Whittle would be expertly questioned. Howard counted on his interrogator being as biased against the man as he was . . ."

"Jiri!" Felicity breathed.

"What was that?"

"Nothing. Go on."

Yeadings considered her, his head tilted, then resumed. "That version of the document wouldn't do for the British, so Howard had to get the authentic writing of the real Hilary. But because he couldn't ask Whittle to sign a second time, he arranged for an expert forger to take Whittle's place."

"The unknown man at Pollards," Hilary offered. "But why the photography?"

"As a record of the event, and to pair with a still taken of the first scene. There he had arranged a hidden camera to be triggered whenever the door opened. It would have worked when Danny went in to collect Felicity. The two men were at the fireplace end of the room, in close conversation over their brandies. Howard had had a mock-up made of the Pollards dining-room, complete with marble facings to the hearth and a cherub-decked ormolu clock, which Felicity described perfectly as being part of the Mayfair room. I take it she hasn't seen the Pollards dining-room yet?"

"No, because it's rather a gloomy place. In summer we usually eat in the garden room, more informally."

"And there was an audio tape running too throughout the first signing. Felicity didn't speak during the important part, just Howard and Whittle.

"Some of these elaborate preparations were intended to authenticate the scene for the Brits, and some were to confound Whittle with his version for the Czechs. Quite a full last day's work for Howard Swaffham."

"And then he went off quietly to bed," Hilary marvelled, "leaving the forger to clear up and get the document and film delivered. But why did Howard want Whittle to follow him out to Pollards?"

"That was all part of his plan to make Whittle's version suspect when he was interrogated about the charming *Ms.* Hilary M.-J. Also, Howard had stage-managed a minor traffic accident on the hill coming out of Henley. I've just phoned through and had our listed RTAs for that night checked. It was even reported in by a patrol car: slight damage to the front nearside wing of a Mercedes, and a small Vauxhall wrapped round a lamp standard. The traffic officer was only involved when the owner of the Mercedes refused at first to reveal to the other man his name and insurance company. Plenty of evidence there that Whittle was in Henley to sign the agreement which he claimed to have signed in London! If our traffic man had thought it important enough to be put into the computer for the same date as the estimated death of Bonnie Hall, we'd also have got to Whittle sooner for the murder."

They both looked dazed. "Whittle did that?" Hilary demanded. "You believe he killed that poor girl?"

"I'm damn sure he did," Yeadings answered. "If we could only get hold of his Mercedes, we might even be able to prove it."

He left them to think over what he'd told them. During the pause the young man was looking intently at Yeadings. "And Harriet?" he asked at last. "What did you learn about her?"

On the disc it had been quite explicit, but no matter for public consumption. Whatever he told them would have to remain sketchy, but Hilary had the right to know that his twin sister's killing had been deliberate.

"There was an import-export merchant who dealt with delicate missions on both sides of the Curtain. Howard's masters had greater faith in this character than he had. He had him watched, not continually but on random occasions. Just over five years back the man—let's call him X—was organizing an illicit arms deal: Czech Skorpions, Russian Kalashnikovs and rocket-launchers, diverted from the Syrians for the IRA. Harriet was one of a pair of agents working then in Cyprus and she got wind of the arms deal when a ship called in for a crew change at Larnaca.

"It was a reconditioned Maltese cargo boat and it took on five Irishmen. Harriet managed to get near two of the men at a *taverna,* and as soon as she heard X's name mentioned she radioed London with the ship's name.

"X flew in the next night from Damascus to give final instructions and caught Harriet on board after dark. She'd been trying to get a look at the cargo. Her partner, on the dock, was supposed to be keeping watch, but there was a rumpus of some kind and he missed seeing the man go on board. When Harriet failed to come back he complained to the dock police that a girl had been abducted, but by the time they were ready to do anything the ship had slipped out, supposedly with a cargo of agricultural machinery for Algiers."

"Surely they sent a patrol boat after the ship?"

"Apparently not. They radioed the skipper, who said he knew of no woman on board and there'd be hell to pay if one of his men had let on a stowaway. He promised to search the whole ship and turn back if he found her. In due course he radioed back that there had been a girl in the crew's quarters prior to sailing, but the first mate had booted her off. She was a prostitute from Nicosia and bad medicine for young lads fresh out of Cork. It seems that that satisfied the Cypriot authorities and they made no attempt to have the ship apprehended.

"Harriet's partner notified London, and surveillance was arranged for the ship by French and British Customs once she had come through the Strait of Gibraltar. Helicopter activity must have alerted the captain to the fact of their being observed. The crew panicked and abandoned ship in a dinghy, making for the coast near Brest. They were picked up shortly after an explosion sank the ship. A circling helicopter recovered Harriet's charred body, but she had been killed by a single shot between the eyes. Rashly they must have dumped the body overboard before the ship went up.

"The Irishmen claimed that a fire had broken out, and that they were completely unaware of the girl's presence on board. Despite rigorous questioning by the French, the crew denied the existence of a Mr. Big, and it could neither be proved that the cargo had consisted of arms nor that the crew were aware of what the ship carried. The captain claimed that they had been diverted to discharge the machinery at Oman, to take on citrus fruits and dates for Cork.

"Because of the change of destination, the lack of a valid manifest and the questionable nature of the explosion, no insurance was paid on vessel or cargo, and London at least had received notification of X having supplied a suspected arms load. Although this man had not been on board when the ship sailed, Howard Swaffham had no doubt that it was X who ordered Harriet to be abducted, so he was responsible for her killing when the project was aborted.

"For reasons unknown—possibly because he was of use to them in another sphere, as well as being an independent arms dealer acceptable to the Czechs—British Intelligence chose to overlook the man's involvement. Howard could not. And that is why he set out finally to destroy him. He waited for his hour of revenge, and both of you helped him to achieve it. The man who was responsible for Harriet's death was the man I too want for murder. A Czech with an Irish mother, he is known in this country as Adrian Whittle.

"We can only imagine what happened in the early hours of May 1st after Whittle parked his Mercedes under the trees half-way up the drive to Pollards. What seems sure is that eventually Bonnie Hall managed to ease the stiff window open and escaped by way of the roof on the kitchen extension. In doing so, she tore her left leg badly enough to be bleeding freely, and she also dislocated her ankle, but her intention was to get away unobserved and to join her boyfriend at the gardener's lodge. She would have been in considerable pain and it would have taken her some time—time during which the young man tired of waiting and drove off without her. When she came on a car under the dark trees, she was ready enough to take it as his, and in no condition to reason that a Mercedes—if she recognized the make—was an unlikely first-buy for a lad of rising twenty.

"It is purely my supposition that she climbed into the passenger seat and there bled so freely as to mark the upholstery beyond redemption. It could be hidden later by covers, but would always come to light when forensic experts got to work.

"What made it inevitable that Whittle must get rid of the car was the fact that when he came upon her he either took her for a car thief in the act, or feared she must be some colleague of Swaffham's who'd caught him out in his own duplicity. I believe he panicked, took her by the throat and shook her. Maybe this time he hadn't intended to kill, but he did. He was obliged to bundle the lifeless body in the car boot until such time as he could organize its disposal."

He ran a hand over his face, sighing. "All supposition, I admit, and there's little hope that we could ever get him into court on a murder charge. At present, I imagine, he will be undergoing rigorous interrogation in Prague."

"He is," said Felicity quietly. "I'm quite sure you'll never get the chance to nail him here. If he does come back it will be like the 'retired' British defector in my father's coffin."